Praise for the *Star Risk, Ltd.,* novels

The Scoundrel Worlds

"The genius of the *Star Risk* series is that it is unrepentant action and fun. . . . *The Scoundrel Worlds* makes for great vacation reading."　　　—SF Site

"Abundant action."　　　—*Booklist*

Star Risk, Ltd.

"Bunch's pacing is superior, his characterization is better than that of most others who produce similar books, and hardware as well as characters display some nice authorial touches. . . . Well up to Bunch's standards for intelligent action sf."　　　—*Booklist*

"Very entertaining."　　　—BookBrowser

continued . . .

And for the *Last Legion* series

"Lovers of military science fiction could hardly find better fare." —Painted Rock Reviews

"The books of Chris Bunch . . . are well-written books with complex plots, intrigue, and great descriptive narratives of battle and combat. *The Last Legion* is no exception. . . . Fans of Bunch's previous books will not be dissatisfied." —SF Site (Featured Review)

"A powerful piece of military science fiction that includes a well-crafted universe that seems starkly real. . . . Bunch's military tone and sense of atmosphere will delight fans of military sf." —*Affaire de Coeur*

"Good fun military science fiction, with many similarities to David Weber's work." —*Community News* (Oregon)

THE DOUBLECROSS PROGRAM

•••••••••••••••••••••••••••••

A Star Risk, Ltd., Novel

Chris Bunch

A ROC BOOK

ROC
Published by New American Library, a division of
Penguin Group (USA) Inc., 375 Hudson Street,
New York, New York 10014, U.S.A.
Penguin Books Ltd, 80 Strand,
London WC2R 0RL, England
Penguin Books Australia Ltd, 250 Camberwell Road,
Camberwell, Victoria 3124, Australia
Penguin Books Canada Ltd, 10 Alcorn Avenue,
Toronto, Ontario, Canada M4V 3B2
Penguin Books (NZ), cnr Airborne and Rosedale Roads,
Albany, Auckland 1310, New Zealand

Penguin Books Ltd, Registered Offices:
80 Strand, London WC2R 0RL, England

First published by Roc, an imprint of New American Library,
a division of Penguin Group (USA) Inc.

First Printing, July 2004
10 9 8 7 6 5 4 3 2 1

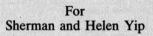

For
Sherman and Helen Yip

ONE

Trimalchio IV lazed under a benevolent sun. All was well on the tropic vacation planet . . . if you were flush.

Star Risk, ltd., was not, at the moment.

"I don't believe it," M'chel Riss snarled. "Howinhells could we be broke? We had two . . . no, three contracts this year that nobody reneged on."

Riss, with her blond hair, green eyes, and statuesque build, could have been a runway model.

Actually, she was an ex-Alliance Marine Corps major who'd resigned her commission after assignments from a line battalion executive officer to advisory slots to covert operations, because of general boredom and a lecherous commanding officer.

Looking for adventure was one thing. Eating regularly was another, which is how she became the second member of Star Risk.

"Not *quite* broke," Jasmine King, Star Risk's general amanuensis, said. She was, improbably, prettier than Riss and had been accused of being a robot. But since she refused to admit one way or another and no one knew of a culture capable of building a robot—actually, an android—as competent and beautiful as King, the matter remained in abeyance.

"But with no income in the offing we'll be on the

welfare rolls—which our beloved Trimalchio doesn't seem to think is necessary—in three months."

"Three months?" Chas Goodnight snorted. "That ain't broke. Broke is when your forwarding address is a shipping crate in an alley somewhere."

He looked pointedly about Star Risk's posh offices on the forty-third floor of an antigrav-supported high-rise.

Goodnight was a highly modified soldier, called a bester, who could, among other things, see in the dark, have reactions three times normal, hear into the FM transmission band. He could—for about fifteen minutes, until the battery at the base of his spine ran dry and he became a wobbling kitten.

Unfortunately, somewhere along the line, Goodnight's moral sense had been amputated, if it had ever existed. The Alliance Army discovered this about the time they arrested him as a jewel thief. Star Risk had rescued him from some forgotten world's death cell.

"I say again my last," Riss said. "How'd we get so broke?"

"Well," King said, consulting one of several screens. "Start with finally being able to repay Grok his loan that got us started—"

"About time, by Ludwig's mustache," the alien, fully named Amanandrala Grokkonomonslf, a furry bulk almost three and a half meters in any direction, growled.

"Keep going," M'chel said.

"There was the cost of your cottage on that out-island," Jasmine went on. "Plus buying the island itself."

M'chel tried to look guilty, failed.

"Not to mention a ten thousand credit advance for your vacation," King said.

Riss nodded reluctantly. It had been a hell of a vacation, three worlds visited, in the company of that Baron. . . . What was his name again? Never mind. It didn't matter. But he was certainly a charmer, and never seemed to need sleep.

"That's for you," King went on. "Mr. Goodnight likes to gamble, as we all know—"

"I just had a long run of bad luck," Goodnight interrupted.

"And then there was that surefire investment Friedrich made."

Friedrich von Baldur, a slender, white-haired, dapper charmer who claimed to have been a colonel in the Alliance but was actually a warrant who resigned just ahead of an investigation of missing supplies, sighed.

"It was, too," he said. "At least by my lights. How was I to know a simple device that made perfect copies of your currency simply for record keeping would be thought of as a counterfeiting tool?" He shook his head at the perfidy of bureaucrats and lawmakers.

"Regardless," King said, "I'm the only one with my nose to the grindstone."

"Wasn't there a small trip to Earth's Tiffany somewhere in there?" Riss said.

"A bauble," King said. "Or a couple or three baubles. Necessary for the old morale and all of that. But we're not pointing fingers here. We're trying to come up with a fast moneymaker." She looked around for ideas. No one said anything.

A long moment crawled past, then the com buzzed.

"Please, God," Riss said. "Let this be a nice, unhappy type who needs a planet overthrown. Or kept from being overthrown."

"One who isn't too bright," Goodnight added.

"And definitely not the taxman," Freddie said, looking piously upward at the heavens.

King waved them to silence, picked up the com.

"Star Risk, limited. This is Operative King. How may we be of service?"

She listened, her face carefully blank. Then she smiled.

"Well, I'm certain we can be of assistance."

Grok growled in pleasure.

"That noise?" King said. "We've had a lot of trouble with line static. Our scramblers, you know. Now, we'll be able to make an appointment for an interview in three weeks . . . no, wait, since you said time was a factor with your problem. It just happens we had a cancellation, and there's a slot that came open tomorrow."

Riss was quite sure the government of Roh Bahtrine wasn't democratic—or else the man who sat across the conference table, Van Hald, was an appointee or a bureaucrat. He was simply too colorless to survive, let alone win, an electoral campaign.

Riss listened, decided he was an appointee, since he referred to the system rulers as the Supreme Council, in capitalized speech.

An appointee, definitely a potential patsy, she concluded.

The members of Star Risk were staring at Van Hald in mild incredulity.

"I must say," von Baldur said, "we've had some . . . unusual assignments. But I can't recall ever having robbed a bank before."

"Oh, no," Van Hald said. "You're not robbing any bank."

"Perhaps I misunderstood," von Baldur said.

"And why couldn't you have just rounded up some local villains to do the smash and grab?" Chas Goodnight asked.

"I said, we don't wish your services in robbing a bank," Van Hald said. "And it's not just any bank, but our system's National Repository."

"Did your campaign funds end up a little short?" Goodnight persisted.

"If all of you will be silent for a moment," Van Hald said waspishly, "I'll give you the precise details and you'll understand why Roh Bahtrine's Supreme Council needs the services of a rather irregular force."

Five years before, Roh Bahtrine had been in a depression, one that hung on and on in spite of the government's best efforts.

In desperation, it finally went to the National Repository and surreptitiously removed about half of the system's liquid assets—mainly the old reliable gold, and the remainder platinum.

"This they used," Van Hald continued, "to, shall we say, encourage outside capital to invest in Roh Bahtrine, and corporations to relocate or open branches in the system."

"You mean bribe them?" Goodnight said.

"Well . . . that's a rather harsh word to use. . . . But yes," Van Hald said.

Now the system was stabilized and its economy prosperous.

"We want your firm to arrange to put the money we, shall we say, borrowed, back, using the guise of a large-scale robbery," Van Hald said.

"Can't you just slither it back, the same way you took it?"

Van Hald hesitated, then shook his head.

"Security measures have been radically changed since then."

"Interesting," Grok said. "An honest government repaying its debts? A true anomaly."

Van Hald didn't reply.

"Well," Friedrich said, "I assume you have details in that pouch."

"I do."

"We'll have our analysts consider them," von Baldur said. "But I can assure you we're interested in this unusual project. Quite interested."

His eyes rested on the rather large, and certified, check on the table between them.

TWO

"All right," Riss said, throwing the projection up on the wall. "This is their capital world—Gentric—and the capital city, Masd.

"Over here is the repository, flanked by two fields, garrisoned with regular troopies, with ground and interplanetary ships in support. *Jane's* says they're supposed to be pretty good.

"So the plan will be to put ourselves next to the repository, try not to kill too many of the guards, try not to get killed ourselves, shovel the gold and platinum bars—that's the shape the geetus is in, by the by—and get out, get paid, and come home.

"Yes, I've already leased some antigrav wheelbarrows. Now, what's the matter with that plan?"

"Do you mean in the design, or in the details?" Goodnight asked.

"I mean the whole idea stinks on ice, as they used to say," Riss said. "It's too frigging easy. Goodnight, you're our resident crook. What's the matter here?"

"I, m'love, was a high-class Raffles, working solo and in the gem trade," Chas said loftily. "I was never part of those vulgar mobs that went around blowing up safes and such. So I know little. But it does stink on ice. I can't believe that a gummint can't figure out a way to put some money back in a drawer without the attendance of loud bangs."

"No," M'chel agreed.

"Are you voting we should pass on the job?" von Baldur asked, looking slightly worried.

"No," M'chel said. "I've gotten as used to feeding off the fatted hog as anybody. I just want to take the job and walk out with my ass semi-intact."

"Well," Jasmine said, "there's only two possibilities for a doublecross I can see: either they plan on letting us put the money back and then drygulching us—I do wonder where that term came from—when we show up to get the rest of our money."

She fell silent.

"And the other possibility?" Goodnight asked.

"I haven't figured out what that can be yet. But I know there must be one."

"Nor do I have any sudden, gut-level Betrayal Flashes," M'chel said. "So we're going to take the job. The way I see it we can do things sneaky, which means tippie-toe in some night with the bags of money and only take out enough guards to make the job possible. Or else we can go in high, wide, and handsome, guns blazing—and why somebody would set fire to a perfectly good blaster is beyond me."

"Normally, I'd argue on the side of subtlety," von Baldur said. "But subtle takes a while, and we are veering toward broke."

"Just so," Riss said. "Not to mention if we play it like crooks, we'll have to recruit some strong-arm experts, us not being well versed in criminality, which means we'll have to split the take, which I'd rather not do. So blazing it is. Jasmine, tell old Van Hald that we're working for him. And ask him for a list of upcoming holidays."

"All right. I assume for a cover?"

"You assume right. And we'll need a crew—say two platoons—of shooters who're good enough to not shoot on the ground. Plus our transport, and some friends to give us a back door."

King was tapping keys on a calculator.

"I make it—if we can do the job in a month—about two million."

"Make it four," von Baldur said. "On the chance they're going to get tricky."

"Plus expenses," Goodnight said.

"Aren't we getting a trifle greedy?" Riss asked.

"Of course," Chas said. "You don't want me to change my lovable ways, now, do you?"

"And how does this look?" Jasmine asked, sliding the screen over.

Riss read it.

"Very sexy," she said. "In three weeks there's a big national holiday, so everybody goes to the shore or somewhere for a couple of days. Plus there's a big airshow over Masd, which should give us a nice cover for any loud bangs since the repository's right outside the city."

"What's it celebrating?" Goodnight said.

Riss shrugged.

"Somebody won—or maybe lost—a war. The fiche is a little vague."

"Definitely lost," Goodnight said. "Victories are tootled with the most mind-numbing detail. Surprised it's a holiday."

"Never mind that," Grok said. "What about our backup?"

"Inbound," Russ said. "The two transports will be in by tomorrow, those two destroyers that are costing us—sorry, I meant Roh Bahtrine—a lot more than they should be paying. . . . Anyway, those two'll be in day after, along with our gunnies."

"Who's running the destroyers?" von Baldur asked.

"A woman named Inchcape."

Friedrich shook his head. "Don't know her."

"Good résumé," Jasmine said. "Actually worked for the same people more than once."

"That's enough for me."

Riss was waiting.

"For our Plan B, which we're not going to mention to our client, of course, and Jasmine's found a way to bury the charges, we've got five spitkits, almost brand new, McG Destroyers," Riss continued. They'll be here on Trimalchio . . . shortly. That's the most I was able to get from the flight leader, an ex-Alliance sort named Vian."

Friedrich von Baldur paled a little.

Grok noticed the expression. "You know him?"

"I do," von Baldur said. "Ironass—pardon me, ladies—Vian. Never known to take a drink or pinch a fanny of any sex. A rigid disciplinarian never known to smile. No. I take that back. A staff officer was making an elaborate presentation to him, waving his arms about, and the staffie stuck his right forefinger in an impeller drive. Blood to hell and breakfast, and a little smile on Vian's face."

"So what is the matter with him as far as you're concerned?" Goodnight asked.

"Unfortunately," von Baldur said, "he was acting depot commander when it became convenient for me to leave the Alliance's service in a bit of a hurry."

"Would he remember you?" Riss asked, amused.

"I don't know," von Baldur said. "I don't propose

to spend much time in his company finding out. He is, as you'd assume, competent. More than."

"So why did he leave the Alliance?" Goodnight asked. "Being as how he's the perfect admiral."

Everyone looked at Jasmine King, who was widely thought to know everything.

"A rather strange case," she said. "He was riding in a hovertrain, going on leave, and there happened to be a young lady in the compartment. No one else. The train went into a tunnel, there were screams, and the young lady claimed that Admiral Vian made an indecent assault on her in the tunnel. For which he was court-martialed and requested to resign his commission."

"How peculiar," Friedrich said. "So he did pinch at least one fanny."

"That's strange," Riss said. "One person's claim, no witnesses, and a highly respected officer?"

"The young lady's father was an Alliance commissioner, and her betrothed was a young fast riser in the Department of State," King said.

"Ah," Riss said. "That'll do it to you every time."

"Lecher Vian," von Baldur said. "Very, very interesting."

"A question," Grok said. "I seem to recall the Destroyer-class ships were supposed to have rather delicate drives."

King nodded.

"The Mark I's were . . . which these are. However, Vian's five have been reengineered after being condemned."

"They'd better be," Goodnight said. "I simply despise being at the center of a loud bang."

THREE

"Whassamattah, Freddie?" Chas Goodnight asked. "You look worried."

"I am," von Baldur said, looking out of the battered hangar at the nearly empty landing field.

The long-abandoned field sat on the far side of one of Gentric's moons, and had been set as the transfer point for the wealth to be returned. On the field were Star Risk's two rented destroyers and the pair of small liners.

"What's to worry?" Goodnight asked. "Jasmine's in place, the transports are here, Riss is ready to pebble and squeak, and we've even got our backdoor men standing by. All we need is a little gold and such, which is inbound."

"I worry," von Baldur said, closing the faceplate on his suit. "Time to dump air. They are inbound."

"You worry," Goodnight said cheerily, "because everything's going too smoothly. Can't you believe in good fortune for once?"

Von Baldur must have had an exterior mike on, for his voice boomed back. "No. I did once. . . . And look where I am now."

Goodnight was about to reply when four destroyers flashed overhead, followed by a trio of heavy cruisers.

"And here's our clients," he said, sealing his own suit. "Trusting bastards that they are."

He bowed to Riss, who turned to the four dozen men and women standing in a ragged formation.

"All right, crew," she ordered. "Time to go breathe vacuum and dot and carry."

"And for me to fade into the woodwork until the clients depart," Goodnight murmured.

Star Risk had deployed carefully.

Jasmine King was the first to leave. She'd altered her appearance to include mousy brown hair, very old-fashioned glasses, and a rare ability to walk knock-kneed that guaranteed there'd be no interested looks from any of the various other sexes.

Jasmine added a face cream that made her look as if she'd been attacked by nuclear acne, and, to make her disguise complete, rubbed a bit of very pungent cheese to the temple plates of her glasses for halitosis's sake.

She coupled that with a nasal voice and a recorder. King arrived on Gentric, announcing herself as a freelance correspondent for Alliance Public Broadcasting, doing a feature on Roh Bahtrine's upcoming Celebration Day, which guaranteed a further lack of interest.

Claiming to have little funds, she took a room in a boardinghouse on the outskirts of Masd, on the main parade route, that not coincidentally had an excellent line of sight on the National Repository.

She then made herself obnoxious by doing buttonhole interviews about what this forthcoming holiday Really Meant to the Man (or Woman) on the Street.

By the time the day arrived, no one, not even the most paranoiac policeman, would do anything except flee in the opposite direction when she approached, and no one had any interest in the bundled electronics that were supposedly part of her craft.

She was the lookout.

The day arrived, and the citizenry of Masd grouped for a parade or, if pacifistic or easily bored, left for anywhere the roar of warships overhead wouldn't be heard.

There were parades and braying announcers and periodic military demonstrations and bands.

King pretended interest, actually kept using a very long lens to make sure nothing untoward was going on at the repository.

The hired guns made wisecracks about the bars of gold and platinum as they transferred them from the cruisers to the liners, although making sure none of them were heard by Van Hald, who was scuttling here and there.

Riss noticed Van Hald appeared nervous, could have attributed it to the utter illegality of what they were doing.

She could have . . . but did not.

Grok's suit made him even more impossibly large. He held in the background, making no effort to help, in spite of the occasional scowls from the loading crew, busy with a tiny calculator.

"That's the end of it," Van Hald announced.

"That's all?" Grok asked.

Van Hald took a moment, trying to read the alien's expression. Even without a space suit, that wasn't possible. He nodded jerkily, lips pursed.

"Very well," Friedrich said. "Let us go un-rob a bank."

"You can lift any time you're ready," Van Hald said.

Friedrich keyed a mike, spoke into it, and the liners closed their ports. Gasses swirled at their drive tubes, and the four Star Risk ships lifted clear of the moon, setting an orbit for Gentric.

The seven Roh Bahtrine ships did the same, apparently setting their course to one of the outworlds.

After a moment, Chas Goodnight came from his hiding place in a shed, and opened his com. "The game's afoot . . . which is very strange," he said without IDing himself. "Come and get me."

Five minutes later, ex-Admiral Vian's five patrol ships appeared around the moon's curvature.

On board one of the liners, Grok was still intent on his calculator. He growled, blanked the screen, and started over.

Van Hald came up. "Might I inquire as to what fascinates you so?"

"Expenses," Grok growled. "My expenses."

Riss was nearby, relaxing against a pile of gold bars. Or so it appeared.

"Your orders?" ex-Admiral Vian asked Goodnight.

He couldn't quite bring himself to "sir" the sandy-haired man in mufti with the low-slung blaster sitting beside him in the copilot's seat with his feet on the control panel.

"Stay with those cruisers," Goodnight asked. "And don't let them spot us."

Vian looked coldly at Goodnight, nodded once without answering.

* * *

Below, on Gentric, another uniformed band tootled its way past Jasmine King.

She repressed a wince, remembering the old saw that military music is to music as military cooking is to escoffier.

Far overhead, she saw contrails as ships broke atmosphere.

She keyed a com. "Clear down here"—and keyed off, without waiting for a response.

"And what do we have here?" Goodnight asked, watching a screen as Vian's ships approached the planet of Gentric.

The Roh Bahtrine ships had altered their orbit.

Vian nodded at his navigator, who touched sensors on a board. "I'd guess," the navigator said, "they're resetting course back toward Gentric."

"The plot sickens," Goodnight said. "You might want to put your crews on full alert. . . . And stay with our friends."

The few men and women who were watching oohed and aahed as four ships, two small destroyers and two liners, flew low over the repository, jetting colorful smoke as they did.

A few cheered, glad that the government was giving a show to the people on the way to the main displays in Masd's city center.

The smoke dropped lazily around the repository.

King saw no signs of disturbance as the anesthetic gas was sucked in by the repository's ventilators.

There still was nothing visibly wrong, but Riss muttered, "by the prickling of my thumbs," and made sure her service blaster was loose in its holster and her three little surprises—a hideout projectile gun, a shock grenade, and an evil little knife—were handy.

King saw the four ships land behind the repository and combat-suited men and women, wearing breather masks, run down the ramps, carrying small parcels that seemed inordinately heavy.

No one else seemed interested.

Riss put small can-opener charges on the outer doors, touched them off, trotted inside, and put another set on the inner doors.

Two guards in a booth, three more on roving patrol, sprawled, snoring loudly.

She reached what Van Hald had described as the main vault entrance. It was closed, but the time lock had been set.

Riss spun the vault knob, a four-knobbed handle, and the door clicked open.

"You're going to blow that one, as well, aren't you?" Van Hald asked.

"Don't worry," Riss said. "We'll cover you. You and your cohorts'll look clean."

She went into the vault, repressing an urge to doff her helmet in reverence. There were still long corridors between piled gold ingots identical to the ones they carried.

"Let's schlep on down," she called.

Grok stood in the middle of the unloading bustle, frowning at his calculator. He hadn't even bothered to remove his suit or open its faceplate.

Suddenly, he grunted an "Ah-hah" and keyed his com.

Without preamble, to all Star Risk coms:

"Hey, Rube," he 'cast. "Plan B."

Van Hald, watching the team replace the gold and plutonium, was standing next to Riss. He heard the transmission from Grok.

"What was that?"

Riss didn't bother to answer, but slammed a hand into the side of his neck.

Van Hald gurgled, went down.

"Abort, abort," Riss shouted. She estimated the liners were half unloaded.

As they'd been ordered, the mercenaries changed tasks. All gold and platinum not already in the vault went back into the liners, and the ships' ramps began closing.

King heard the crack of sonic barriers, looked up, saw the seven Roh Bahtrine ships enter atmosphere. A missile curled from one, shot downward, and smashed into the ground between the road and the repository.

There were screams.

King, unhurriedly, went back to the boardinghouse and picked up a small case.

In it was another, far sexier outfit, and wipes to get rid of the cheese stink and cream.

She piled her electronics gear in her suitcase and hit a timer. It would tick down and melt everything in her case, without flames or that much of a smell.

King made her way to a large department store in the suburbs and got rid of her false identity, then headed for the spaceport.

She had her own extraction plan.

*   *   *

The heavy cruisers dove at the still-grounded liners, springing their doublecross. . . . And then Vian's patrol ships bounced them.

"A Bahtrinian sandwich," Goodnight said.

Vian touched his mike: "All ships . . . lock on your targets. . . . Make sure no collateral damage. . . . Fire at will!"

Missiles shot from the patrol ships' launch tubes down at the Roh Bahtrinian warships, who hadn't seen anything above them, intent on stopping the "robbers."

One cruiser took two hits, tucked, and pinwheeled into the ground; the second was struck three times. It broke off, careening through the air.

One Bahtrinian destroyer tried to keep up the attack, was hit once in the drive tubes, and made a hard but survivable landing.

The two liners were clear of the ground, their escorting destroyers above them.

At full drive, they made for space.

"Two jumps," Friedrich ordered, and the navigators of the liners fed prearranged settings into their drive computers.

The starships vanished into N-space, quickly followed by their destroyers.

"Very good, Admiral," Goodnight said. "Now take us home."

The RP—rendezvous point, predetermined—was repressed glee. The for-hires were paid off, in gold from the liners, plus a hefty bonus, and went on their way, swearing that if ever Star Risk needed anything—anything, including their first born—they had but to ask.

Even the frosty Vian allowed that he'd had a most satisfactory experience, for the least time spent and without any casualties, and hoped they'd keep him in mind for the future.

The only one missing was Jasmine King, and she made her own way back to Trimalchio IV before the others arrived.

"Hokay," Goodnight said. "Now that the smoke's cleared, and little ears have gone about their business, what the hell happened? Obviously, this was a crook run from the beginning. But why?"

"Messr. Grok?" Riss indicated.

"I had looked up a few estimates of what was supposed to be in the Roh Bahtrinian Repository," the alien said. "I decided to keep a running count on the amount of gold and such . . . if no other reason, if the Bahtrinians accused us, after the fact, of having sticky fingers. I counted only about half, perhaps two-thirds, of the estimates, and decided something had gone wrong."

"It had," Riss said.

"I still don't get it," Goodnight said. "Why the robbery—phony robbery?"

"Messr. von Baldur?" Riss said.

"Chas, sometimes I suspect you of simplemindedness," Friedrich said, a touch smugly. "Obviously, they borrowed the treasury some time ago, as they told us. What they didn't bother to add is that while that treasury was being hidden wherever it was being hidden, someone, or more likely several someones, made unauthorized withdrawals from that money, probably without telling their fellow politicians.

"When it was time to pay up, full accounting, those someones could not, or did not want to, make restitution. So they came up with the story that the repository now had additional security, and that the robbery was the best way to handle things.

"Of course, what they intended was to have their naval units hit us in midpayback, and then, in the course of the blood and slaughter, they would report that one ship managed to escape, which is where the missing loot was off to."

"That's not that bad a plan," said Goodnight.

"No," King said. "If you assume the people you're going to pull it on aren't very bright."

"Still," Goodnight said. "It's pretty damned unique."

"Aren't they all," Riss said, yawning and thinking about a tall, cool drink on her island. "Aren't they all. But once again, truth, justice, and the suspicious way of life triumph."

FOUR

M'chel Riss was fully engaged, without her usual ally, Jasmine King, for tech support in her War against Whatever Color Her Toenails Used to Be.

She was alone on the tiny islet she'd bought, near the fringes of the cluster that sprayed out from Trimalchio IV's main continent, and enjoying the solitude immensely.

Between eyeing the two different shades warring it out on her big toes and trying to make a decision as to which was favored, she was considering whether to lift into "civilization" for dinner or whap something together out of the freezer and continue reading *Beyond String Theory and Other Amusements*.

She rather thought she'd go into town—tonight didn't feel like a time for mathematics—when her com buzzed.

Riss fielded it.

"Go."

It was Jasmine, at the Star Risk offices.

"There's somebody here who wants to talk to you."

"Does he look like I owe him money?"

"If you do," King said, "it'd be worth every penny. Yum."

"I hope," M'chel said, "you're wearing a whisper mike."

Jasmine activated a pickup.

For a very long instant, the stars swung in their orbits, and she remembered a brief Temporary Duty, back when she was still in the marines.

The man was a little older and had a little more silver at his temples, and maybe a few more smile lines, since she'd last seen him.

Lieutenant Colonel Dov Lanchester, Alliance Marine Corps.

Once, very briefly, they'd been lovers, when they'd attended a Planetary Insertion course. Nothing came of it except some wonderful memories, and they went separate ways to new assignments.

The next time, he'd been fast-tracked to captain and she was still a first lieutenant. Worse, he was her temporary CO, which meant nothing was supposed to happen—and didn't. Stupidly, Riss often thought, when the lonelies struck.

Now she rather wished that Lanchester had been her CO on her last assignment, instead of that cockless pickleface who'd tried to weasel her into bed and was the biggest reason for her resignation from the Alliance Marines.

But as the military phrase correctly pointed out, you can wish in one hand, and shit in the other and see which one fills up first. . . .

"Uh . . ." she managed.

"Major Riss," Lanchester said. Like everything else about him, Riss thought his deep voice damned near perfect.

"M'chel," she said. "How are you, Colonel?"

"Dov," he said. "I'm still in, you're out, which the Alliance should regret every damned minute."

"Maybe they should," M'chel said. "*I* don't."

"I tracked you down, since I'm between assignments, to see if I might buy you dinner," Lanchester said.

M'chel nodded.

"Shall I pick you up?"

Riss started to say no, bethought herself, and nodded.

"At seven?"

Again she nodded.

"Now, if you'll give me coordinates to your tropic paradise . . ."

Trimalchio IV was going through a fascination with antigravity. Chas had the theory the drives were popular since so many citizens of Trimalchio also seemed to exist without visible means of support.

The restaurant tables were roboticized booths floating out and back on preset courses, over the ocean, with waiter call sensors.

The waves were small, all three moons were out, the breeze was warm, and the wine was correctly chilled.

It was most romantic.

Dov was looking up at the sky.

"Three moons," he mused. "Just like on . . . what was it—Myrmidion II? Do you remember—"

"I do," Riss said. "My damned tent leaked."

"You should have complained," Lanchester said. "Other arrangements . . . could have been made."

M'chel carefully arched an eyebrow, didn't reply, but changed the subject.

"So what assignment—assuming you can talk about it—brings you my way?" she asked.

"I can talk about it," he said. "It's advisory. . . . And that's not a cover. It's the Khelat-Shaoki Systems, generally called the Khelat Cluster. Twenty-seven worlds belong to the Khelat, fourteen to the Shaoki, and they've been fighting each other for half a dozen generations."

"Who's the Alliance backing?"

"Khelat."

"Why?"

"Uh . . . because us killer marines support honesty, love, and the Alliance Way?"

M'chel snorted and drank wine.

"Khelat is the main source for *maln*."

"Which is?"

"A mildly stimulating, mildly addictive tea that's become the new fad in the civilized worlds. *Maln* is controlled by Omni Foods, which indirectly controls six seats in the Alliance Parliament."

He shook his head.

"I wonder what would happen if the flag-wavers ever figured out that we spend half our time fighting for the Stock Exchange?"

"So why'd you take the slot?" Riss asked.

"Got some good men and women aboard . . . including an old friend of yours, Bev Wycliffe, as my XO. And because this'll give me a leg up on getting my star."

"You're still ambitious."

"I am," Lanchester said. "Growing less so the creakier my joints get." He shrugged. "Enough of that. Can we order? Having no idea of what these furrin devils consider gourmet, I plan on eating nothing but underdone beef or its equivalent until I've got to go back on combat rats."

They were back on Riss's island, and it was very late.

Lanchester drained the last of a respectable Vegan brandy in his snifter and got to his feet.

"I suppose I should get back to my hotel, if you still want to be out and about tomorrow."

"You should," M'chel agreed, wondering why her voice was getting a little throaty. She got up and led him to the door.

They were close, very close, and Lanchester suddenly kissed her.

Flames flared inside Riss, and she kissed him back, arms going around him.

"You kiss even better than I remember," Dov said.

"Less talk," Riss managed. "And more bedroom. Down that hall."

Neither of them, during the next five days, seemed much interested in going into the city or doing anything other than being in each other's company.

Lanchester, in spite of Riss's growls, insisted on going over the briefing material, and inadvertently M'chel learned more than she wanted to know about the Khelat-Shaoki cluster.

The Khelat and Shaoki came from the same Earthmigrant culture that'd split in half a very long time ago, over what nobody was sure.

There were differences:

The Khelat had basically claimed near-desert worlds and irrigated them toward fertility.

The Shaoki preferred less arid, if now less productive, planets.

The Khelat were ruled by an extended royal family; the Shaoki by a large military council.

There was one minorly bright note. The war had gone on forever, it hadn't been that much of a disaster.

"They seem to like to skirmish and pose," Lanchester said. "And break off when things tend to get serious. The soldiers, the confidential briefing said, can be impossibly brave. The officers tend to take care of each other and themselves."

"So you'll teach the Khelat how to go for the throat?" Riss asked, amused.

"I suppose so. At least," he went on, "I won't have to worry about nukes. The Alliance Control Commission seems to have done a pretty good job of watchdogging. Plus, they're not prone to radioactivity, since they both want each other's real estate.

"Oh yes," Lanchester said. "The Khelat are claiming there are Shaoki-supported rebels on their worlds."

"In the hills, of course," Riss said.

"Of course," Lanchester agreed. "Where else would any self-respecting bandit hang his hat?"

Once, lying entwined on the beach, Lanchester said, "It's kind of a pity."

"What is?" Riss asked.

"That I'm in the damned marines, and you're doing . . . well, what you're doing."

"Why?"

"It makes it hard to think about anything . . . anything more than tomorrow, considering the way that assignments and reassignments work."

"But if it hadn't been for the marines," M'chel pointed out logically, "we never would have met. Right?"

"You don't believe in fate and foreordained lovers and things like that?"

"Not lately."

"Oh, well." And he kissed her.

Both of them were glad the subject changed, but

that night, their last night before he transshipped, Riss lay awake, wondering.

Half an E-month later, the dreams died.

M'chel, to her considerable surprise, found herself writing Dov Lanchester through a military post office almost twice a week, messages not terribly sentimental but lightly coded, to keep off the nosies.

Slightly as astonishing was that Dov replied frequently.

Then an E-transmission was returned, with the automated reply:

CANNOT DELIVER. ADDRESSEE DECEASED.

FIVE

"I want," M'chel Riss said evenly, "to hire Star Risk, limited."

She ignored the surprise from the other four, who'd been wondering why she wanted a formal meeting of the firm.

"Here is a list of my current assets, as well as a properly witnessed promissory note for half my share of future commissions until whatever is due is paid."

"But . . . but . . . that's like gambling with your own money!" a shocked Friedrich von Baldur said.

"And their deck," Chas Goodnight added.

"Just what do you wish our services for?" Grok wondered.

"To investigate the death of one Lieutenant Colonel Dov Lanchester, Alliance Marine Corps, while serving in the Khelat Cluster as a military advisor, and to provide, shall we say, proper retribution."

"M'chel," Jasmine King said gently, "you've been glowering around here for the past three weeks about Colonel Lanchester's death. People, soldiers, do get killed. Don't you think you're behaving a little . . . aberrantly?"

"No," Riss said shortly. "Because there's something

very strange going on. Here's the evidence I've gotten so far:

"I sent a letter to my friend on the team—she wasn't really a friend, but a close acquaintance—and got an automated response back.

"The Alliance advisors were withdrawn from the Khelat Systems shortly after Dov's death."

"That *is* a little strange," Goodnight said. "Have you found out anything about their assignment? Were the advisors pissing in somebody big's ear or something?"

"That's number two. I went to another friend, who's an archivist. The final report of the advisory team is sealed."

"Oh?" Friedrich said, arching his eyebrows. "Stranger and stranger."

"Then," Riss continued, "I finally got a response back from Bev Wycliffe, who'd been XO on the team. She didn't give me any details about how Dov died, but suggested I stay way out of it."

"Which definitely suggests something's stinky," Goodnight said.

"Which is why I want to hire Star Risk," Riss said.

"No advisors," Friedrich mused. "But some kind of situation that required them. Hmmm."

"I have heard," Grok put in, "that capitalism abhors a vacuum."

"Well said," von Baldur said. "Jasmine, would you like, once again, to be the companion of an aging roué?"

"Going where?" King said. "As if I didn't know."

"For a small vacation," Friedrich said. "To the Khelat Cluster."

Two weeks after King and von Baldur left, a message en clair came back:

COME ON IN. THE WATER'S FINE.

SIX

The posh lifter that had been waiting for the Star Risk team flew along the coast from Khelat II's main spaceport toward the capital.

Chas Goodnight was flipping through the Mich guide, muttering aloud: "Five continents . . . three temperate . . . former deserts . . . now irrigated from numerous artesian wells and desalinization plants . . . some mineral wealth . . . extensive plantings of *maln*—dash—see glossary . . . two arctic continents . . . bah!" He looked up.

"Tell me something interesting, Grok."

"The irrigation system was devised by an Earth consortium of the Dutch and the Israelis," the alien said.

"Gaad, fascinating," Goodnight snorted, and pointedly looked out the lifter's port.

"They've got *how* many frigging princes?" Goodnight asked, as the buildings of the capital, Rafar City, rose from the desert.

"At least three hundred fifty," Grok said. "Why didn't you do your homework on the flight out?"

"I did my language condit," Goodnight said. "Other than that, I was busy."

"We noticed," Riss said.

"She was lovely, wasn't she?"

"And married to one of those princes," M'chel said. "I checked the manifest, and figured that was the only reason you bothered to learn the language."

"Ah, well," Goodnight said. "While the mice is away, or however that goes. At least I took the time for the language conditioning."

"Is it not interesting," Grok said, "that they left their central city in the desert, rather than making the lands around beautiful?"

"Perhaps it reminds them of their roots," M'chel suggested. "As I recall, they came from a desert planet to begin with."

"I shall never understand humans," Grok decided. "It is also interesting, that they sited their capital at a distance from a spaceport. That is hardly convenient."

"Unless you're used to being invaded by transports," M'chel suggested.

"Princes . . . and a king," Chas murmured, still considering the social system. "How bizarre."

Rafar City was laid out in broad avenues, as if a highway engineer was its main architect.

The buildings were spotless, and high-rise buildings dotted the city.

The Rafar Arms Hotel, rather than being a tower, was a sprawl of low buildings that mimicked the higher buildings around it, set in vast gardens.

Riss, although having no objections after years of bunkers and barracks, had once wondered why Friedrich insisted on luxury hotels whenever possible.

"Other than you obviously like it," she had added.

Friedrich had said something pompous about expecting his surroundings to match his capabilities.

Jasmine had added, "besides, it makes the client, stunned by all the extravagance, hold still for the outrageous fees we charge."

Waiting in the main lobby of the hotel were von Baldur, King, and an expensively khaki-uniformed man with a finger-line mustache. His epaulettes carried a ring of six stars. Riss didn't know what rank that made him—the highest the Alliance went was four, and that was for the Commander of the Forces.

Friedrich introduced him as Prince Barab, Minister of Defense.

The man blinked at Grok, then bowed to the others.

"You have honored me, and my worlds, by taking the time to consider yourself with our small problems. I welcome you to the Khelat Worlds."

"And we are equally honored," Riss said smoothly, "that you consider us worthy."

The man smiled as if he really meant it.

"Your leader, General von Baldur, has presented your capabilities, and I am much impressed."

Riss noted that von Baldur had given himself a promotion, most likely to keep pace with Six-Star Barab.

She also noticed that Barab didn't speak in the local language, but in Alliance lingua franca.

"Unfortunately," Barab went on, sighing deeply, "such a decision can only be made by his Most Royal Highness, the King. And unfortunately, he is in his spring quarters."

"What might those be?" Grok said. "If I'm not asking an unseemly question."

"Each year," Barab said, "His Highness and certain specially honored members of the Royal Family go deep into the wastelands to remind themselves of our roots and to ensure humility."

"Ah," Grok said.

Chas Goodnight had a bit of trouble keeping a straight face.

"You mean you go camping . . . when you don't *have* to?"

"Now, now," von Baldur said smoothly. "Each culture has its own practices."

"Thank you, Friedrich, for your understanding," Barab said. He frowned.

"But I spoke hastily. Our situation seems to be worsening by the day.

"Perhaps we should seize the horn of expediency and allow you the great privilege of visiting his Royal Highness, when he may choose to discuss this matter."

"We would be delighted," Friedrich said.

"Give us a chance to wash and change," Riss said, "and we'll be ready within the hour."

"Good, good." Barab took von Baldur by the sleeve, drew him aside.

"But I assume you'll wish to leave that alien behind. . . . Although I mean no discrimination."

"Of course you do not," Friedrich said. "But I must add that without his unique capabilities our fees will almost certainly increase radically."

"By how much?" Barab asked, a worried note in his voice. "I have already notified the king of your quotes."

"But that was with my fully integrated team present," von Baldur said. "Without Grok, we'll have to go onto the open market. . . . I, quite frankly, can't think of anyone I've heard of with his qualifications."

Riss had overheard this, as had the other members of the team, all of whom pretended sudden deafness.

"I would guess . . . probably double," von Baldur said.

Riss noted that Barab wanted desperately to ask

just what Grok brought to the operation, but wasn't forceful enough.

"Very well," he said, still worried. "These are unusual times, and we must all allow for this, mustn't we?"

Friedrich smiled at him.

Riss thought the smile was very much like the ones she'd seen of Earth tigers, closing in for the kill.

It took them less than half an hour to clean up and change. All of them now wore dark green outfits that closely resembled uniforms, and Grok had his weapons belt on.

Prince Barab's personal lifter was a sleek Rolls-Bell, just what a prince should appear in. It was fitted with every plush item imaginable, from real wood paneling to leather upholstery to a concealed bar.

But being a military vehicle, it was also equipped with a chaingun, accessed through a moon roof, and had blast-proof glass.

And it was painted in camouflage.

"Now this," Goodnight drawled, "would be *just* the thing to putt around Trimalchio in."

Barab looked at him.

"Do you have that great a problem with terrorists?"

Chas shook his head, stopped himself from asking "Do you?"

Barab ordered the pilot to divert over a military post to show them the systems' mailed fist.

Riss observed closely.

New barracks. State-of-the-art Alliance lifters. Modern patrol ships and a couple of destroyers, also current-supply Alliance. Huge hangars.

But the barracks already needed paint, and the lifters and other ships looked very short of maintenance and were arrayed in a haphazard style on the base's three fields.

M'chel was not impressed.

Friedrich, however, made nice on the unit below, and Barab beamed.

"Hoo," Goodnight breathed to Riss as the lifter settled down into the king's camp. "We wuz doing it wrong back when we wuz sojer boys and girls."

The tents were solid sided and fitted with bulges that looked like auxiliary power for temperature control units.

There was a heavy scatter of lifters, but all of them were luxury items.

The camp was aswarm with servants carrying things here, there, and the only ones doing anything resembling work.

Such, evidently, was one of the privileges royalty gave you. Goodnight decided he might have liked bivouacking in the army if someone had made an arrangement like that for him.

Riss noted armed men trotting toward the lifter as it landed and saw they were very smartly dressed, and, from their precision movements, well trained.

She corrected the "trained" to "drilled," as the soldiers, clearly bodyguards, jumped back in dismay when they saw Grok and fumbled about, while their officers bayed orders that made no sense.

All of the Star Risk people stood quite still until the guards were sorted out and brought back under control. They knew the dangers of an incompetent with a gun, and there appeared to be almost two dozen of them about.

The operatives were taken into the largest tent, told to wait for a moment until the king was ready to be honored with their presence, and offered refreshments.

None of them wanted alcohol. Drink and duty seldom mixed.

"So you think you can help me?" King Saleph asked, in the Alliance diplomatic tongue.

Goodnight was watching him with great interest, this being the first king he'd ever come upon.

Saleph had moon-pool eyes that looked to Riss like those of a penned predator, driven mad by his cage.

He was very thin, and the smile on his long face kept vanishing, as if slipping off, to be hastily put back on.

"I know we can, Your Highness," Friedrich said firmly.

"But your prices," Saleph almost whined. He kept eyeing Grok, as if afraid the hulking alien might eat him.

"Cheap, if we are able to end this war, aren't we?"

The king squirmed. "You're not the only foreign soldiers in our employ who've promised the same thing . . . without results."

"One of the first tasks we'll undertake," von Baldur said, "is to evaluate your other, uh, advisors, and make appropriate recommendations."

The king brightened, as if the thought of a war among mercenaries was quite attractive.

"Also, we propose to carry the battle to the enemy as soon as possible," von Baldur said in ringing tones.

Riss decided Freddie should always walk point for them, since nobody else would be able to think of such horseshit, let alone talk about it convincingly.

"That is good," the King said, an edge of excitement in his voice.

"We can begin immediately," von Baldur said.

"To have Khelat at peace," King Saleph said dreamily. "Something my father and my father's father were unable to accomplish.

"Peace . . . and utter obliteration for those damned Shaoki!"

The hilltop was about the only relief in a sea of green.

King Saleph had insisted that someone from Star Risk must see the new root of the Khelat riches, and why the war was being fought.

As Lanchester had said, it was *maln*.

M'chel Riss had agreed to be the Star Risk representative. Her escort was a Prince Wahfer, who looked like all self-respecting warrior-type princes should: tall, well muscled, curly hair with a thin mustache, wearing combat fatigues, a pistol, and an elaborately worked dagger.

He wore three rings, two too many to Riss's sometimes puritanical thinking, and an old-fashioned bejeweled watch on one wrist.

Wahfer had piloted his own lifter, without even a bodyguard, and they'd flown for about an hour east before setting down in this plantation.

The bush grew about two meters high and wide. Its leaf was broad and dark green.

The bushes stretched in neat rows to the horizon. Below were mobile irrigation pumps and automated weeders.

A tiny lifter with some sort of supervisor darted here and there, from pumps to robots, but there was nothing else to be seen.

"Quite impressive," Riss said.

"Yes." Wahfer walked to the edge of the hilltop and plucked one leaf.

"This, dried and crumbled, will sell in the Alliance for about half a credit."

Riss tried to do the math about what the plantation was worth, failed, looked impressed.

"As far as I know," Wahfer said, "with the exception of tea, coffee, and certain illegal drugs, *maln* provides the most credits per kilo of any natural substance. *Maln* will make Khelat very, very rich. Once this damned war is over and Shaoki is put in its proper place."

"Which is?" M'chel asked.

"Their inhabitable worlds, for the most part, have more surface water than ours. Proper use of the land will mean creating plantations even vaster than the ones here."

He frowned.

"You don't look happy about that," M'chel said.

"Truthfully, I am not," he said. "Not that I am one of those absurd peace seekers. I think, like you do, war should be fought for its own rewards, a testing of a man . . . and woman's . . . bravery and a system's resolve."

Riss didn't argue with him.

"How long would this plantation have been here?" she asked, deliberately changing the subject.

"Oh, five or six years," Wahfer said.

"And before that?"

The Prince shrugged. "Some sort of farming land. Probably there would have been a village or two or three for the farmers to live on. But since all land belongs to the king, when His Majesty determined the proper purpose for this property, the people would have been relocated."

"To where?" M'chel asked.

Wahfer shrugged. "To a city . . . to another plot of earth . . . It matters not, now, does it?"

"Exactly as you'll do to the Shaoki?"

Wahfer smiled, a killer's smile.

"When the war is finished, I doubt if there shall be that many of them to relocate."

"Since we have not had time to check for eavesdroppers," von Baldur said, and nodded to Grok.

They were back in the suite at the Rafar Arms Hotel.

Grok turned on a random-noise generator and went back to sit down.

"So," von Baldur said. "This is an initial briefing, since we have not handled a contract this large yet, and want to ensure we play our cards correctly. What are our goals?"

"To be considerably richer than before," Goodnight said.

"Of course," von Baldur said. "And the steps thereto?"

"We'll need to get whatever prime intelligence the Khelat have on our enemies," Jasmine said. Friedrich nodded.

"First on the Shaoki," Riss said. "But certainly on how much of a myth or threat these bandits in the hills actually are."

Again, a nod.

"I think we need to assess the troopies on our side," Goodnight said. "I wonder if any of them are any good, and if not, let's fire the bastards and steal the money for ourselves . . . and for the people we're going to need to hire."

"Correct," von Baldur said.

"One other thing," Riss said. "We should be figuring out some nice, spectacular things that'll knock the socks they don't seem to wear off our clients."

"An excellent thought," Friedrich said. "That will unquestionably make a demand for increased funding or expenses more palatable. With all that established," he continued, "then it shall be time to launch an offensive or two against the Shaoki. Maybe that will be enough to produce peace."

"Maybe," Grok said skeptically. "But this is very close to a civil war in this cluster, and civil wars among you humans, I've read, generally aren't over until things escalate to total butchery."

"They can do that," von Baldur said indifferently, "after we're paid and gone. I have little interest in genocide."

"It pays so shittily," Goodnight said.

Riss smiled slightly.

"And one other goal, just to keep things open and aboveboard, for me at least, is finding out who was responsible for Lanchester's death, and getting his ass on toast."

SEVEN

There were almost six hundred of them, in full dress uniform of their commander's design, in rigid rows.

"Your men parade well," M'chel Riss told the CO, Joch Rohm, yet another man who rated himself a general. In the Alliance, command of half a thousand men might get someone a colonelcy. But this was mercenarying.

"Thank you, uh . . ." Rohm looked for rank tabs on Riss's deliberately blank dark green coveralls.

"Miss Riss," M'chel said. "However, we're not running parades. Please dismiss your men, and have them fall out within the next half hour in patrolling uniform."

"Uh . . . yes. Miss."

It took an hour before the mercenary force was back on the parade ground. They didn't look nearly as perfect—their field gear, for the most part, looked as if it had just been issued and never worn.

Riss walked down the ranks.

"You . . . Sergeant. Front and center."

The noncom paled a little but doubled up to her.

"What are the five blocks in a patrol order?"

The man looked blank.

"Pull your team out and move them into the woods in open formation."

"Yes . . . ma'am."

Ten men and women obeyed, moving as if they'd barely learned their lessons from a book.

Riss watched them trot away.

"General, what's the size of your marksmanship training team?"

"We don't have one."

"Communications training team?"

"We have technicians who could teach, I suppose."

"What about ground-to-air light missile training."

"I'm sure we could assemble some of my experts into a team."

Riss nodded.

"How many hours do your men have in zero-G hand-to-hand?"

"That's an area we haven't been training on."

"How many of your men have an instructor rating from the Alliance, or an equivalent?"

"I don't have that figure handy, I'm afraid."

"Guess, General."

"Maybe a dozen . . . maybe two dozen."

"How many men are experienced at in-space transfer under hostile conditions?"

"Well, my warriors have been more trained at hands-on, on-planet conventional warfare."

"I see," Riss said. "If you'd step over here, away from your aides?"

The man obeyed.

"Your contract has another month to run," Riss told him. "When it expires, it will not be renewed."

"But . . . why?"

"This planet needs teachers, not more cannon fodder. General, I'll give you a bit of advice. Mercenarying is primarily either instruction, techies, spaceship crews, or special ops these days. The local lads provide the blood and the charges. People who're good at chucking spears around rate very low on the employment roster.

"That's all."

"Your troops," von Baldur said smoothly to Prince Barab, "are somewhat lacking in basic intelligence toward the enemy."

Barab looked as if he was about to lose his temper, changed his mind.

"Yes," he said. "That is a criticism that's been leveled before. That was one of the things the recently departed Alliance advisors were intending to help us with. The problem is that the Khelat are instinctive warriors, not particularly respecting the professions of espionage and such.

"I shall continue to have my staff search for any accumulated information about the Shaoki."

Von Baldur made politeness, cut off, as Jasmine came in with a handful of microfiches.

"Anything?"

"Not much," King admitted. "M'chel managed to find some reports about smuggling orbits into various of the Khelat worlds, if you want them."

"Now, what would the Khelat want to worry about . . ." Friedrich changed his mind. "No. Ship them over. At this point a thin something is better than a fat nothing."

"Colorful," Chas Goodnight said, voice dripping with scorn.

He and Grok stood outside a ramshackle barracks. Behind them were one hundred of the king's bodyguards that Goodnight had borrowed, calling the group a "potential teaching aid."

"Aren't they," Grok agreed, without sarcasm, looking at the fifty men in a ragged formation. "The First Commandos, is that correct?"

"That's what they call themselves." Goodnight shook his head. "Are any two of them carrying the same weapon? That'll make resupply interesting.

"Come to think," he said, "are any of them carrying any less than three weapons? Not counting hideouts, sleeve guns, armpit daggers, and shit like that. I guess they need those just to show how baaaaaaad they are. And let's not even talk about their uniforms or strong need for baths."

Grok didn't answer.

"A goddamned disgrace to mercenarying," Chas grumbled. "Every damned unit we've looked at so far is either spit and stupidity or steel-teethed commandos. Disgusting."

"You make a jest," Grok said. "You think soldiering for hire is a calling for a high moral standing?"

Goodnight grunted, having temporarily lost his sense of humor.

The leader of the rabble ambled forward, and threw a most casual greeting that he might have intended as a salute at Charles.

"I am Captain Gorgio Pantakos, and we are at your service."

Quite suddenly, Chas recognized him.

"I remember your name being Dedan a few years back, correct?"

Pantakos jolted.

"No. You are thinking of someone else."

"Right," Goodnight said. "Somebody who got involved in some little war and decided to settle things out by turning a bunch of the local yokels with flame-throwers loose on a medium-sized village. And there wasn't an unfriendly troop within parsecs."

"That wasn't me," Pantakos insisted.

"Yeh, it was," Goodnight said flatly. "As if war wasn't a shitty enough deal. I wanted to have a look at your team . . . which doesn't seem to have accomplished anything, other than tearing up some bars and terrorizing whores.

"Now I have.

"Even without recognizing you, Dedan, I was pretty sure I was going to terminate your contracts, if I didn't get reasons to change my mind. Of which there don't seem to be any. This poor goddamned cluster's got enough problems without sociopaths who can't hold it under control.

"You and your crew are restricted to barracks, are to be disarmed immediately and transshipped back to whatever sewer the poor goddamned Khelat found you in."

Pantakos/Dedan flushed, and, perhaps thinking he could still intimidate, moved his hand to a heavy service blaster, worn crossdraw.

It was an incorrect response.

Goodnight touched his cheek, went bester. Before Pantakos's hand touched the butt of his blaster, Goodnight had it in his own grip. He twisted, and the bone snapped.

Goodnight came out of bester in time to hear Pantakos yelp in agony.

Goodnight spun him about and kicked him hard in the butt. Pantakos stumbled forward, fell on his face in front of his formation.

One man reached for his gun, froze seeing Grok

leveling down on him and the bodyguards unslinging their blast rifles.

"As I have read from ancient Earth, you are a daisy if you do not," the alien growled.

No one moved for a long moment, then the group turned, started back inside.

No one bothered, until Goodnight shouted, to pick up the moaning Pantakos from the dirt.

"What the hell was that about being a daisy?" Goodnight asked.

"I read about some Earth gunman named Doc Earp saying it at a battle called the KO Corral."

"Find a leetle more macho line next time, all right?" Goodnight said.

"I cannot believe," Grok said, without replying to Chas's insult, eyes never leaving the retreating motlies, "that you have just turned moral on me, Chas."

"Sorry," Goodnight said. "I didn't sleep very well last night. I won't disappoint you again."

"I mean no insult, lady," the man in the oil-stained boilersuit said. "But *you're* evaluating my team's performance?"

Jasmine King could have, possibly should have, lost her temper. Instead, she found it funny.

They were in the cramped, rather littered office in a monstrous hangar, almost full of small patrol ships with various crimps or parts of their skin missing, and women and men with tools bustling about.

"You mean someone who looks like I do can't know anything about technicals?"

Jasmine wore a dark-colored, skintight coverall, slash-cut high boots, and a stylishly small pistol, carried in a shiny rig that matched her outfit.

"Oh, no. Oh, dear no," the stubby man said, coloring. "That'd be dumb thinking, just to start with. What I meant was, well, us techies are generally at the shitty—sorry for the language—end of the stick when it comes to everything. And, uh, you, uh . . ." his voice trailed off.

"I'm not sure I believe you, Mr. Ells," Jasmine said, grinning. "But I'll accept what you say. For the moment.

"My team, as you might have heard, will be overseeing the freelance military people in the Khelat System. Which includes your Maintenance and Operations Section."

"I hope, to be frank, that you're better than the Khelat," Ells said. "Because they've got the damndest assortment of for-hire idiots soldiering for them that I've ever seen. . . . And then there'll be nobody in other slots where there should be someone."

"Such as?"

"Those half-wits that call themselves commandos just for openers, who shouldn't be allowed a kid's knife, for fear they'll cut themselves."

"They're gone."

Ells eyes rounded.

"That's a good start. Now, what about hiring some pilots? The Khelat, may they be forever blessed, think that all it takes to push a starship around is to be a member of royalty."

"I've seen the scrap heap," King said.

"They can wreck 'em faster than we can fix 'em, and that's the pure truth."

"That's something we'll have to look at."

"I don't know if we're gonna run out of princes or TAC ships first," Ells said. "By the way, did you notice that the easy way to tell a prince—other than he's got more jewels than anybody—is he generally speaks Alliance instead of Khelat?"

"I've noticed that," Jasmine said. "And wondered why."

"I'm not real sure," Ells said. "But I think it makes them superior to the other swine they're ordering around. And nobody's wising them up to the fact that makes the silly bastards strangers in their own land."

He shook his head.

"I've gone through your people's fiches, and also the maintenance records," King said, changing the subject. "I figure you're putting in, each, about sixty hours per local week. You need more time off."

"Sixty hours is what's on the clock, about right," Ells said. "They get pissy when we bill what we really do."

"That'll change," King said. "From now on, straight time bills . . . or we can flip you all to salary."

"Salary," the man said in wonderment. "Just like the sojer boys and girls what wear the pretty suits with all the rank. My, my. I'll have to talk to my people."

"Get back to me," King said. "Now, a question, or maybe the start of questions. What's your biggest complaint about the Khelat?"

"Well, they're likable enough. But they're rock stubborn. And, well, I can't say they're lazy. But they seem to have the opinion that some god decided they didn't have to work. Especially not when it comes to manual labor.

"Which is why my team's so damned big. We're supposed to be training them to do their own wrenching, their own electronics design and such. . . . But we're the boys and girls who do the work, most times. And if there's any kind of error, and one of us is anywhere close, it's our fault.

"They're brave enough, I suppose. As long as things are going their way, and then it's fanny bar the door and get out from under the bugout.

"Or so I've been told. I keep myself away from what should be called the front lines. Not that there's been a whole lot of real fighting in the year I've been on this contract."

Jasmine nodded slowly.

"I just wanted to show up, introduce myself, and give you a new indent number for anything you need. . . . And I'm a hell of a system analyst, I should warn you."

"Lady . . . sorry . . . I've never padded a contract. At least not yet. Although these Khelat have made me think about it."

"Very well," Friedrich von Baldur said. "We have rid ourselves of the deadwood and figured out, tentatively, who we'll be keeping."

The team had taken up quarters, at least temporarily, in a wing of the Rafar Arms.

"I might add that Jasmine has discovered our contract cuts almost equal what we're charging these Khelat, so that should make them happy.

"It appears that it is now time to show our employers that we have another set of teeth. We should be committing to something a bit spectacular, somewhat lethal, and, needless to say, not purposelessly hazardous.

"And then it shall be time to hire some competent underlings of our own."

EIGHT

"Target, target, gimme a stinking target," Riss chanted as she scanned the seven lit screens set up in the hotel suite.

"I'm having trouble believing this," King said. "The Khelat have been at war with the Shaoki for at least five generations, so you think they'd keep close tabs on their enemies, right? Wrong. I can't find anything that looks interesting to take out that'll irk the Shaoki and knock the socks off the Khelat that's not based on data at least five E-years old. Even here in the outback, people move their assets around . . . especially once they've been scoped."

"Lemme see the old stuff," Riss asked.

"Well . . . up there, screen C . . . I'll throw this up."

The holo showed a rather ornate building, block-wide, in the center of a city.

"This is a still of a high-speed run a recon ship made just about five years ago in the Shaoki III system on the fourth world, which is Irdis, the Shaoki capital, over the planet's second city, and military capital, Berfan."

King touched buttons.

"If you look carefully, you can see two antiaircraft sites on the roof. . . . Plus down here, on all four corners, armored lifters on standby, which suggests a possible target of importance."

She keyed another sensor, and the recon's record ran, blurring passage over a very large city with towering buildings.

"The Shaoki build close together," King added as an aside. "Not nearly as much money as the Khelat. Or maybe they're just friendlier.

"That recon ship had a Khelat pilot, but I suspect he was the front man and some for-hire sort was the real driver.

"Two years later, for some unknown reason, they decided to make another pass over Berfan. They used, according to the records, the same approach the previous recon had plotted, and got blown out of the sky for their laziness. If laziness it was."

"Hmm," M'chel said. "If that building's still there, and still in use, I'd think it was probably important . . . at least to one of their chiefs.

"Now, to figure out a way in . . . and a way out. I suspect I need to put Grok and you in motion."

The prisoner was ushered into the small, bare holding room.

"This is the Shaoki agent, Toas," the prison officer said.

"I am not—"

The officer, without looking disturbed, slammed Toas into the wall, headfirst.

"That is enough," Friedrich said.

The officer looked surprised but obeyed. He crossed his arms and took a position against one wall.

"I will talk to him alone, if you please," von Baldur said.

The officer started to object.

"I have permission from your deputy warden."

The officer nodded and marched out.

Toas looked at him with scorn.

"Sit down," Friedrich said, extending a hand to the other chair in the room, on the other side of the table, bare except for a solid-sided suitcase, Friedrich sat at.

"I'll stand."

"Suit yourself," Friedrich said indifferently.

Toas looked puzzled.

"I want to talk to you about the Shaoki beliefs," von Baldur said.

"I know of none."

Von Baldur nodded, as if expecting that answer. He touched the side of his briefcase twice.

"There are, as I am sure you've guessed, listening devices in this cell. Now they are receiving nothing but static. You can speak honestly."

"Why should I trust you?"

"A good question. I surely would not, if I were you."

Toas's puzzlement grew.

"You come from the village of Jahka?" Friedrich asked.

"There is no longer such a village."

"What happened to it?"

"It was leveled and those people who did not flee to the city were named bandits. Like me."

"Why?"

"Because . . ." Toas looked about, then firmed his lips. "Because Prince Quan wanted our land that we had held for generations, for a *maln* plantation."

"Of course," Friedrich said.

Toas blinked.

"You believe me?"

"I believe you," von Baldur said. "You are not the

first, nor the tenth, farmer I have seen called a bandit because he stood against a rich man. Have you ever met a real bandit?"

"No," Toas said, then hesitated. "Yes, yes, I have. Once, when I was a boy. The villagers had taken him when he was lying drunk, after having raped one of our women. They hanged him to a harvester's top brace."

"Good," von Baldur said, standing. "That is all I need."

"Wait," Toas said. "Can you help me?"

"Do you want me to?" von Baldur said. "That attracts attention."

"I do not care," Toas said. "I was just ready to kill myself when you called me out. I do not care what happens to me, especially if there is some way you can help me get revenge on Prince Quan."

"For yourself?"

"For myself . . . for my family . . . for my village."

"I shall see what I can do," Friedrich said. "Perhaps have you paroled to me as being particularly helpful in understanding the ways of the Shaoki."

A smile that wasn't humorous came to Toas.

"You are a devious man."

"I try to be."

The lifter moved slowly toward the guard shack. There were two sentries.

One stepped out of the booth, saw the stanchion flag with the twin stars of a general, waved the lifter into the compound, and stiffened into a salute, not seeing the three outlanders—Jasmine, Grok, and Riss—in the opaque rear.

The lifter moved past the booth.

"Interesting," Grok said softly. "He didn't bother

looking inside, nor checking our ID. 'Sloppy' is the word for it, I suspect, which is somewhat frightening, considering this compound is one of the main arms depots."

"Umm," Riss agreed. She was looking back through the rear window. The sentry lowered his blaster and stared with a look of utter hatred at the lifter.

"The people really love their royalty, don't they?" she said. "Since the guard couldn't see through the tinted plex, he must've assumed we're some sort of prince."

"Or else he just hates generals," Grok said.

"There is that," Riss agreed. "So what do you have for me?"

"You shall see."

The three walked down the waist-high stacks of missiles. The warehouse was dimly lit, but she could make out the stenciling on the crates.

"Ten . . . fifteen years old, Alliance issue," she said. "Remote Pilot Vehicles. Not the fastest around, as I recall. Nuclear option, which isn't what I'm thinking of. Yet. I remember seeing some of these back when I was a 'cruit."

"These are supposedly out-atmosphere fitted," Jasmine said.

"I guess for this part of the world," Riss said, "they must be state of the art. Have you had a tech find out if they're still in banging order?"

"No," Grok said. "I wanted you to see them first and decide if they further your scheme."

"I'm not sure," Riss said. "No. I do have a bit of an idea. Assuming Chas comes through with what we need."

*   *   *

It was Chas Goodnight's first trip to Boyington, a spaceflight recruitment center for that part of the First Galaxy.

He'd always thought that he loved a party; the wilder the better. Unfortunately, the craziness on Boyington reminded him more of the way he used to carry on as a teenage recruit.

Pilots, engineers, and navigators filled the hotel bars, and it seemed the screaming and hollering went on all day and night.

Fortunately, Goodnight had made his connections before he lost his temper at anyone, and was negotiating with them in a drawing room of the Bishop Inn.

He decided that two out of three contacts wasn't bad.

Redon Spada, the super patrol ship pilot, had taken an assignment, no one quite knew where.

Tough, Goodnight figured. The flier, who seemed about half in love with Riss, could nurse his broken heart—and depleted bank account—when he got back.

Besides, Goodnight thought, Riss probably wasn't in the mood for anyone making calf eyes at her, as she was still recovering from her jarhead colonel's death.

At least he'd tracked down Inchcape, who'd run the destroyers on Gentric, and Vian, with his patrol ships.

"All right," Goodnight said briskly. "We need both of you and your ships, plus anybody you know who happens to have a spare cruiser up her sleeve, and enough armed transports to mount a smallish sort of invasion. Plus, Star Risk will want you to double the number of ships you brought last time."

"This one sounds fat," Inchcape, who was stocky and no-nonsense, said, a touch of greed in her voice.

"It is," Goodnight said. "We're working for a legit

planetary government, and we aren't doing anything that might piss the Alliance off.

"We'll go either ten thousand plus real expenses per day per ship, or a flat rate of a hundred g's per week. Plus combat bonus, insurance, and compensation for injuries or death. Don't bother trying to bargain. I don't have time to footle around."

"I can round up another three or four more DDs," Inchcape said. "And I'll take the daily rate. I'm cautious."

"The same rate for patrol ships as for destroyers?" Vian asked suspiciously.

"Yep," Goodnight said. "We'll be putting you into stickier places, and more of them. You'll earn it."

"Let me try one," Vian said. "I'll tentatively accept the day rate like Captain Inchcape here. . . . But I want a clause that I can renegotiate after, say, six weeks, when I've had a chance to personally evaluate the situation."

"I'll put it in the contract," Goodnight said. "But you'll swing by your toes before you get a raise."

Vian looked closely at Goodnight, then reluctantly nodded.

"And I'll be able to round up four more of the McGees," he said. "But they'll be delayed, since they've still got the Mark I power plant, and I want them refitted before I'll trust them."

"You'd better set to, then," Goodnight said. "Now, I'll transfer, say, a million to each of your accounts as earnest money as soon as the contracts are signed. You'll be paid weekly, money deposited to your accounts offworld. We're not having people staggering around, waving credits in all directions on the client worlds. Not that there's much worth buying, anyway."

Goodnight felt satisfied. He'd gotten everything and everyone that was on the shopping list.

Then something struck him.

"Man does not live by air strikes alone," he muttered.

"Pardon me?" asked Vian.

"Never mind," Goodnight said. "Something I seem to have forgotten."

"I am sorry," the official said, very clearly showing no sorrow at all, "but the prisoner Toas cannot be released to your company."

Friedrich glowered into the pickup.

"I must remind you that I speak with the highest authority!"

"I am not questioning that," the official said. "However, the prisoner Toas was killed yesterday. Shot while attempting to escape."

He almost smiled.

Von Baldur decided not to say anything. He was damned if he would let this pissant little murderer get his goat.

He nodded brusquely, cut off the connection, and mentally made a note of the official's name.

Friedrich was a firm believer in the old saw that what goes around comes around.

Mik Hore's battalion was a little more what Star Risk needed.

"Strictly advisory?" Hore asked into the screen. He was an older man, balding, stocky, and looked more like a prosperous banker than a warrior.

"Of course not," Riss said. "If somebody shoots at you, you better damned well shoot back."

"What's the ROE?" Hore said.

"The Rules of Engagement are very simple," M'chel said. "Anybody who's got a gun and isn't Khelat is to be assumed as the enemy. If somebody has a gun, waving it in any of your people's general direction, don't become a target.

"But, on the other hand, if no gun, your troopie might get his or her contract broken. Or worse case, if it's an obvious fraud, they could be turned over to the locals."

"I don't like that," Hore said.

M'chel didn't respond, and there was nothing but the hum of the N-space transmission for a moment.

"However," Hore said, "we've been a time without a contract. These damned fools around my part of the sector seem to want to hire killers rather than people who specialize in building killers."

"That's why they're hiring mercenaries, not training their own," Riss said.

"I guess so," Hore said.

Again, he considered.

"I'll admit that your terms are more than generous," he said. "And if we've got to be under the local law . . . I guess we can live with it. As soon as we can hire some horses, we'll be riding on over."

"You might want to wait until I can give you an escort," Riss said. "We've got a DD squadron under a woman named Inchcape we'll run over to you. Be a shame to have your asses blown off before you even get issued the local uniform."

M'chel found, and hired, two more tightly knit and well-trained units before reporting her successes to Prince Barab.

Jasmine considered the mercenaries she personally had hired and decided that none of them would be worth, in Goodnight's phrase, sour owl crud in a firefight.

Which was exactly what she wanted, since the dozen women and men were the part of the military that never gets mentioned in the romances.

These were highly skilled clerks, some payroll, others inventory, all cross-trained, most of them formerly part of the Alliance military bureaucracy.

Jasmine realized Star Risk was coming up in the world, since she had never needed more than one clerk to take care of payroll and such before. But then, Star Risk had never taken on a good chunk of a galactic cluster as a client and brought their own logistical support before, either.

"Since I'm in charge of your division," King said, "I guess I'm supposed to give you the welcome aboard speech. Consider it given.

"I'll be through in a minute, and you'll get shown where your quarters and mess are here in the hotel. By the way, we now occupy most of it, and it's secure. Other than that, I'll give you two cautions:

"First, your sort of soldiering doesn't include killing or getting killed. This is one reason you're going to stay in mufti, so nobody thinks of you as an instant target. You'll be issued gas guns and grenades for self-protection in the event of an emergency. There isn't much of a threat here on Khelat II, but there are a few people who don't seem to like outsiders. Stay where the bright lights are, and keep a low profile.

"Second, and most important: You are working for the woman or man with a gun, at the sharp end. Don't ever, ever forget it, or you'll have your contract broken and be on the way back to wherever you came from.

"Some paper shufflers seem to feel that it's their money that's being spent, and think it delightful to make life difficult. Don't become one of them.

"That's all. You're dismissed."

Jasmine decided she wanted a drink. Making speeches wasn't her forte.

The patrol boats came in low over Rafar City, lifted, and set neatly down, holding a diamond formation.

The Khelat had barely reassured themselves that they weren't Shaoki when, an hour later, Inchcape's five destroyers, with Goodnight aboard the lead ship, came in for a landing, a little less showily than Vian's troops.

Behind them, in hastily leased transports, came Hore's battalion, six hundred strong.

M'chel was one step closer to her showing of the flag raid.

Riss took time off from planning her raid to put Hore's mercenaries and the other units to work.

As promised, she broke them down into squad-sized units, assigned each of those tiny units to a Khelat infantry or artillery unit.

"So where do you want us to begin teaching?" Hore asked.

"This is a blaster," Riss said. "It goes bang. It goes bang out this end. . . ."

"That bad?"

"I always assume the worst," M'chel said.

The huge, fur-covered being on screen surveyed his caller.

"Being Grokkonomonslf. It is a surprise."

"And for me, as well," Grok said in the unpronounceable-by-humans language. "How do you like being in a world of nonthinkers?"

"I am quite enjoying it," the other replied. "I can study their illogic back through the ages and wonder yet again why they are a dominant culture."

"I attempted the same enlightenment through study of their philosophy," Grok said. "And am getting nowhere. Perhaps I should have followed your lead, and considered history."

"I do not know about that," the other one said. "For I'm as baffled now as I was when I began my research. Maybe I should have taken a position with a university instead of working for the Alliance, and also undertaken civilian matters rather than the military. But the credits were excellent, and I thought the soldiers would be a trifle simpler to understand. I think I was mistaken.

"But I assume you made this com not to commiserate with me."

"True," Grok said. "I need a small favor."

"For which you are prepared to indebt yourself?"

"I am," Grok said. "But not myself to a great deal, although the client's money is readily available."

"What is it you need?"

"The after-action report, fairly recent, on what occurred to an Alliance planetary advisory team. It is classified."

The other being held out his paws, palm up, a gesture learned from humans that he was somewhat proud of.

"Now, what do you and I care about classifications? What I have in mind for my fee, for performing such a simple task as going to the archives and pawing about, is a certain piece of what the humans called sculpture, which is their term for shaped and polished rock. It is fairly old, and is what is known as a fingering piece, by a human named Moore. But it is expensive."

"I am not concerned about that," Grok said. "I am well compensated for what I am doing."

The other one growled in pleasure.

"Then we have, I think, what humans call a deal."

"Have you ever done any suicide bombing before?" Technician Ells asked Riss.

"Once," she answered. "I didn't like it much."

"Didn't the cutout work?"

"It did. But still."

No rational being likes killing himself, even if that "death" is merely experienced through a guidance helmet on an Remote Pilot Vehicle. But there's still a shock. Alliance programmers found this out a very long time ago, and so the piloting helmet was equipped with an automatic cutoff for when the RPV was in its final target dive or when it was hit.

But it still "hurt," and there were psychiatric casualty wards specializing in slow and gentle retrieval of "pilots' souls."

"I've done a little rewiring," Ells went on. "You'll have a sensor in your hand. When you hit it, you'll be tossed back into the next RPV. Two clicks and you'll be back aboard whatever ship you're basing yourself from. All right?"

M'chel took a deep breath.

"All right. Load everything onto one of the destroyers, and let's start the ball downhill."

"I must say," the prince, who wore old-fashioned eyeglasses, said, "one advantage of your mercenary service, General, is that you do not insist on delving into, and criticizing, the customs of my people."

He smiled, ingratiatingly.

Friedrich looked blank.

The hidden bud in his ear had suddenly whispered into life. It was Goodnight's voice:

"Riss, her two DDs, and three patrol ships are off."

"Am I boring you, General?"

Von Baldur brought himself back.

"Of course not, Prince Jer," he said. "I'm just putting your thoughts together with what I already know of your system."

"These are not mere thoughts," Jer said, "but well-proven principles of ruling."

"Of course. Go on."

"At one time, our cluster was peaceful, happy, until Shaoki embraced apostasy and fell easily into their present anarchic state. Naturally, like all disbelievers in the natural order of things, they insisted on looking for converts, which is why they support those dissidents we have hired you to suppress in the hills.

"Of course, what these bandits purport to believe—that they want a louder voice in our government—is not true, since they wish a complete change, and want to become Shaoki quislings when our government is toppled.

"But that shall never happen."

Friedrich von Baldur looked into the prince's glittering eyes. The gleam was not a reflection from his glasses.

"Of course not," Friedrich agreed.

"Let's give it a go," Riss said, pulling on the pilot helmet on board Inchcape's flagship, the *Fletcher*. Ells had added two com inputs, one linked to the bridge, the other to a link with Vian aboard his patrol ships.

There were two realities then, one a little ghostlike, from the nose of one missile "looking" at blank steel, the other Riss's perspective aboard the ship.

"Launch me," she said.

The door slid open and she was forced out into normal space. Just "below" was the Shaoki world of Irdis.

"Launch one," a voice said. "Launch two . . . launch three . . ."

She "pushed," and the missile drive sent her downward, on a preset homing on the city of Berfan. She had a chance to relax for a few minutes, which she didn't like. There was no reason to feel claustrophobic, she reminded herself, since she was very much aware of reality and she was leaning back in a comfortable chair aboard the *Fletcher*.

She definitely didn't like being a bomb, even though all logic told her she was full of ham hocks.

Riss touched a sensor, added an external mike aboard the missile to her audio display, heard the crackle of metal heating, then the hiss of atmosphere.

She keyed her helmet to a GPS, made sure the missile was still on target, then checked a prox detector, which told her she was about eighteen miles above the planetary surface.

Her hands, back aboard the *Fletcher,* overlaid the course the recon ship had taken years earlier.

She jumped as an alarm shrilled.

A voice in her ear told her she had been acquired on radar.

"I'd guess," the *Fletcher*'s weapons officer said, "we'll have an alpha-alpha launch in about. . . . We do have a launch."

"Give me a slow count," Riss said.

"Forty-seven . . . forty . . . thirty-two . . . I'd think about getting out of there . . . eighteen . . ." the voice said calmly.

"On my way." M'chel hit her sensor, and suddenly she was in the second missile, behind the one she'd been piloting.

"Eight . . . five . . . four . . . three . . . impact!"

Just ahead of her, the Shaoki countermissile exploded, and there was nothing left of her first missile but an expanding ball of hot gas.

Riss concentrated on closing on the target.

"I want another count," she said.

"Twenty seconds to impact . . . fifteen . . . ten . . . get out of there . . . five . . ."

Again, Riss "jumped" to the third missile that had been launched.

But it wasn't necessary. The Shaoki battery that had attacked the first launch wasn't responding. The second missile, set to echo the first's course, had blasted through the impact cloud from the first, and Shaoki Target Acquisition hadn't picked it up.

That missile smashed into the target building and set off a perfectly satisfactory explosion.

"*Something* was in there besides shredded wheat," she muttered, and brought the third missile up into a low orbit over the city.

She scanned hastily for another target, saw a temptingly large building on the horizon, thought about it for a minute.

"Naah," she growled. "With my luck it'd be an orphanage, not an army headquarters."

She hit the self-detonate button and pulled out just before the third missile went off, and she was back aboard the *Fletcher*.

"Good going," the weapons officer said.

"I went and said it very clear/I went and shouted in their ear," Riss recited.

"One for Dov," she said to herself, and went looking for the officers' mess.

NINE

"I have been pondering this matter of the building you blew up on Irdis," Grok said to Riss. It was a week after she'd returned from her raid.

"Which," Jasmine put in, "turns out, I've found, through the miserable monitoring system the Khelat have, to have been the central secret police station for the planet."

"There must be some people wanting to buy you a sufficiency of drunkenness for that," Goodnight said. "Hell, I'd buy you a shot or two. A dead cop—especially a secret-type cop—is a blessing of the gods."

"And so speaks the forces of law and order," Friedrich said.

Goodnight shrugged. "Speaking of which"—and he held out an evidence bag with two pistols in it—"here's a couple of bangsticks picked up in local raids. Maybe we can figure something out to lead to the six bandits the Khelat are always chasing around."

Von Baldur took them, examined them, and passed them to Jasmine.

"Perhaps the serial numbers might give us something?"

They were in the Star Risk suite in the Rafar Arms, surrounded by electronics and weaponry—a typical setting for the five. Piled around one com were copies of congratulatory messages from everyone from the king on down.

"We are all being ever so clever," Riss said, "and ignoring the fact that Grok has a point. . . . At least I assume he does."

"I do," the alien said. "Having little to do with the target."

He looked pompous, which is fairly hard for a fur-covered monster almost 2.5 meters tall who looks like he belongs on a homicidal rampage.

"I have been puzzled by the fact that there was only one—two, counting the failed attempt—recon of what should be considered an important division of Khelat's enemy. I applied the standard Vance-Sapir-Whorf equations to the situation—"

"Might I ask what they are?" Riss inquired.

"Briefly, they posit some analytical parameters to judge the behavior of a culture, working from the premise that language is not only a way of reporting experience, but also a way of defining experience."

"Say again your last," Goodnight said. "I don't understand. Also, I don't see how a set of equations bears on our young asses."

"Ah, but it does, it does," Grok said. "Consider this—the Khelat language is composed mostly of verbs in the imperfect form. So is Shaoki, by the way, since they come from a common root. You'll have noticed this, since there's a certain tendency for the Khelat to plan and schedule things most carelessly."

"Hoboy, is it ever," Riss said. "I was supposed to have a meet with Prince Barab this afternoon. He didn't show, and I commed his office. His aide was surprised at my getting a little upset. Perhaps, the aide said, he meant tomorrow afternoon."

"A good example," Grok agreed. "Now, if we extend this into practice, it can also mean that an action contemplated for the future can easily slip into the past. In other words, something that is going to be done, unless reality introduces, can be taken as done."

"Like recon jobs or raids," Riss said. "The Khelat thought about doing something about that ugly chunk of real estate I ended up leveling, never quite got around to it, but somehow, magically, it was taken care of."

"Exactly," Grok said, growling in pleasure.

"My paws and whiskers," von Baldur murmured. "That also means that if we send Force A out to take care of Situation B, and they report things are well flattened, they may or may not be telling the truth."

"In fact," Goodnight said, "from what we've seen, it means almost certainly not. So watch your flanks."

"And truth itself becomes a variable," King added. "Just as in subparticle physics."

"I still don't have a clue," Goodnight said. "And am damned glad I don't. Thank the god of evil bastards that I pray to that I also brought back, in addition to all these goddamned pilots wandering around wiggling their hands in the air, some headbangers."

"Oh?" King said. "I didn't catch that. Where did you bury their cost?"

"Ah-hah," Goodnight gloated. "You see, even though you're super with the figures, sometimes somebody can slither one past you.

"I'll show you directly. . . . As soon as I get back from doing a little dirty all my very own that I picked up. You don't get to have all the fun, M'chel."

He put a computer fiche on the biggest screen in the room, and the other four studied it carefully.

"You can see," Goodnight said, "I'll need your help, Grok."

"Given," the alien rumbled. "But only if I get to go along."

"I thought you'd say something like that."

Von Baldur nodded slowly.

"Good, Chas. We do need a follow-up to M'chel's little bit of nastiness. However . . . we are supposedly working to educate our Khelat brethren, correct?"

"Uh-oh."

"Take at least a handful of them with you, leading from the front and all that. There'll be a bonus for you. Do not, please, attempt to fool me by leaving them in the rear, and taking only a manifest with you."

"But Friedrich. This is going to be deep-space work, which requires a bit of experience."

"You never get experience without experience," von Baldur said, a bit sententiously.

"I gotta?" Goodnight said mournfully.

"As you would put it, you gotta," Friedrich said.

"You surely know how to ruin a good time."

"One more thing," von Baldur said. "*Do* try not to get killed."

"I'll do that little thing," Goodnight said. "Death spoils fun even more than you do."

TEN

The ship smelled mightily of used feet.

It wasn't because of slobbery.

Goodnight's mercenaries, in their earlier incarnation as regular soldiers, had been made familiar with soap. The Khelat were notoriously sanitary people.

The cause was stuffing far too many beings into a patrol ship intended to fit four or five fairly friendly people. Plus suits, plus gear, plus rations. Extra water was in an auxiliary pack bolted to each patrol ship's skin.

Goodnight had forty-three raiders to choose from, and had chosen thirty. For his mission, he thought more than that would just get in the way.

In addition, there was Grok, his large tool kits, and ten Khelat.

They were officer cadets, which Goodnight found meant they were connected to the royal family in one way or another.

He didn't like it, felt he was setting himself up, but didn't have much of a choice, especially since Prince Barab had publicly proclaimed, without, fortunately, being specific, the Best and Brightest of Khelat were Fighting Back.

"They'd damned well better," Goodnight said. "Costing us enough in fuel."

No one bothered to remind him that he wasn't picking up the bill.

Grok and Goodnight had spent two weeks in space deep inside the Shaoki sphere of control, alternating their watch with one or another of Vian's patrol ships. They couldn't assign the task out, because they had only an idea of what kind of target they were looking for . . . and a very vague one at that.

Unsurprisingly, Jasmine King found it for them, making an intercept of a propaganda 'cast from the Shaoki worlds on the might and majesty of the Shaoki fleet.

She'd frame-by-framed the 'cast and found an awesome shot of the Shaoki battle fleet, ready and waiting.

The holo shot had been awesome enough for her to triangulate the location of the fleet, hanging in space off the capital world of the Shaoki II system, Thur. She made the assumption that the fleet wouldn't be kept in the boondocks but close at hand, for easy self-stroking by the Shaoki council.

Vian took out a patrol ship and found the fleet just where Jasmine had said it would be.

Goodnight was starting to get elaborate ideas, and decided the Shaoki fleet wasn't a target—they didn't have enough warships for a direct confrontation—but a tool.

Monitoring from the patrol ship found a lot of signals from the starships sent to a single location on Thur, below them.

That gave them a target.

And that put the raid in motion.

All Goodnight wanted was one lousy Shaoki ship to become his tool, a weapon.

The raiders went out, in their four ships, with a single destroyer stationed at the last jump point before entering the Shaoki sector, covering their back door and exit.

The four patrol ships made the final jump, one at a time. Goodnight was assuming that none of the Shaoki electronic lookouts would be ready for something that gave the radar signature of a 2 cm ball bearing.

The McGee ships were very stealthy.

Goodnight was right—unless the Shaoki were stealthy in a very different way, and had set a trap.

Again, they waited, but only for a day or two, to verify their original observations, plus to confirm the general times when work craft came up from the planet.

That established, the four ships crept toward the rough globe formation that was the heavy Shaoki craft orbital station.

"We might as well suit up," Goodnight ordered. "At least it'll smell better."

There were two blasters on Friedrich von Baldur's desk that had been given him by Jasmine. They were current-issue Alliance, a little battered.

Von Baldur rechecked the serial number on the first against a list of numbers. No match. He did the same with the second pistol; found no match again.

He did the same with another list; found nothing.

Most interesting. Those two pistols had been taken from the corpses of "bandits" by Khelat soldiers. Yet their numbers weren't on the list of pistols stolen or taken from the Khelat, nor on the list of weaponry brought in by the recent advisory team.

So where did they come from?

While Jasmine was pawing around, she'd also found something interesting in the government accounting office, made a copy.

Von Baldur thumbed through a printout, admiring the work.

It was very neat.

Somebody had been stealing the military blind.

Von Baldur, as an ex-supply officer and a most experienced thief, knew when and where to go looking.

There were some questions:

Was the thief or were the thieves part of the mercenary operation or was the thief or were the thieves Khelat?

If they were Khelat, how high did the thievery go? Von Baldur wasn't a damned fool, and if it went to the king, he wasn't going to make a lot of noise.

In fact, part of him wanted to link up with the thieves, in exchange for a good piece of the action.

He decided he'd have Grok look into the matter when he finished tarting about with Goodnight.

"All right," Goodnight said. "Move out."

Vian's patrol ship hung in space, three kilometers from the hulking battle cruiser Goodnight had picked for a target. He'd chosen it because it was positioned sloppily in the globe formation, and he hoped carelessness in one thing meant they'd be slack in other areas.

Also because it was one of the few surplus Alliance ships he was sure he could find in *Jane's*, which gave him a fairly good blueprint of what lay inside.

Vian cycled atmosphere back into the patrol ship's tanks, killed the artificial gravity, and opened both locks.

A bit of paper, forgotten on a bulkhead table, was whipped out into space with the last trace of air.

Goodnight motioned, and Grok and his troops fed themselves out into space, immediately clipping on to one another as they exited.

One soldier lagged behind.

That figured, Goodnight thought. One of the two Khelat trainees with his team.

He beckoned impatiently, and the soldier reluctantly clambered out of the lock, and, forgetting to clip on, started to float away.

A soldier grabbed the man by his air cycler and clipped a lead on him. Fine, Goodnight thought. He can go into battle on a leash. We won't tell anyone afterward, unless he really screws up.

The Shaoki battle cruiser, big, graceful, old-fashioned, almost two kilometers long, was close.

Goodnight passed a line to the others, and they spread out.

"Behind" him, other raiders were debouching from the other four ships.

All mikes were open. Goodnight had given orders that no one was to break silence except to give an alarm.

He said, unconsciously whispering, "After me."

Steam boiled from low-power jets, and the ragged formation of roped men moved steadily toward the cruiser's stern.

Goodnight killed what little speed he'd amassed, and the raiders mostly touched down silently near the stern of the huge ship.

Goodnight had planned for that, figuring the drive area of the ship would be the noisiest and the least likely to be listening to odd clangs on the skin.

He pointed to five of his men, who deployed just below the cruiser's top fins.

In normal wartime, they would have found an entrance through a port or even through the drive, although that had always given Goodnight the kohlrobbies, figuring someone was about to light it off just when he was making his crawl. Although, if someone did, he certainly wouldn't know about it.

Instead, since Goodnight had no interest in capturing the cruiser, shaped charges were positioned in a rectangle, tied together with det cord, and a line was led off a few dozen meters to a hellbox.

The mercenary demo specialist bowed, handed the box to Goodnight.

Chas took off the two safeties, touched the sensor.

The results were more than satisfactory.

The charges went off as planned, tearing a rectangle out of the double ship's skin and lifting it back like a sardine can's lid.

Air roared out into space, and water crystals became ice and curled into nothing.

Goodnight wondered how many men and women he'd just killed, but didn't have time for mawkishness.

He leapt down, the cruiser's artificial gravity still working, into a large hydraulic control space.

Goodnight beckoned his warriors inside. They poured down and spread out.

Except for one man, who huddled back against a bulkhead. It was the same Khelat that'd hesitated on the patrol ship.

Goodnight clicked on an exterior speaker.

"Let's go, let's go, let's go!" he chanted, and the men ran toward two ports.

Except for that Khelat.

"Move out, troop!" he shouted.

The man whimpered, made no move.

"The hell with you," Goodnight shouted, never that calm in the best of times, let alone in an assault. "Damned coward!"

He made for the port, letting his blast rifle down into firing position, but something made him turn.

The Khelat was moving, pointing his own rifle at Goodnight.

Goodnight didn't bother talking, but blew a fist-sized hole in the man's suit and chest.

Then he went out, after his men.

The cruiser's automatic damage-control doors hadn't worked, or weren't turned on.

The cruiser was entirely in a vacuum, and its skeleton crew had died, most without realizing it.

They made their way through the ship, found no one living.

In the control room, Grok had set down his tool chests and was considering the navigation area.

"If I recollect," he rumbled, holding out a power wrench, "the overrides should be in here. Now, Chas, if you'll give a hand with these panel fasteners . . ."

"We don't have that kind of time," Goodnight said, and sent four quick blaster bolts into the panel corners.

It clanged free to the deck.

"How terribly direct," Grok said, peering inside.

"Ah yes," he said. "Here and here are the sensors to keep one from setting a course into the heart of his own sun. If you would do the honors, Mr. Goodnight?"

Chas obeyed, his rifle flashing twice.

"Now, if you care to set the course you've prepared . . ."

Goodnight had prepared a fiche that should work on any Alliance nav computer, and went to a control couch and fired up the device, ever grateful the Alliance built its electronics for worst-case scenarios.

Such as trying to operate in a vacuum with gauntlets.

He fed the fiche into the proper slot. The computer beeped complainingly, and lights lit.

Goodnight considered them, touched sensors.

Slowly, the objecting lights went out as Goodnight corrected the fiche's preset present position to match the cruiser's actual location.

"Hey, Skip," one of the mercenaries sent. "Somebody's trying to talk to us."

"Ignore them," Goodnight said. "Loose lips sink ships and all that. They'll worry more and shoot less—for awhile—if nobody's talking back to them."

He turned back to the computer.

"I think," he muttered, "that's about it. Power on, and to commence to traveling in . . . oh, five minutes.

"Hokay, troopies," he 'cast. "Time to hit the bricks. Momma's going home."

The thirty-nine women and men went, as ordered, to the center air lock, intended for mass debarkation.

Goodnight touched controls, said, "It should be on its way," and helped Grok with one of his toolboxes to the air lock and the others.

A noncom made a head count.

"Sir, we're short one man," he reported.

"We took one casualty," Chas said.

The sergeant frowned, waited for an explanation, then realized one wasn't coming.

"Out of here," Goodnight ordered, and the raiders went into the lock and cycled out into space.

They'd returned to the patrol ships when the cruiser stirred, the nav program cut in, and it swung, pointing down toward Thur.

Whatever the fleet had been transmitting to below on the planet was now ground zero for the cruiser, as it accelerated "downward" on secondary drive.

Maybe the target would be a nice, fat command Center, filled with nice, fat commanders.

"Now that should make quite a bang," Goodnight said. "Dov two, baddies zero."

But he was preoccupied with thoughts of that dead Khelat, who broke under pressure but still had enough courage to try to murder Goodnight.

For what? Being called a coward?

Stranger and stranger, Goodnight thought.

ELEVEN

"And here you have it," the alien told Grok. "Transmission under way, two items."

"Two?"

"The after-action report from the Alliance Advisory Team to the Khelat Systems, as requested. And a page from the Boanerges Fine Arts catalog on Earth. They specialize in Moores.

"I think you'll be interested in the report. . . . There is certainly something strange about the death of the advisory team's commanding officer.

"And the price on the Moore I want is circled."

"How expensive is it?"

"Now," the being said, "why do you care? You'll pass the price along to your client."

"Strong point," Grok agreed.

"I think," Friedrich von Baldur said, "it is time for us to prepare an Offensive against Shaoki." He deliberately put capital letters in his voice.

King Saleph looked nervous. Beside him, Prince Barab twitched a little in unconscious agreement with Saleph's hesitation.

"Do you think we're ready?" the king said. "The Alliance advisors—the gods rest their souls—seemed to think we were at least a year distant from any significant attacks on Shaoki."

"As, no doubt," von Baldur replied, "did the mercenaries we have replaced. Star Risk, unlike governments and firms that are first interested in building their bank account and secondarily in the needs of their client, believes in solving a problem as soon as possible. Therefore, we shall swing into action immediately."

"And what's this?" M'chel Riss asked as she yawned, very early, into the main Star Risk suite.

"This" was an ornately wrapped package with Riss's name on it.

"A bomb?" she asked.

"No," Jasmine said. "We've swept it."

"And?"

Neither of the other two responded.

"Awright," Riss snarled; tore the package open. It held a surprisingly tasteful bracelet, with gems worked in strange shapes. There was a note:

Perhaps we might see each other again without the confines of duty.

Wahfer

"How nice," Jasmine said.

M'chel put it on. "I guess so," she said. "I suppose it would be a good idea . . . professionally . . . to accept."

"Is he good-looking?"

"That has nothing to do with it!" Riss snapped.

She finally met Jasmine's eyes, and the two of them broke into laughter.

* * *

The call did come, and M'chel accepted.

The prince arrived in a long, dark lifter, with two bodyguards and a pilot.

He asked if she wanted to eat "real Earth food," and Riss declined, suppressing a shudder. She'd been trapped into real Earth food on too many worlds, always wondering why anyone bothered. The only people on Earth who ate well, as far as she could tell, were the French and the Chinese.

She said she was curious about the Khelat diet. Wahfer took her to an ostentatiously expensive restaurant. Haute cuisine consisted of many, many dishes on small plates, surprisingly spicy, eaten with the fingers.

Wahfer said it was customary to honor a guest by feeding him or her, and Riss, lying, said it was forbidden on her own worlds.

Wahfer, as the first course arrived, accompanied by a spiced wine that M'chel just sipped at, asked what she thought of his worlds.

"Why is it everyone here on Khelat always asks that question?" M'chel said.

Wahfer thought.

"I could be honest and say that it's politeness to care about the opinion of visitors, but honestly, it's because, I suspect, we are so far from the center of things that it really matters."

Riss nodded. That sounded honest, and she said that so far she found things interesting.

"One question, though," she said. "With all of the princes in your family, isn't there a certain amount of . . . let me call it competition?"

"Of course," Wahfer said. "That is the way the universe is designed, is it not? Each man strives to succeed, and it is not enough just for your own success, but you must have an equal or better's failure to compare it to."

"Ah," Riss said.

Two waiters changed their plates.

"By happenstance," she said, "did you have any dealings with the Alliance advisory team that was withdrawn?"

There was just a moment of hesitation, then Wahfer said, "No, not really."

Riss caught that moment, filed it.

The evening continued on an amiable note, if not, at least on Riss's part, with any romance.

Wahfer and one bodyguard escorted Riss to the Star Risk suite, and they were not invited in.

So, she thought as she rinsed her mouth of the spiced wine's taste with a shot of clean brandy, then poured herself a small decanter for a nightcap, Wahfer knows something was wrong with things.

That could be a contact worth developing.

TWELVE

Jasmine King wandered through the shopping district. Part of her mind was looking for something; another part was giggling gently about the way the romances portrayed "going undercover."

Certainly, she thought. Easy. Not a problem. Except when everybody around is dark complected, or perhaps of Earth-Asian descent.

And we'll ignore what happens when you're trying to look unobtrusive and all about you have tentacles. . . .

King slid through the crowded arcade streets, appearing to look at nothing, seeing everything.

She went in a shop here, a shop there, found an example of what she was looking for in a store that sold everything from jewelry to rice.

The item was in a corner, next to three or four exotically ugly statuettes. She was staring at a sealed case of Alliance-issue rations. Or so the packing stamp, with a serial number, had it.

But another serial number had been stamped over on the case.

She memorized both numbers as the shopkeeper approached.

"Missy is homesick for Alliance food?"

"Not particularly," Jasmine said. "I'm just curious where this came from."

"I do not remember very clearly," the shopkeeper started.

King took a bill from her pocket, extended it toward the man.

"Ah," he said, but no more.

King added a second bill.

The man's smile, lacking a few teeth, beamed.

"I am happy to be of service to the beautiful woman," he began.

The rations came from a warehouse with a camouflaged roof, sitting in a small valley about a kilometer outside Rafar City.

There was a long line of battered or economy lifters, ground vehicles, and people on foot, and a cluster of soldiers at the entrance. The warehouse was surrounded by razor wire, and there were perimeter alerts.

King sat in her lifter, about a half kilometer away, watching through binocs.

A customer would approach, talk to a soldier. Money would change hands, and crated goods would be brought out.

King was about to pull out and put in a full electronic surveillance when three military lifters flew low overhead, grounded at the rear of the warehouse, and soldiers started unloading crates and cases.

They moved fast, faster than King had seen soldiers move on Khelat so far, and in minutes the lifters were empty and took off.

King, feeling very naked without backup, followed at a good distance.

*   *   *

"I shall be happy to be of service," Grok told Jasmine. "My smoking gun turns out to be not as smoky as I'd wished, and needs further work. I would like an excuse to get out in the open air and do some honest work."

"Like killing people?"

"If the opportunity presents itself."

The lifter slid carefully down an alley, briefly onto a thoroughfare, then followed a freight-loading route. Grok, at the controls, went very low and very slow, without his lights, using an amplified-light headset to navigate.

The area was dark and little strewn. There was only an occasional movement, and neither of the lifter's occupants could tell if it was this world's version of rats or people intent on their own errands.

"This is the kind of district a man can get his head bashed in for him," Chas Goodnight observed.

"Or anyone else," Grok said. "Jasmine is getting too bold in following strange lifters about."

"Or else she's been doing better with the ol' marksmanship training than I thought," Goodnight said.

"I think I'm going to set it down here," Grok said. "That second warehouse she found is just around the corner, and I'll bet there's watchguards out."

"Shall I put the alarm on?" Grok said as he grounded the lifter.

"Either that or we're liable to come back to a stripper and have to hike home," Goodnight said. "But put the remote on vibrate, hey? It'd bother my nerves if it went off in the middle of a lovely bit of sneakery."

Goodnight wore black light-absorbing coveralls, and Grok depended on his dark fur and nightmare appearance to keep him safe.

Both beings wore weapons harnesses in the open. If they were stopped by anyone, they'd decided to shoot, rather than talk, their way out.

They slid around a corner, saw the storage building they wanted.

Goodnight, being the better second-story man, carefully checked the top of the razored fence.

There was a sensor about every ten meters.

Grok examined the nearest one closely. It was, surprisingly, clean and maintained. He rumbled in his throat.

Goodnight was considering the guard shacks spaced at regular intervals around the building. He took out a tiny pair of binocs, set them to normal light, and swept the area.

It was a bit brisk that night, a wind coming off the desert, and he saw no guards moving beyond the cozy security of the shacks.

That was good. He considered the sensors atop the razor wire, and took a shorter from a belt pouch to "wire" around the alarm.

Grok tapped him on the shoulder, shaking his head disapprovingly. Goodnight leaned closer. The alien's breath smelled, interestingly enough, of flowers.

"They've put all their eggs on one wire," Grok explained.

Chas puzzled.

Grok took wire cutters from his pouch, made two vertical cuts in the razor wire, starting from the ground, up about a meter, the two cuts about two meters apart. He carefully rolled up the wire until there was a door-sized opening.

Goodnight now understood. Grok wasn't being malapropistic—the Khelat had put all their caution on that upper wire and ignored what lay below it.

Brute force worked better than subtlety.

The two went through the hole in the wire, and, crouching, went to the building.

No faces looked out of the nearest guard shack.

Grok bowed to Chas, who considered the wall. A few meters away was the box that must have been some sort of interior alarm, most likely a motion detector.

Chas pointed to it, gave Grok a shorter.

The alien spliced a pair of wires to each side, working carefully, unhurriedly, and took the alarm out of circuit.

Goodnight went to the nearest door, sneered at the lock, picked it with four easy motions, and the two were inside.

They slid infrared goggles down, and Chas took a flash from his pouch, turned it on.

His other hand was on his gun, an old-fashioned but very silent single-shot projectile weapon.

The flash slid across crates and cases. All of them had Alliance supply numbers on them, some of them with a second set of numbers stenciled next to them.

Chas nodded. It was clear what was—

Overhead lights flared on, and the ambush was sprung.

"Sunnabeech," Goodnight yelled reflexively, going flat as a crew-served weapon on a landing chattered a burst across the crates.

Another fully automatic blaster opened up from another upper grid. The two were in a cross fire.

For one instant. Then Goodnight touched the bester switch in his cheek and accelerated. Now the blaster rounds came at him slowly, and there was more than enough time to roll out of the way before the bolts blew fist-sized holes in the concrete behind him.

He cursed at the puny suppressed weapon but aimed and shot the gunner of one weapon, who lolled out of the way, tilting the gun up, finger frozen on the trigger, shooting chunks out of the ceiling.

Grok had his enormous blaster out and shot out four of the overhead lights, then lofted a grenade toward the second auto weapon.

It went off short, but the loader jerked in terror and fed a belt crossways into the feeding trough.

The gun jammed.

Goodnight was running, zigging, as he reloaded his popgun.

There was a soldier at the steps leading up with a nice, lovely blaster.

Chas killed him, sent a grenade spinning up toward the crew-served gun, and had the man's blaster. Four more shots and the warehouse was back in darkness.

Goodnight's eyes took less than a second to adapt to the dark as he went flat.

Bolts crashed over his head, and Chas heard somebody scream as a grenade went off at the other side of the building.

Then he was up, doubling up the steps, and cut the two survivors of the crew-served down.

He scanned across the warehouse in time to see Grok's huge bulk hurtle over a railing, claws tearing at the other gunners.

Chas went back down the steps to the main floor.

A door came open, and there was a soldier with a portable spotlight.

Goodnight shot him, had the light as Grok, impossibly agile for his bulk, came down to the main floor.

"Come on," Goodnight shouted. "I think they might be on to us."

"As you have been known to say," Grok said unhurriedly. "No shiteedah."

A day later, at Friedrich's request, Star Risk, less Grok, assembled in one of their suite's living rooms. Antibugs were at full blast.

By now, Star Risk had taken over the entire wing of the hotel, and it was starting to look less like a luxury hotel than a highranker's barracks.

"Where's Grok?" von Baldur asked.

"I am here," Grok's voice came from a small transceiver. "In spirit and witness, if not the flesh. My apologies, but I am quite busy digging out some interesting data."

Friedrich frowned, then forgot about it.

"Here is what I have on this whole Alliance supplies situation. I first got interested because I was trying to find out just how crooked the Khelat government is, and thought these disappearing supplies, not to mention these unrecorded guns, might be."

"In the fond hopes," Goodnight put in, from where he sprawled on a sofa, "of maybe being able to cut ourselves in on the profits."

"The thought did occur to me," von Baldur admitted. "But I thought the risk might be inordinate.

"The closer I looked, it appeared as if it is a private swindle that someone is running on their own. An indication is that the supplies are being sold directly to the public. If the government were involved, I would guess they might find a more direct, and more profitable, way.

"I thought it might be interesting to find out who is running this. That produced the firefight of night before last. I sent in some of our troops—the ones we'd hired—to see what happened on the morning after.

"That warehouse had been cleaned up. It was empty, thoroughly cleaned. No blood, no torn-up crates, no bodies, no guns, but here and there on the walls were fresh splotches of paint.

"None of the guards on duty that night reported hearing or seeing anything.

"I went to the government's secret police. Again, nothing had happened of note.

"I made a couple of assumptions at this point—one that the conspirator or conspirators have high-level connections within the government, and that we would be well advised to back out of the matter to avoid personal risk."

"This," Goodnight said, "is after I almost get my young ass shot off. Let's make those kind of assumptions a little earlier next time, all right?"

Friedrich smiled briefly.

"What a shitty contract we did take," Riss said. "I say so, even if it was my idea."

"This is," von Baldur said gently, "the sort of things mercenaries learn to expect, my dear."

"But I don't have to like it," M'chel insisted.

"No," Jasmine agreed. "And if we can assume the situation might well get worse, I think we should keep a bag packed and a back door oiled."

"That is not a bad idea," Friedrich said.

M'chel came into the suite with a wheeze late the next afternoon.

Grok and Jasmine were waiting for her.

"Great gods, but it's hot out there." She went to a sideboard, poured down two glasses of ice water. "Too hot even for beer."

Grok handed Riss a folder.

"What is this, my birthday?"

"Hardly," the alien said. "This is the final after-action report of the Alliance Advisory Team assigned to these worlds."

Riss stiffened.

"It is yours," Grok said. "I procured it through a fellow who is studying in the Alliance Archives."

"What does it have about the late General Lanchester's death?" M'chel said, her voice suddenly cold.

"I can give you a précis," Grok said. "General Lanchester was killed on a low-level mission, sweeping for bandits in and around the village of Jaku. You can read the details that the senior Khelat, a Prince Jer, provided. He was a witness to the tragedy.

"However, there are other items of interest.

"The comment by the team executive officer, Major Wycliffe, after the report, and evidently added at a later date, says, and I quote, 'Due to the circumstances surrounding General Lanchester's death, we were withdrawn after reporting the details to First Mar Div headquarters.' "

"Which are?"

"Which are not in the report," Jasmine said, "and getting them is what took Grok so long. What is in the report is that Lanchester was in the field that day with a unit called Special Detachment 43. Which was commanded by Prince Jer, now strategic advisor to the king. A rather high-level officer for a seventy-five-man unit, created to work closely in the field with the Alliance Advisors. I tried to contact this unit, and found it had been dissolved. About a week after Lanchester's death."

"So something stinks to heaven, but nobody's around to talk," Riss said grimly.

"Not necessarily," Jasmine went on. "We had a few names in the report of soldiers in that unit. One of them, a team leader, was—is—named Kae Plamen. General Lanchester's communications man.

"I thought, given the details of the action in which Lanchester was killed—that his three-man lifter was in front of the screen when an enemy rocketeer fired on him . . . there might have been other casualties. So there were. His gunner was killed, and Team Leader Plamen badly wounded.

"I did a little digging and found he'd been wounded badly enough to be invalided out of the service."

"Another dead end?" Riss asked.

"The good Plamen receives a pension from his government, and I managed to find his address without, I think, alerting the government," Jasmine said.

"Most skillful." Grok nodded his approval.

"It still stinks," Riss said. "If there was something dirty about Dov's death—which there's no doubt of— why didn't they just take this Plamen out in the desert and put a few rounds in his back?"

"Undoubtedly, they wanted to," Jasmine said. "But his father is head of his guild, and any disappearance would cause trouble. Besides, I don't think his killer figured anyone would pursue the matter."

"I just want to have a chat with this Plamen," M'chel said, trying to sound calm, feeling blood pulse in her temples.

"Your wish is our command," Jasmine said. "He waits in the suite dining room. I spirited him in, crouched in a photo analysis computer crate, so he won't have to worry about having been spotted. Shall we go chat with him?"

"As I've already heard a tape of what he had to

say to Jasmine," Grok said, "you'll excuse me. I am in the middle of finding out something Friedrich wants."

Ex-Team Leader Plamen was about as thoroughly crippled as anyone Riss had ever seen. One eye was gone, replaced by a black patch, his face was terribly scarred, he had no right arm below the elbow, and moved sufferingly slowly.

She guessed he might have been good-looking once.

Riss wondered why he hadn't been fitted with prosthetics—Khelat was rich enough and once had ties with the Alliance.

Then she realized he was nothing more than a worker. Certainly, no one of the royal family would have been allowed to walk about with wounds that ghastly.

"Good evening," Jasmine said in Khelat.

Plamen nodded his head nervously.

"This is Colonel M'chel Riss," she went on. "One of my teammates, and a good friend of General Lanchester."

Plamen looked at M'chel carefully.

"I do not like her," he said. "She has killer's eyes."

Jasmine forced a laugh.

"If you are right, that is hardly the way to render her harmless."

Plamen shrugged. "I care what people do or think but little, since I was wounded."

"Let me be frank," Riss said. "We do not believe that General Lanchester was shot by a bandit at all."

Plamen hesitated.

"I must tell you how good it feels to have an out-lander speak fluently in my tongue."

"It is the only way for people to understand each other," Riss said sententiously.

"If you were a member of my royal family," Plamen said, "you would be speaking Alliance and using an interpreter, as if you, too, were one of the offworld elite."

"I am hardly elite," Riss said. "I was born poor, and joined the military to better myself. Like you."

"Yes, like me." Plamen made a face. "And see how successful I have become."

"If you agree to help us and answer our questions," Jasmine said, "you will be well reimbursed."

"I should demand no pay. . . . But I shall take it," Plamen said. "Credits do much to make me more handsome to some women."

"You were General Lanchester's communications specialist," Riss asked.

"And very proud to be chosen," he said. "Just as I had been proud to be chosen a member of Special Detachment 43, which was established as a liaison between the Alliance team and our military, which is why Prince Jer commanded it. And I had dreams of further promotion."

"What happened on the day General Lanchester was killed?" Riss said. "The true story. He and I were very good friends."

Plamen looked deeply into Riss's eyes, then nodded.

"We had gone out on a sweep in lifters that the Alliance had provided. We were covering the area around Jaku. . . . Do you know it?"

"I know of it."

"We had been told by our commander, Prince Jer, that Intelligence had said there was a company or more of bandits staying in the ruins of the village.

"We took not only the men in our detachment, but two companies of infantry, as well. Prince Jer led from the front, as officers are supposed to do, until we reached the village. We were moving very, very slowly, and General Lanchester was becoming angry. He was on the com almost constantly, chiding the formation's officers to move more quickly. Sometimes he used language that I do not think princes are used to.

"As I say, we regrouped in the village, prepared to continue the sweep on the far side. Then someone— I don't know who—a villager, a bandit . . . shot at Jer's lifter, which was flying the royal colors, hardly indistinguishable. He immediately ordered his pilot to turn and return to the village, but for the rest of us to find the bandits.

"That was enough for my general. He swore at Prince Jer, and, even worse, told him to stand up like a true prince and defend his king, and stop behaving like a coward.

"Jer made no answer, and Lanchester turned back to the others.

"I happened to be watching toward the rear, where Jer's lifter was, and saw the prince push his gunner out of the way and aim the craft's rocket launcher at us. I tried to shout a warning to my general, but it was too late. It hit us square. I was lucky that General Lanchester's body was between me and the strike.

"He was obliterated. . . . I am sorry, Colonel, but you wanted the truth . . . and our driver was killed, as well.

"I recovered in the hospital, and knew I should pretend to have seen nothing. But I still think that my family's importance is what really kept me alive."

"You swear this?" Jasmine King asked.

"I swear this by everything that is holy, and will gladly agree to be tested on one of the Alliance's lie machines.

"Prince Jer, the one who was closest to General

Lanchester and to the king, murdered my general, your friend."

It was quite late the next evening when Riss tapped on Friedrich's door. He checked his security box, saw who it was, and hit the remote to unlock the door.

Ever the old-fashioned sort, he offered Riss a drink, some of the herbal tea he was supping, or something from room service.

M'chel declined.

"Very well, then," von Baldur said. "What is it I can help you with?"

"First, a question," Riss said. "Am I still your client?"

"Well . . ." Friedrich's voice trailed off. "It is a little complicated, but let us assume so."

"That actually simplifies matters," Riss said.

"With this information Grok got, about my friend's murder, plus other things that've happened, at first I was going to ask for a leave of absence, not wanting to help these goddamned Khelat anymore.

"I have a scheme."

Friedrich's mouth opened in surprise, and he held up a hand.

Riss shook her head.

"Not until I'm finished. I decided I couldn't walk out on the team when you're stuck with these smarmy bastards. But I sure didn't want to rub them to my bosom. So I thought a minute, and decided what I want to do about the situation.

"Either I can step out—which I don't want to do— or else you can maybe take a little trip with me."

"To where?"

"To the capital worlds of the Shaoki."

"Oh, my," von Baldur said.

"We've made an impression on them already, with Chas's and my raids," Riss said. "Now I propose we doublecross our clients—if we can get more credits—and go to work for the Shaoki and help them win the war. My idea seems to fight right in with the way these Khelat think."

"Well, dear me," Friedrich murmured.

THIRTEEN

The first step in doublecrossing the Khelat was to get out of the cluster.

The rest of Star Risk were told what was in the offing. Almost equally disgusted with their clients, and assuming von Baldur and Riss could improve on their deal with the Shaoki, the vote was unanimous.

The pair took the first commercial transport out of the cluster, not much caring where it took them.

It was strange to arrive in a system that was not only at peace, but also didn't even have an army, letting their police force deal with any problems.

Riss instantly realized Star Risk would never be retained by such an aberrant culture.

They booked into a plush hotel and sent a message to their banker at Alliance Credit, back on Trimalchio IV, to go to Star Risk's safety-deposit box, withdraw envelopes 43 and 11, and send them, by courier, to the pair.

The banker didn't know, or need to know, the envelopes contained false identities.

While they waited, Riss caught up on her sleep and Friedrich found some nice, honest, dumb gamblers to pass the time.

He was considerably enriched when the envelopes

arrived, and Riss had snored her way through some of her exhaustion backlog, almost as far as when she first joined Star Risk.

They bought tickets back into the Khelat-Shaoki cluster, but this time to Irdis, the Shaoki capital world.

"Now," Friedrich explained, "we are prepared to open negotiations with the Shaoki."

"Under what name?" Riss asked.

"Why, our own, of course."

"If we're going to do that," Riss asked, "why'd we fribbit around with phony ID?"

"Because we might want to have a fast exit if the negotiations collapse."

Irdis was the richest of the Shaoki worlds. It had an abandon of small continents, not particularly fertile but all irrigated.

The Shaoki must've used less talented irrigation engineers than the Khelat, for the land was still poor and crops weren't that rich.

On the other hand, the Shaoki hadn't given in to the temptation of a single-crop economy, unlike the Khelat, so they were still self-supporting.

There was far more water on Irdis than Khelat, and so there was fishing, a deal of shipping, and such.

M'chel, reading the encyclopedia entry, didn't much want to live under either power.

It took almost four days for the Shaoki to approach them.

M'chel grumbled, "Supposing we *were* traitors, ready to sell out a Khelat Grand Offensive just moments away?"

"Well," von Baldur said, "by the time they returned our messages, I suppose the Khelat would be bringing in their occupation forces. Which really shows how much they need Star Risk, does it not?"

M'chel growled, went to a window, looked far down at the Shaoki city.

That wasn't improving her mood any.

The Shaoki not only weren't as rich as the Khelat; they evidently liked living in each others' laps.

They'd revived, from Riss knew not where, the ancient belief in putting up their buildings to be self-contained, from waking to sleep. Their "hotel" also held offices, several restaurants, clothing shops, other boutiques, possibly even a funeral home, so no one had to go out of doors.

Which was just as well.

Pollution didn't seem to bother the Shaoki very much. The rich had air-conditioning; the poor had emphysema.

No one went into the countryside unless they had to, so there was no Shaoki custom like the absurd Khelat one of going out to commune with the desert.

Not that most worlds had much of a desert. There was plenty of salt marsh, shallow oceans, and rocky barrens. But no sand, or at least M'chel hadn't seen any.

She hadn't looked very hard, but busied herself with preparing a potential back door, from the hotel to the spaceport, in case things fell apart.

Finally, their coms were returned, and they were notified that two ranking members of the council would come calling.

The pair held the rank of colonel.

Diaya, male, was middle-aged, going to paunch, and his hair transplants weren't taking.

His superior, Suiyahr, was about ten years younger. She had the pursed lips of a fanatic, and could have done with another ten kilos anywhere on her overly athletic body.

"Our intelligence reports you are two of the principals of a firm calling itself Star Risk," Suiyahr said coldly. "You've been responsible for the escalation of the war, from our estimates, and some estimates consider you, or your underlings, guilty of war crimes."

"Possibly," von Baldur agreed.

"And now you wish to betray your employers."

Friedrich shrugged. "We are mercenaries," he said. "We work for the credit, and let others worry about patriotism."

"Hardly admirable," Diaya said.

Von Baldur looked at him, decided that to reply that he personally thought anyone willing to endanger his life for a flag or a medal was a fool was hardly politic, said nothing.

"If we decided to have you arrested, and bring you to trial on certainly capital charges," Suiyahr said, "wouldn't we have crippled the Khelat war effort considerably and saved ourselves a great deal of money? I rather imagine you are quite expensive."

"Quite," Friedrich said amiably. "But that would hardly be the wisest of decisions, since it would certainly anger our colleagues and make them more intent on your conquest.

"Not to mention that the presence of Star Risk, working for the Shaoki instead of the Khelat, with our strategies and advisors, could bring this war to an end.

"With a victory for the Shaoki!"

Riss was admiring von Baldur's logic in keeping them out of a deathcell, and was starting to relax when she noticed his fingers, under the table, were crossed and white.

"A *final* victory," Diaya said, and Riss saw a glitter

in his eyes, just as she'd seen it from King Saleph. "Something our predecessors on the council were unable to realize!"

"Peace," Suiyahr agreed, sounding hungry, "and a final settlement with the Khelat!"

M'chel did relax then.

From here on out, it would be nothing but wrangling about the numbers.

FOURTEEN

"No," Technician Ells said to Riss, "we'll not be leaving with you."

"Why not?"

"We made a contract with the benighted Khelat before your arrival, and we'll stick by it."

"Will your men and women back you?"

"I'll not ask them," he said. "Not because I'm afraid of their vote, but because of consideration for you."

"Oh?"

"People talk," Ells said. "And I doubt our peerless princes and king would think kindly of being abandoned if they found out. But thank you for giving us the option."

Two of the mercenary units also determined to stay.

"They're thinking," Hore said, in some amusement, "that with you gone, somebody'll have to be the head mother, and it might as well be them."

"They think," Goodnight said, also finding it funny, "they can just tippie-toe in and get the same contract we did?"

"A better joke," Hore said, watching the last of his men file onto waiting transports, "is that we're talking about soldiers for hire and thinking in the same breath. Now *that's* funny."

The next dawn found a lot of emptiness around various worlds of the Khelat.

Star Risk was gone, with its clerks and specialists, as were Hore's command and Inchcape's destroyers and Vian's patrol ships.

Khelat had suffered only half a dozen casualties in Star Risk's leaving, all of them overly ambitious security people, none of them fatal.

King Saleph raged in vain to Princes Barab and Jer.

FIFTEEN

There were almost six hundred members of the council. All but a handful were assembled in a grand hall, listening to Friedrich von Baldur, who wore a rather grandiose uniform of his own design. He was about three-quarters through his speech.

Over the hall patrolled not only Shaoki ships, but Inchcape's destroyers on the fringes of the atmosphere and, closer in, Vian's patrol ships.

The hall was too juicy a target to not cover thoroughly, even though no one in Star Risk was convinced the Khelat even knew they'd switched sides, let alone be able to mount an attack at short notice.

Still . . .

"We shall assist your cause on two fronts," von Baldur said. "The first is helping your officers and soldiers realize their full potential.

"The second, which I believe, in the long run, is the most important, is economic. Not only does Star Risk believe the Shaoki have been denied their place in the sun for far too long, but we also feel the Shaoki should dominate the riches of this cluster.

"With such domination, the systems and worlds

which remain barren can be developed, and every man of the Shaoki be a prince!"

There were cheers. Von Baldur bowed.

"But we are men and women of action," he went on. "Not words. So when I next appear before you, I want to have concrete accomplishments to show you. Now is the time for work!"

Again, cheers, and again, a bow.

Von Baldur, smiling, left the stage, where the others of Star Risk waited.

"What's this two-front deal?" Goodnight asked. "What've you got in mind, besides beating the Khelat bum?"

"Later," von Baldur said. "I—or rather M'chel—shall explain, in a quieter place. Right now, as I said, let us put the boys to work."

"Awright," Goodnight said. "Grok's put the antibugs in place. . . . So what's this second front we're supposed to open?"

Von Baldur was still busy critically surveying the amenities of their quarters.

The Shaoki called it a mansion, but in their building scheme it was actually three floors in one of the ultrahigh-rises. Star Risk had specified a pair of elevators that went nowhere but to their lodgings, put in security on the floor above and below their three.

Jasmine had asked who'd been the previous occupant, was told it was a council member whose "performance had been lacking."

"Since it's my idea," Riss said, "I'll explain.

"Dov . . . the late General Lanchester . . . happened to mention that a corporation named Omni Foods has the whip hand on half a dozen members of the Alliance Parliament."

"So?" Goodnight snorted. "What's new about corporations buying politicos?"

"Nothing," M'chel said. "However, Omni Foods is the main buyer of the Khelat *maln,* that spicy tea that I think should be used to wash toilets."

"I say again my last," Goodnight said. "So?"

"So we're going to hire ourselves a lobbyist back on Earth who can figure out who these six are. We'll contact them and inform them that there's a power struggle going on out in the Khelat-Shaoki cluster.

"I still don't get it."

"If we are winning," Friedrich put in, "we surely don't want a few battalions of Alliance Marines showing up on the Khelat side to even the odds."

"Oh," Goodnight said. "That has been known to happen."

"It has," Riss said. "I was on a couple of those expeditionary forces.

"The other benefit it has is for one or another of those six politicos to put the word back to Omni Foods that there may be a change in who controls the *maln.* Omni Foods will get the word, and unquestionably want to be in on the ground floor if the Shaoki control things."

"Which means bribes, I would guess," Grok said.

"Channeled through us," Goodnight said. "Now I get it. So that'll keep the Alliance off our asses, put some money inbound, which'll make the Shaoki Council happy, and we get a rake-off. Not bad, Major."

"*I* thought it was downright sneaky."

I have never done this before, Jasmine thought, but didn't show any sign of her uncertainty.

She looked up and down the gigantic range, at the two hundred Shaoki soldiers in prone firing position behind their blasters, and nodded as arrogantly as she knew how to the Shaoki officer.

"You may order your troops to open fire, sir."

The Shaoki keyed a throat mike.

"Make ready . . . take aim . . . fire!"

The range erupted in explosions.

A hundred meters downrange, large targets, carefully made to be almost unmissable, swayed and shook as blaster bolts impacted.

The sound crescendoed, then died to a few hesitant cracks as either the sluggish or the most precise emptied their magazines.

Jasmine had her binocs up, sweeping the targets.

If the Khelat soldiery were about twice the size of Grok, she might have been impressed.

But she showed no sign of displeasure.

There were about fifty Shaoki officers in the small amphitheater-classroom, listening to Grok.

"Now," the monster said, "remember what we learned yesterday, that all intelligence taken in is to be evaluated carefully, not on whether or not it bears with your opinions, but on its raw dependability."

The officers, all assigned to intelligence staffs of various Shaoki divisions, hung on Grok's every word.

But he didn't think he was really communicating.

"One way to evaluate an intelligence report," he went on, "is considering how accurate is the source, from someone who's provided valuable data in the past to someone known to be a liar; then how accurate the datum itself is, from personally witnessed to an unreliable rumor."

He still didn't think he was getting through, but kept on hammering.

*   *   *

Colonel, now de facto General, Mik Hore considered his battalion.

It had changed considerably.

It had doubled in size, the additional men and women Shaoki. Supposedly, they were fully trained, and were attached to Hore for positional training.

Every mercenary ammo bearer had a Shaoki partner, as did every squad leader, every platoon leader, company commander.

Each Shaoki would hopefully learn what it was like to be part of a combat battalion, then, when the hurried training was finished, would train other battalions. Like oil on water, this initial knowledge would spread throughout the Shaoki army.

Which, Hore thought sourly, would be fine.

Until the first day of combat, when everything would fall apart.

As it always did.

Goodnight listened to his own breathing's echo in the suit recycler.

He and thirty Shaoki were crouched in the dust of one of Shaoki IV's moons. They were atop a low rise. Ahead of them was a low concrete building.

He extended a com lead to the Shaoki officer beside him, who touched it to a contact.

"Now, Major," Goodnight said. "From here, we do what, having spotted that possible enemy position down there?"

"I would send a section down that draw, to verify that it is hostile."

"Not quite," Chas said. "First, you send a com section back down the hill, and, with a directional mike, report your discovery to your ship in its orbit. You can make the probable assumption that it's unfriendly, since you're reconning a Khelat world, remember?"

"Ah. Yes. I just forgot. But after I send the report, then I put forward a team, right?"

Goodnight shook his head.

Sometimes it was like pounding sand.

"Not unless you're in a hurry," he said. "It's better if you put the position under observation for a while first. Meantime, spread out your force so that you've got a complete field of fire, as well. If you then observe movement, engage the target."

"But suppose the target is civilian?"

"If you feel humanitarian," he said patiently, "send out a sacrificial lamb or two to take prisoners. But don't expect them to be grateful for your kindness."

Pounding sand . . .

"Now, here you are," Riss told the battery commander.

There were four multiple rocket launchers positioned in the draw between hills.

"Enemy forces advance toward you, up the draw."

Robot tracks swung into view.

The officer issued brisk orders, and rockets crashed out, screamed toward the robots, impacted around them. The officer was about to issue orders for another firing when Riss interrupted.

"To your surprise," she said, "a second force comes over the hilltop here."

She pointed, and the artilleryman saw another group of small robots wheel into sight.

"Fire mission!" the officer shouted. "As previous, advancing enemy tracks—"

"What about this new enemy?" Riss asked. "They're closer, and a bigger threat."

"We were ordered to stop an attack up the draw," the officer said stubbornly. "One mission at a time."

There were a dozen ranking staff officers in the domed chamber, sitting around von Baldur.

In front of them hung a sun and four planets and their moons.

Von Baldur touched a sensor, and the scene shifted to a close shot of two of the moons, the planet just on the edge of the picture.

"The situation is quite simple," he said. "Your unit has been using this moon as a mask to close on the world. As you are coming out . . ."

Small red dots that were ships sprang to life.

". . . getting ready for your attack on the main world, which were your orders, you're ambushed."

Other dots, these blue, moved from behind the other moon.

"You are outnumbered," von Baldur continued. "Admiral Fregnard, what is your response?"

"We break from our attack formation, swing until we are facing the new enemy," the officer said briskly. "Then we attack."

"I remind you, you are outnumbered."

"That does not matter! No unit I lead will ever retreat!"

Von Baldur sighed.

It was late. Jasmine made silent rounds before shutting down for the night.

All was quiet, all was still.

Friedrich von Baldur sat in one of the living rooms, glooming at a decanter and an untouched snifter.

He looked up as Jasmine entered, forced a smile.

"What's the matter?"

"Nothing," he said. "Everything."

"Such as?"

"Perhaps we took on too great a task in this system. The Khelat are worthless, and the Shaoki are worse. We could be training them for the next century, and I do not think they would still make candidates for the rear rank."

"That's one sort of job security," Jasmine suggested, sitting down, sliding the snifter over, and sipping.

"That is not what I wanted with Star Risk," von Baldur said. "Not what any of us wanted."

"True."

"I always considered the probability of being killed, but it would be a damned crime to be killed working for these morons," Friedrich said.

"I was thinking about that lobbyist we are going to hire. He probably makes twice what we do, without any danger. I could have been him, could have done that."

"Freddie," Jasmine put in, her voice a little sharp, "you're chasing your own tail."

Von Baldur grunted, got to his feet.

"You are right, of course. I shall stop brooding."

"Damned well better," Jasmine said.

Von Baldur left, and Jasmine nursed the rest of his brandy. At last, she decided it was time to consult with M'chel

"I think," Riss said, the next evening before dinner, when the team assembled for its customary drink, "it's time that we do something drastic."

"Such as?" von Baldur said. He appeared a little more chipper than he had the previous night.

"I could call it going out and setting an example.

But I'll be honest. We're getting a little stale and need a morale boost."

"I could do with a breather from all this talking," Goodnight admitted.

"And a chance for real blood," Grok seconded.

Riss held a hand out to Jasmine.

"Well," King said, "it just so happens I have just found an interesting target. I think."

SIXTEEN

Once the land had been arid desert, with villages and scrub grazing led here and there.

But then the workers had come. First, artesian wells were driven, and the villagers praised the princes and king of Khelat for improving their lot.

But the hosannas didn't last for long, and the villagers, their scant belongings, and livestock, were driven off the land, relocated to an equally dry district half a world away.

The villages were put to the torch, then pumps were installed atop the wells and ditches and pipeline run. Here and there, prefabricated maintenance sheds were put together.

The land was plowed, disked, and irrigated, then *maln* cuttings planted and fertilized.

They grew quickly into mature bushes, and harvesters were brought in for festive summer camps.

The *maln* leaves were dried, baled, then, in sealed containers, they went offworld, toward the great warehouse and shipping planets.

The land was quiet, except for the gentle rustling of occasional winds, and the gurgle of the automatic irrigators.

A few wild creatures came out of the wastelands,

but found the land too foreign for anything other than hunting expeditions and water.

Just before dawn one day, the air shuddered with the whine of starships' secondary drive. Three destroyers plummeted down, swept over the huge plantation, and none of their detection apparati found life.

Four patrol ships flashed over the fields, then slowed, making a slow check.

Again, nothing.

Coms were sent into space, and the next arrivals were two huge transports, which settled down for a landing, crushing fields of *maln*.

Air locks irised open, and landing ramps slid down. Lightly armed troops ran out. Half of them were mercenaries from Hore's battalion, the other half Shaoki trainees.

There appeared no need, but a pair of crew-served blasters were set up at the bow and stern of each transport, and two batteries of air-to-ground missiles unloaded and made ready.

The troops, once they realized they were unopposed, behaved as if the raid was a holiday. Men with sledges ran down the rows, smashing the heads of the irrigation pumps or putting small charges at their base. Small explosions cracked here and there, as other cracklings of flame came as the maintenance sheds were fired. Necklace charges were laid around the pipelines, cross-connected, and set off.

Water sprayed here and there, formed pools.

The soldiers ran back to the transports, chivvied by their noncoms, boarded, and the ships lifted off.

Once all the men and women were safe aboard, Vian's patrol ships, modified with external sprayers such as crop dusters used, came back.

Clouds of bitter-smelling defoliants hissed out, settled down on the *maln* plants. Almost instantly, they curled, withered.

Alarms gonged on the bridges of the destroyers, now hanging five miles overhead.

"I have them," a weapons officer reported. "Six . . . no, seven patrol ships incoming. ID'd as Khelat."

"Vian Zero, this is Inchcape," the destroyer leader commed.

"Vian. Go," came from the leader of the patrol ship formation.

"Do you have the unfriendlies?"

"On-screen. For a long time."

Von Baldur, beside Inchcape, took the mike.

"This is Star Risk Zed," he said. "Do you need help?"

"Negative."

"Bounce them, then," von Baldur said. His voice was harsh.

Vian's ships came down, at speed, in a head-on attack at the Khelat.

Three of the onrushing Khelats flinched aside, and air-to-air missiles smashed them.

The other, braver, four, held courses.

Two were exploded before they reached Vian's formation. The other two flashed past, their missiles fired too late, or acquired early and spoofed into destruction.

Two Star Risk patrol ships spun, then, at full drive, went after the surviving pair.

At full emergency, the Khelat tried to flee.

Neither of them survived for longer than a minute.

Von Baldur swung a pickup back on the destroyed *maln* plantation, smiled tightly.

Jasmine unstrapped herself from the auxiliary seat behind the pilot's seat, stood.

She saw the smile on Friedrich's face.

"Feel better now?" she asked.

"Yes," he said thoughtfully. "Yes, I do, as a matter of fact."

Over the next five days, ten *maln* plantations on various planets were also put to the torch.

SEVENTEEN

Even Grok's eyes got tired after a day of plumbing microcircuitry.

He decided to go for a walk, and perhaps a meal. There were cooks aplenty in Star Risk's quarter, but he felt cussedly independent, strapping on his blaster and a couple of grenade pouches before he went out into the madding throng.

Even the open corridors of his own building weren't enough, and so he went out into the open air and the curving sidewalks. Here and there separate businesses had sprung up, generally of hasty and shoddy construction.

The Shaoki goggled at the huge alien and got out of his way as quickly as possible. Grok paid no attention, growling happily as he strolled.

He paused a moment to read the menu of one small café, and the proprietor was instantly outside, beaming a beckoning smile, no doubt anticipating how much he imagined Grok could eat.

"Welcome, welcome, welcome," he said. "Please come in and try my humble fare."

Grok considered, then held out his palms in a why-not gesture.

The man escorted him to a table and a seat, which creaked alarmingly but held.

"You are one of the beings who have come to help us win our war," the man said.

"I am one of the beings who've come to help you with certain technical matters," Grok advised, politically. "The Shaoki need no training in bravery."

"With your help, I know we shall conquer! I have seen the holos!"

"Which you believe."

"Of course," the man said, a trace indignantly. "They wouldn't be allowed to print them if they weren't true, would they?"

Grok made an agreeable noise.

"Let me ask you something," he said. "If Shaoki wins, what will be the advantage to you? Personally, I mean."

The man was taken aback.

"Why . . . the riches we take from the Khelat. And . . . and maybe, with the increase in the worlds that will be Shaoki, it will be as the government says, with every man a prince."

Grok suppressed amusement at just how quickly Friedrich's phrase had been co-opted by the Shaoki Council.

"I can see it clear," the restaurant owner said dreamily. "I'll have not just one restaurant, but many, scattered through the Khelat worlds, and I shall never have to enter a kitchen or dining room—no offense, sir, and I do not mean to insult the wares I offer—unless I wish.

"All my employees, except, of course, for the head cooks, will be Khelat, and I can pay them a hundredth of what I must pay here on Irdis.

"Or, perhaps, if they are condemned labor, which I think all of the Khelat who serve in their armed forces should be, not pay them anything but allow them to keep their tips, since I am a kindly man, and give them transportation back to their barracks each night."

"Do you think that will make them peaceable, willing to stand behind a Shaoki occupation?"

"Of course," the man said. "For haven't we been told of the evils of the Khelat princes and king? Besides, if they do object, there is always prison or worse."

Grok grunted. "Ah," he muttered. "The voice of democracy in action."

EIGHTEEN

There was a com for M'chel from the spaceport.

A courier from Alliance Credit, their bank on Trimalchio IV had arrived with an emergency message for her.

"From whom?"

"Uh . . . I'm not supposed to tell you, but deliver it personally."

Riss gave the courier instructions to their complex, disconnected.

"I don't suppose," she told Friedrich, "this is about my overdraft. It isn't *that* big."

"And for you only," von Baldur said. "Curiouser and curiouser."

The courier was little more than a teenager, and Riss wondered why young people kept getting younger every year.

The message was on a fiche, keyed to her print only.

"The man who gave us this asked if we could stamp it like that," he explained. "I . . . I mean, we, the bank, didn't think you'd object."

M'chel nodded, excused herself into another room.

First she ran the package through a portable sniffer, detected no sign of any conventional explosives. Nor did a fluoroscope show anything unpleasantly resembling a potential bang.

She carefully opened the small package using none of the easy-open tabs, although it wasn't likely the package contained a bomb, since Alliance Credit had sealed it.

It was a standard fiche.

Riss fed it into a com, touched the play sensor, still ready to dive for cover if it hissed or ticked like proper bombs were supposed to do.

A man appeared in midair.

It was Khelat Prince Wahfer in ceremonial robes.

"Uh . . . Colonel Riss . . . M'chel . . . I'm sending this to you the only way I can think of, since Alliance Credit is how we were paying Star Risk. There's been a frightful misunderstanding, and no one can understand why you left us so precipitately.

"Since I thought—think—of you as a friend, I'm trying to reach you, to ask you if we can meet . . . perhaps on some neutral world . . . and discuss our misunderstanding.

"This message has been approved by His Most Royal Highness.

"There is a private com number I've attached to this, and there'll be a machine or myself there to answer it all the time.

"I'm sure this matter can be resolved to our mutual advantage."

"Right," M'chel snarled. "How dumb do you think I am?"

Then she thought for a minute. "Maybe I am that dumb, after all. But not quite yet," she muttered to herself.

Her smile was not pleasant.

* * *

Riss took the com to von Baldur, who played it through twice.

"Very interesting," he mused. "What is a double-doublecross?"

"Just what I thought might be needed down the road," M'chel said.

"Yes, indeed," Friedrich said. "We might, indeed, need the good prince in the fullness of time. Now, allow me to return to my musing about a certain Khelat world that I was worried about, when we were in their employ, as being woefully underdefended."

NINETEEN

The world was named Hastati, and was the eighth world orbiting around a vast, dying red star, part of the Shaoki-Khelat-occupied cluster.

It was sparsely settled and almost completely undefended, with its single moon ungarrisoned, nor had any orbital fortresses been hung around it. There were two battalions of the local planetary guard, originally customs guards, with only three patrol ships capable of out-atmosphere work.

Hastati had some mineral deposits, including one that when added to an iron compound produced steel with an amazingly high Rockwell rating. Even better, the mineral, while molten, was fairly easy to work.

Its second claim was that it purported to be the original world the settlers of the cluster had landed on.

Von Baldur doubted that—almost no one would be desperate to settle a world just barely habitable, with only two continents and those in the far northern and southern hemispheres, especially around a sun that might go *pfft* at any time.

But both the Khelat and Shaoki believed the myth.

Friedrich had Jasmine do a little basic research, discovered that no one was sure what system was first colonized, let alone what specific world. But Hastati was regarded as vaguely sacred, which was another reason it hadn't been fortified. Neither side thought the other would dare.

For von Baldur, Hastati's ultimate importance was that it could offer a nice base to attack a "neighboring" system. . . . If you had a rather grandish fleet for the operation.

He didn't when Star Risk was working for the Khelat, nor now.

But Hastati offered possibilities. . . .

The council was suitably horrified when he proposed an invasion of Hastati with no bombardment from space.

But they acceded.

Von Baldur and Goodnight, with his battle-analysis mind on full less-than-bester tilt, crept into Hastati's system, made quick decisions, returned to Irdis, and sent in the troops.

A dozen large transports escorted by Star Risk's destroyers and patrol craft, which had been piggybacked into the system to save the crews for combat instead of wearing them out in their cramped quarters, hit Hastati.

The Shaoki troops, again, were leavened with Hore's mercenaries.

Riss had made sure that all of the mercs were drilled: "Kill only those you have to," and, in turn, passed the antislaughter policy along to the Shaoki troops, who seemed a trifle disappointed.

The capital held for two days, the Shrine of First Arrival for one more, then Hastati fell.

The thousand or so Khelat soldiers were taken to hastily constructed prisoner of war cages.

Grok reported a transmission from the shrine, which

was allowed to go out. Von Baldur didn't bother having it decoded, since it would obviously be a scream for help.

He then clamped down with blanket jamming on all Khelat wavelengths. Only one constant transmission was permitted: a visual of a FREE KHELAT banner that Jasmine had designed, flying over the Shrine of First Arrival.

"That oughta ass them nigh onto tears," Goodnight said. "Keep 'em from thinking too clearly."

"Not," Riss said, "that they've been guilty of that so far."

They waited for the counterattack.

It took two weeks in the coming, and by then the Shaoki on the ground were dining on their fingernails. Star Risk, wondering what was taking the Khelat so long, wasn't in much better shape.

But a snitch satellite, planted on the fringes of the system, eventually sounded, and Star Risk's second stage was implemented, as Khelat ships blipped into real space from hyperdrive.

The Shaoki and Hore's mercenaries boarded the waiting transports and lifted off. They used the moon for a mask, jumped for N-space and eventually home.

The Khelat closed in on the desecrated, conquered, and occupied world.

"Interesting," Goodnight said. "Not as big a fleet as we'd expected."

Star Risk, less King back on Irdis, were in the command center of Inchcape's destroyer. They and the other mercenary ships, plus a carefully selected group of Shaoki's best warships.

"More interesting," Grok said. "The transmissions my techs have intercepted are from normal line units, not the Khelat assault divisions you would've thought to have been committed to a major battle."

"And where are they?" Riss wondered.

"Dunno," Goodnight said. "But let's take what we got while we got 'em."

"Patience," von Baldur said. "I think Inchcape can best determine when she's ready to grab them by the throat."

"Madam," Inchcape said to her com officer. "Make a signal to all ships. . . . Set ordered synchronization to this ship."

"We're within range," she said. "Now, let them get a few millimeters closer. . . . *Goddamit!*"

One of the Shaoki cruisers had launched a volley of missiles.

"Oh, well," she said, nodding to von Baldur. "We always forget about first-timers and amateurs. You may start the battle, if you wish, Miss."

"This is Star Risk Control," Friedrich said into a throat mike. "All units, all units. You may fire when ready."

He grinned bashfully.

"I always wanted to say that, from when I was a child."

"You forgot to say 'Gridley,'" Goodnight suggested.

Grok looked at him in astonishment.

"You know where the saying came from?"

"Probably the only thing I remember about history," Goodnight said. "I saw it in a holo once, about old-timey water ships."

Inchcape was paying no attention, listening to her weapons officer report targets acquired, being tracked, and missiles launched.

The Khelat had no idea that there were warships off Hastati on full alert until the first missile flashed on the screen of a Khelat destroyer, less than a second before impact. The destroyer's entire nose section vanished in a flare, then the rest of the ship blew up.

On one of Inchcape's screens, blips flared, vanished. Each was a Khelat warship, and its crew, dying.

Riss doubted if, in spite of orders, many of the Khelat had put on the bulky, clumsy suits.

"Prepare to jump on my synch," Inchcape said. "Four . . . three . . . two . . . *now!*"

The Shaoki fleet made a one-second in-out into N-space, reappeared "above" the ecliptic and the Khelat ships.

Riss fancied she saw the lead elements shaking their heads back and forth, like hounds who've lost the scent.

"All ships," Inchcape said. "Acquire targets and fire."

Again missiles spat out, and more Khelat died.

"All units," Inchcape said. "Cease fire and jump for home."

All but two Shaoki cruisers obeyed, and those two became the only Shaoki casualties of the battle, spraying missiles at any target even as they died.

Inchcape's destroyer came out of N-space, surrounded by other ships.

Their coms were yammering at each other.

Riss made out a blurt from the Shaoki flagship, someone shouting about fifty, maybe more, Khelat destroyed.

"I made it seventeen ships," Vian's weapons officer said.

"Any bets," Goodnight said, "that it'll be a hundred by the time we get back to Irdis?"

There were no takers.

"Pretty good short, sharp shock," Riss said.

"It is. What worries me," von Baldur said, "is where the hell their elite units have gotten off to."

They found out within the week.

TWENTY

"Uh," the scar-faced man said, twisting his garrison cap nervously, "we've got a problem, Miss King."

Jasmine held back a smile. The mercenary, Llaros, one of Hore's artillery specialists, must have seen a dozen wars, but was behaving like a raw recruit.

There were three of his fellows behind him.

"It's about my contract," he said. "Or rather, my money."

The others nodded.

"I'm only drawing twenty percent due me," he explained. "The rest the Shaoki are supposed to send home . . . to my mother. And she hasn't seen any allotments in four pay cycles."

"Oh." Jasmine cursed to herself. She'd gone for the easy and let the Shaoki payroll departments take care of all monies sent out-system. She should have known better.

"Are you sure they've got the right transfer address?"

"Yes'm," the man said. "And when I asked what was wrong, their finance department didn't seem to give a . . . give a hang. And these other fellers have problems the same."

"We can't have that," King said.

She was about to summon one of her clerks and put her in motion, on a priority, when the general alarm went off in loud clangs.

"All troops, all troops, man your emergency positions. This is no drill. This is no drill."

The four mercenaries spun and doubled out.

Jasmine shrugged on the weapons harness that hung behind her computer station, went for Star Risk Central.

Thur, the capital of Shaoki II, was being attacked by the Khelat.

This wasn't a raid, but an invasion.

Banks of coms were being trundled into Central and tuned in by technicians.

Von Baldur sat in the middle of chaos, seemingly imperturbable.

On the two center screens were Colonel Suiyahr of the Shaoki Council and a beribboned general.

"We must strike now," Suiyahr was saying. "Hit them with everything."

"Yes," the general agreed. "First, give me soldiers on the ground to hold my city, drive them back before they seize all of Shaoki II."

"Maybe," von Baldur said in a neutral voice.

"Look," Suiyahr said. "Screen eleven. They're deploying on the ground, and they're in the open. Hit them now."

"Yes," the general agreed.

"Very well," von Baldur said. "Bring in your air."

Both Shaoki started issuing orders.

"You," von Baldur said to one of the techs. "Put screen eleven on the master."

The technician nodded, and the street scene in Thur filled the three-meter-wide screen in the center of the room.

Riss was just coming into the room, buckling her combat harness, saw what was wrong instantly, as did von Baldur.

"Cancel that order," he snapped, not pretending to be just an advisor.

But he was too late.

Two Shaoki destroyers came in on high cover, and half a dozen patrol ships roared in underneath them. One of them was part of Vian's unit, the others were Shaoki.

The thin wave of Khelat infantry on-screen carried no blasters, but had small ground-to-air missile launchers.

They didn't seem shaken by the ships attacking them, but rather aimed carefully. The sky was suddenly filled with missiles reaching up.

They were too small to be acquired by the patrol ships' countermissile system, no more than a meter long, but big enough to destroy their enemy.

Four patrol ships were hit, tried to lift away. Two exploded in midair; the other two wobbled, lost control, and smashed into the ground.

That was the patrol ship that was part of Vian's unit.

There were more missileers in sight now, their launchers being aimed, and the screen suddenly zigzagged, went blank.

"Get eleven back," von Baldur said.

"Trying, sir," a technician said. "Can't. We've lost contact with the pickup man. I think he's hit."

Von Baldur scanned his assortment of images, chose another. A distant view of the battlefield bloomed on the center screen.

One of the Shaoki destroyers had taken a hit and was limping away, and there was no sign of the patrol ships.

"Give me a scan," von Baldur said. "And put up a radar picture of Thur."

"Yessir."

The radar sweep was spotty, broken, and there was no sign of any ships in the air. Then a wave of blips soared into sight.

"IFF them," von Baldur ordered. A technician touched a sensor for the Identification, Friend or Foe, and all of the blips glowed red.

"Shit," von Baldur muttered under his breath, then forced control.

"The Khelat appear to have air superiority," he reported to Suiyahr. The screen with the general on it fuzzed to black suddenly.

"They've hit our command post!" Suiyahr said. There was an edge of panic in her voice.

"So it appears," von Baldur agreed. He slid out of his chair. Behind him were the other members of Star Risk.

All of them wore Shaoki uniforms—it does not pay to look special in combat unless you have to—but had current Alliance harness and weaponry.

"Chas . . . I think we could do with a little analysis. I may be missing something, and do not want to be cowboying around unnecessarily."

Goodnight nodded, touched his cheek as he sank into a chair, went bester.

"Current situation," he said. "I would suspect the Khelat, with air superiority, now will continue bringing in troops, and moving them into contact. I would anticipate other landings shortly, as soon as Thur appears to be secured."

"I could have guessed that," Riss said.

"How about strength?" von Baldur said.

"Thin on the ground," Goodnight said tonelessly.

"It looks as if they put in the missile crews without much in the way of backup, from what I see on-screen. If we hit them now and drive them back, we have the advantage. If they can hold Thur, the situation may be in doubt, so we need to put a rod up the arse of the Shaoki without any delay."

"Come on out," von Baldur said, and Goodnight unbestered.

"What a crock," Chas said wryly. "For this I let the Alliance rewire me? Any sojer could've figured that out. Even a marine."

Riss was about to respond, and von Baldur held up a hand.

"I think," he said, "it is, unfortunately, time to go be brave in a public place. I don't think we'll have time for anything but noble inspiration. Try not to get killed."

Two waves of armed transports had crashed into Thur's center, where a great park provided an excellent landing field.

The Khelat landed a command and control ship in the midst of the assault wave, and three very large cruisers orbited above it.

Star Risk had made quick decisions, was deploying.

All of them except King had gotten instantly airborne—von Baldur to the central Shaoki command center, Riss to a armored lifter unit, Chas to a commando team. Both units were in motion toward Thur, and the Star Risk operatives had their lifters drop them on the units without ceremony.

Grok should have taken charge of the overall communications division, had growled a refusal, and was just landing at a self-propelled artillery unit, already rumbling into Thur's outskirts.

Jasmine had wanted to go to Vian's patrol leader ship, but Grok's independent action had stuck her at the com center.

She promised herself some sort of revenge on the furry alien, paced back and forth as dusk fell, watching screens change to available light, infrared, or radar, and the flurry of commo specialists.

The Khelat should have pressed their attack.

But they did not, as if they weren't sure what part of their success to pursue.

Their launcher teams took shelter where they could, without much infantry backup.

At least, Chas Goodnight thought, these commandos were half-trained.

Which was better than nothing.

They'd infiltrated through the fragmented Khelat positions into the rear.

He took two "volunteers," crept forward on a compass course. It felt good, he thought, to be back doing what he'd been trained to do, sliding through darkness, moving silently, slowly.

He didn't need any of his bester skills.

Goodnight crouched regularly, looked around for man-shaped lumps in the darkness.

He saw a pair of soldiers and a almost man-length launching tube.

A dagger slid into his hand.

Goodnight waited, breathed, then rushed the two.

One managed a gurgle as Chas slit his throat; the other was struck speechless.

He died, as well.

Goodnight motioned his backup onward.

Ahead of them, just where it should be, was a sharp

rise, with two or three shattered apartment buildings atop it.

That would be his new home.

"I think," Friedrich said calmly, seemingly unbothered by the confusion around him in the Shaoki command center, the semihysterical orders being shouted by various members of the council and the unfolding defeat on screens around him, "it might be time to consider sending in your air."

"With what target?" Suiyahr demanded.

"Why, I'd suggest the nice fat transports and C&C in downtown," Friedrich drawled.

"But . . . what about the Khelat ships in space?"

"They are not bothering us at the moment, so let us not bother them."

"But—"

"I am sending in my own forces," von Baldur said. "Your naval elements are welcome to accompany them. . . . Your commanders have my signal operating instructions."

"But . . . very well," Suiyahr said dubiously.

"Fire mission," Grok said, gave coordinates, and the SP battery around him fired on command.

The range was very close—less than a thousand meters. The rounds barely armed themselves before impacting.

One tube was a little late in firing, and Grok sent the battery commander over to wreak havoc on the gun captain.

He wished he had another ten—no, make it a hundred—guns that he could put track to track and level the terrain in front of him.

Or else a forward observer with some courage that

would give him hard targets, instead of this firing into nowhere, hopefully over the heads of the Shaoki infantry in hasty positions ahead of him.

"Now," Suiyahr said, "the council has decided that, since we have our forces in position, we will attack."

"At night?" von Baldur asked.

"We will have artillery illumination," Suiyahr said. "Plus the lighting from the ships overhead."

"Don't you think it wise to wait until dawn, after we've hopefully taken out the Khelat air?"

"Later is maybe," Suiyahr said impatiently. "Now is for sure."

Von Baldur was about to protest more, saw the look on Suiyahr's face, kept silent.

Goodnight and his two men clambered up through the wrecked apartment building as high as they could go.

Below and beyond them was the park, very poorly blacked out. He could identify two—no, three—landed ships with his naked eyeballs.

What a strange image, he thought. Whoever saw an eyeball in formal dress?

He unslung the laser designator, turned it on, but didn't "fire" the device. Instead he swept the area, making sure no one was waiting in ambush with his own pickup.

Nothing.

Very good.

He flipped the sensor on, and target heaven spread below him.

Now all he needed was a Device of Ruination.

He flipped on his com and heard nothing but confusion and unfamiliar signs.

Goodnight sent a com back to the commando unit,

got no answer. He tried again, and got nothing but overriding chatter.

I suppose they went out for a glass of tea, he thought.

The fog of war was settling fast this night.

"Up," officers shouted. "For Shaoki we die!"

The line troops weren't either commando or night trained.

They reluctantly came out of their nice, safe hide-outs, driven by warrants and officers.

There was—had to be—safety in numbers, and in spite of the ravings of their commanders, they unconsciously moved closer together, three long ragged lines of more than a thousand soldiers, advancing into Thur.

The Khelat awaiting them weren't much better trained, but they had the advantage of the day's victory behind them, and were fighting from cover.

They saw movement in front, hesitated, then artillery flares bloomed overhead and the attacking Shaoki were silhouetted.

Rather than freeze, they dove for cover, or started to, and that was enough for the Khelat to open fire.

A few Khelat had targets, the rest practiced the old infantry tactic of point, pray, and shoot.

The first line of Shaoki hesitated, and another volley slammed into them.

Khelat rockets and mortars dropped down around them, and the pavement of Thur gave little shelter.

"Fall back," someone shouted—no one ever confessed—and then there were other shouts of "Retreat."

The Shaoki line broke, moving back first at a walk, then a trot.

Their noncoms and officers were shouting at them

to stop, then the panic caught them, too, and they broke and ran, crashing into the second wave. It, too, began a disorderly retreat.

The night attack had made it only a few hundred meters when it shattered.

The Shaoki fell back through their old positions and kept going. Some, but not many, of the soldiers kept their weapons. Others threw them away, along with their weapons harnesses and even uniforms.

Riss was sitting in the gunner's hatch of the lead armored lifter when she heard shouting, screams, even over the drive whine and the noise of shell fire and explosions.

She grabbed a pair of binocs, swept the area in front of the column of lifters, and gaped.

Riss had heard of units breaking under fire, but it had been her good fortune to never have it happen to her. She knew any unit can panic, no matter how experienced, but that green units were more likely to break.

She also knew the book solution, had hoped not to ever use it. But here it was, in front of her.

She reached down inside the lifter, grabbed two blast carbines from their rack, tossed one to the Shaoki commander.

"Come on," she said. "Ground this pig, unass the lifter, and play hero."

Riss was sliding down from the turret as it landed on the torn pavement.

Evidently, the commander knew the drill, as well, because he was talking into his throat mike, and the other lifters behind them grounded, too.

Riss didn't need amplified light to see the men and women running toward her.

She fed a magazine into her blaster and sent bolts shattering into the roadway in front of her. Her fire was echoed by the Shaoki lifter commander.

That stopped them.

For an instant.

Then someone shouted that the Khelat were just behind them, pushed through, ran toward Riss. The mob started to roll forward again.

She took a deep breath and cut him down.

That stopped them again . . . for more than an instant.

Riss jumped back on the lifter, was behind a crew-served blaster, and ran half a magazine into the emptiness between the rabble.

"You men," and she needed no loudspeaker to be heard. "Get back to where you belong."

"They're comin'," someone shouted.

"Then don't get shot in the back," Riss called. "Come on. We're going forward." She motioned to the lifter commander, who gave orders.

The column of massive assault lifters took off, just centimeters off the ground, and moved forward slowly.

The broken unit had to get out of the way. They crowded off the road as the column bulled its way toward the Khelat. The pause had given some of them time to think, take a breath, and, rather shamefacedly, find arms of one sort or another.

Less then a third of the soldiers who'd broken kept retreating. Riss thought that was very good, and felt proud of herself.

She didn't allow herself to think about the unarmed man who lay sprawled, dead in the road, that she'd shot.

* * *

"You had best get reinforcements in a hurry," von Baldur "suggested" to Suiyahr.

The woman looked away.

"Yes, yes," she said. "In good time. They are assembling even as we speak."

Von Baldur had the grave suspicion that no Shaoki commanders were willing to get near what looked to becoming a serious debacle.

It figured.

Goodnight kept himself from swearing. Here, under his thumb—or laser, at any rate—was one of the fattest targets ever.

The only problem was, was nobody seemed to be interested in talking to him.

He decided on desperation, clicked his com on. "Any station able to ID Goodnight's eye color, please respond."

He knew there had to be spoofers out there, but who knew about eyes?

His two cohorts looked at him oddly but said nothing.

Goodnight made another 'cast.

Jasmine King was listening to a com sweep while she watched the shift change around the com sets. Boring was the mildest description she was thinking.

Something caught her:

". . . Goodnight's eye color, please respond."

She grinned, listened to the 'cast again.

Jasmine wondered if she should respond. Knowing somebody might have Chas tied to a chair and pulling his fingernails out, she decided to take the chance.

"Unknown station, this is Jasmine. Over."

"This is Goodnight" came back at her. "Gimme an ID."

"Rude bastard," King said. "You give *me* one, Brown Eyes."

"You used to work for the dog from hell."

Jasmine laughed out loud. That was, indeed, Cerberus.

"It *is* you. What do you need?"

"I need some bangsticks. Big ones," the 'cast came back. "Also, if there's anything in the air, I'd like them to do a fast flyover over the beeg park downtown, with bangs on the pad and laser pickups on."

"I've got both," King said. "Hold on."

She remembered the call sign of the artillery unit Grok was piggybacking, commed it.

Grok got on the other end.

"We have laser-targeting capability," he said. "Give me a launch time. Over."

"Stand by. Over."

She motioned to a tech, who handed her another microphone.

"Star Risk Inchcape, this is Star Risk Control."

"Star Risk Inchcape here. Over."

"Can you put your ships over that park in city center? I have someone in place with a laser painter. Over."

"On the way. Inchcape out."

"This is Star Risk Vian. Monitored your last. Do you want me to do the same?"

"That's affirmative," King said, feeling very much like a general.

Eat your heart out, Grok.

Speaking of whom . . .

"This is Star Risk Control," she 'cast on Grok's

frequency. "Stand by with your fire mission until air incoming clears your space."

"Standing by."

The starships whistled in. A few missiles came up, but the Khelat gunners either weren't trained or didn't have night sights, and they missed badly.

Chas Goodnight "painted" the obvious C&C ship with his laser designator.

High above, Inchcape's weapon's officer saw the target, "told" a missile where to strike, sent it on its way, then locked it.

Goodnight's designator beeped, and he switched to another target. Again, after an instant, his designator beeped, telling him the target was acquired.

He wasn't aware that he was grinning as he aimed at a third ship.

"The air is clear," Grok reported as the ships passed. "Fire mission!"

The tubes chugged on full auto.

Now, this, he thought, would be a killing.

Rated . . .

He remembered a word he'd read in some ancient book, thought it fit.

Frabjous.

Yes, frabjous.

Riss ignored protocol, ignored the unit commander, and took it upon herself to order the lifters forward.

No one objected, and the monsters lifted and went toward the flaming wreckage of the park.

Khelat were coming out of their hasty positions with

improvised white flags. Riss ordered the column on, not to stop for prisoners. She hoped the soldiers in the lifters didn't misunderstand her commands.

A hasty com told Grok to raise his artillery fire as the lifters, infantry running behind them, entered the park, or its wreckage.

There wasn't much more than a sniper here and there, and crew-served weapons took care of them, as well as whatever building they'd taken cover in.

One of Goodnight's commandos, seeing the lifters, got up and started cheering and waving.

Chas knocked him down, lay across him as somebody sent a burst just over their heads.

"It's dumb to get killed," he hissed into the man's ear. It's even dumber if it's your own side doing the killing."

At dawn, the reinforcements arrived. But there weren't many Khelat soldiers to worry about.

It was, as they say, a famous victory.

TWENTY-ONE

Colonel Suiyahr tried a smile, found it didn't suit her, and looked at Friedrich von Baldur as if he were a subaltern who'd been found embezzling the mess funds.

If it was intended to quail Friedrich, it didn't work. She wasn't the first to put on that expression to Freddie, nor the most justified.

"Of course, we're impressed with the way Star Risk helped us win the great victory on Shaoki II," she said, as if by rote. "And we hope there are many more in the future."

"So what is the problem, then?" von Baldur asked.

"Frankly, it is the fees you're charging us," Suiyahr said.

"Oh? I was about to inquire about the possibility of a bonus, given our performance on Shaoki II, which certainly was not of a sort specified in our contract."

"You jest, of course," she said. "We of the council feel that your rates are quite exorbitant, and having done some research, feel that the contract should be revised to be more in keeping with what other firms elsewhere in the galaxy charge for equivalent or even superior service."

"Might I ask what firms you've contacted to get such figures?"

"That isn't the point," Suiyahr said. "What is the point is that the council leads the Shaoki worlds, and considers itself responsible for the financial welfare of the people."

Von Baldur sighed. He could have mentioned the luxuries the council members lavished on themselves, knew better. As it was, it was shaping to be a very long afternoon.

The adjutant of Hore's battalion recognized Jasmine King.

"I'm honored," she said, a bit sarcastically. "I'm trying to contact one of your troopers . . . an artilleryman named Llaros," Jasmine said. "He's been having trouble with his pay. It appears the Shaoki are at fault."

"Hold on," the adjutant said, turned to a computer keyboard, hit keys.

"Right," she said. "Here he is. But I'll have to take a message. His whole battery is on a detail."

"Who'd they get on the wrong side of?" King asked incuriously.

"Nobody," the adjutant said. "We're just setting up our own armory. And I see there's an entry on him in the unit diary, said everything's straightened out."

"Good," King said. "But leave a message that I got back to him. We don't want anyone thinking we're turning into a bureaucracy. "King, out."

Jasmine frowned for an instant, then lost the thought just as Vian came into the suite.

"You said something about wanting to learn how to drive a starship," he said with a smile. "I volunteered. You want to make a swift run over to Khelat II and raise a little hell, strafing? A day or so gone."

Jasmine did, but wasn't sure she should. She glanced at her assistant, who held out his hands.

"We *can* manage without you," he said, with a bit of hauteur.

"Then we're on our way," King said, standing and reaching for her combat harness hanging on the wall behind her.

"You won't need that," Vian said. "We're the clean-fingernails sort, not hand-to-hand."

Jasmine started to replace the rig, caught herself, remembering Riss, who supposedly took her showers with her harness on.

"The only time you won't wear it," M'chel had said, her tones those of a high priestess, "is the one time it could have saved your ass."

Jasmine shrugged into the harness.

"I'd be lost without it."

Vian didn't argue, just grinned.

"I am thinking," von Baldur said to Goodnight and Grok, "after that snooty little interview with Her Ever So Arrogant Liaison with the Council, that we had best come up with a nice, spectacular target to keep the checks rolling in."

"I hear you, boss. I'll check with the crew," Goodnight said. "See what's whuppin'."

"So here we are," Vian announced as the three patrol ships broke out of hyperspace. "And the planet below should be Khelat IV's third world."

Jasmine realized her palms were wet from worry that her awkward navigation wouldn't even be close.

"And what would have happened if something else was there?" she asked, knowing the answer.

"It depends," Vian said. "If it were a sun, we'd go up like a spider in a candle flame. Another planet, and we'd calculate where we were and where we went wrong. If we were in the middle of nothingness, without a clue, we might have to embarrass ourselves and jump back to where we came from. But you plotted well, King. Just as I thought you would.

"Now if you'll slide out of the way, I'll take it in-atmosphere and the shooting can start."

Jasmine unsnapped her safety belt, slid back into the supernumerary's seat. She was slightly proud of herself, and also surprised that Vian had turned out to be a patient instructor.

"Next time," Vian said over his shoulder, "you can take it in. And you can try a landing when we go back home."

"Maybe," Jasmine said. "That will be my third."

The other two had been in yachts, with Riss as instructor.

"All right," Vian said to the others on board. "We're going in."

The patrol ship shuddered as it bounced into the outer atmosphere. Its wings glowed a bit red.

On a nearby screen, she saw the other two ships flanking her.

The target, on the far side of the world, was a resort area favored by the Khelat royalty. It was what Riss called a "piss-off target" intended to get the Khelat princes grinding their teeth at being subjected to such inhumanities. Angry war leaders generally aren't thinking coherently.

Vian's three ships had deliberately come in on the "far side" of things. Vian didn't really believe the Khelat were so totally inept as to not "see" the raiders. Hopefully, they'd launch whatever AA missiles they had at long range, thinking the target was Rafar City, and miss, leaving the three mercenary ships open targets.

Vian, as he brought the ship down toward the surface, yoinked it at irregular intervals.

That should further shake up whatever Khelat defense forces there were.

Jasmine had chosen the target on Riss's recommendations. She'd noted the resort when Star Risk was still on the Khelat payroll, but wasn't sure just how much they had in the way of defenses.

Since the resort was a third- or fourth-choice vacation, she assumed the security would be fairly light.

Everyone was almost right.

Jasmine was concentrating on holding on to her stomach. Even though the antigravity was on, the world spinning below her, getting closer by the instant, was still unsettling.

"I don't like this," Vian muttered, keyed his mike. "All Risk elements, this is Control. This is getting too easy."

There were twin mike clicks back at him, acknowledging his 'cast.

"The bastards should have started shooting," he said.

Vian's plan had been to bring the raiders straight down to about five thousand meters, flare out, streak for the capital like that was a target, then divert around Rafar City, which would be far too strongly defended, and fly over the deck along the shoreline to the resort.

They were at about ten thousand meters when a screen blipped.

"They've acquired us," Vian's weapons officer said. "Three, no, four sites."

There was a pause, silent except for the now-loud hiss of atmosphere against the ship's skin.

"We have a launch, sir. Six launches. All homing."

Vian growled, and the patrol ship's jinking became more furious.

"Closing . . ." the weapons officer reported. "Dumping chaff, firing countermissiles . . . three missiles fired . . . two acquired targets . . . closing . . ."

There were two bright flashes on a screen.

Jasmine took a deep breath.

She never saw the missile that exploded less than twenty meters away from the ship.

The craft bucked, rolled about its own axis, and spun down and down, toward the suddenly too-close planet.

Vian was fighting the controls, and the ship stabilized.

Khelat II's surface was veering up at them.

Jasmine King wanted to scream, but controlled herself.

The patrol ship was level, then spinning, still dropping, and Jasmine saw a flicker of land. Then there was nothing but water on-screen around them.

And then they hit.

TWENTY-TWO

Riss had lost friends before in combat and accidents, but somehow Jasmine's loss hit her particularly hard.

Illogically her mind told her it was her fault—if she hadn't wanted vengeance for Dov Lanchester, Jasmine would still be alive.

She thought about some kind of memorial service, then realized she hadn't the foggiest idea of what Jasmine King believed or disbelieved in.

It was a greater shock to realize she knew just as little about the other Star Risk members. Other than their obvious vices and virtues, they kept to themselves.

It was a lonely life. By choice.

She put those gloomy thoughts away. All she wanted was out of this goddamned cluster, and solitude and quiet.

"Nonsense," von Baldur said briskly. "We are not going to limp away licking our wounds."

"No," Goodnight agreed. "We're going to tear an enormous strip or two off the Khelat."

Grok snorted agreement.

"I think we will all feel better if we go out and break something."

M'chel considered for an instant.

"We will," she agreed reluctantly. "A very big frigging strip."

"Well, then," Goodnight said. "Shall we commence to plotting?"

Another message, this one in a simple business code, came from Alliance Credit, this one just saying that the previous person who wanted to establish contact with M'chel Riss had sent another message, repeating the first.

Riss thought about it, still didn't know how to play the card with Prince Wahfer, so let it lie.

Besides, she was busy plotting blood and slaughter.

There was a war on, but the Khelat rulers hadn't found it necessary to call for night shifts.

The huge shipyard was still, with only necessary maintenance machinery running, and the occasional two-man patrol, more to keep out thieves than anything else.

Star Risk wanted no mistakes, so there were none of Hore's infantrymen, nor any Shaoki on the raid.

One of Vian's patrol ships slipped in-atmosphere. The ship grounded at the spaceport attached to the yard, amid rusting and wrecked ships, and the four Star Risk operatives moved out.

They looked more like an equipment-repair crew than saboteurs, laden with strange packs, welding gear, and computers.

They cut their way through the double layer of wire at the rear of the plant, easily avoiding the alarm sensors, then found an easily jimmied door and went inside.

The building stretched for almost ten kilometers, and appeared impregnable.

Chas Goodnight licked his lips.

* * *

Grok eyed a huge hull-plate rolling mill, saw its weak spot. He tucked one of the demolition packs he was carrying into the huge gears at one side.

When the charge went, it would not only shatter the gears, but badly dislocate the great rollers, as well.

Friedrich von Baldur decided he felt like a ten-year-old again, as he kicked in the door labeled PRECISION MEASUREMENT DIVISION.

The shelves inside were stacked high with various gauges and calipers.

Friedrich went to work lustily with a large hammer he'd found, then set incendiary charges.

Riss struggled into a heat suit and sealed it.

Nearby roared two of the great smelters, kept running under robot control night and day. She opened one of the smelter doors, involuntarily jumped back as the flames reached out toward her.

Then she threw a boxful of floor sweepings into one smelter, then the next. Those contaminates should ruin this run, she thought.

Just to make sure, she put a small det charge on each of the doors' hinges.

Grok grumbled as he pushed the sliding door open, into the plant's central control room.

It hung from the roof of the yard building, all glass walls, looking down on the rows of machines and ships under construction.

He set to work, smashing here, cutting contacts there, zeroing out running computers over there.

Grok froze for an instant, seeing something move in a reflection in front of him. He whirled, and there was a watchman just outside the control room, a look of utter horror on his face, seeing the monster.

The man forgot about the blaster holstered at his hip.

Grok grabbed a table and hurled it through the glass at the man.

It hit him and he staggered back, over the metal railing outside the room, and fell 150 meters to the concrete below.

Grok went back to his destruction, thinking once, wistfully, how he wished Jasmine King were with him, to do a more thorough and subtle job.

Chas Goodnight sat at a computer terminal, tapping keys. He nodded satisfaction, looked out at the assembly floor.

Robot welders were moving, their torches glowing, as they set to work fastening themselves to each other and to the floor.

Damn, he thought. It *does* work. I never got a chance to try out my conditioning the Alliance gave me before.

Flame spurted here, and Goodnight decided it was time to be about his business.

Riss trotted down the corridor, between huge machines, sowing demo charges like a crazed planter.

She flung the last, and ran for the door they'd come in through.

The patrol ship was about five hundred meters up when flames gouted out the windows of the plant, and explosions shattered the assembly lines.

Von Baldur watched the screen with satisfaction.

"Well, a bit of revenge for our Jasmine," he said.

"Just a bit," Riss said coldly.

TWENTY-THREE

Riss looked at the stack of papers, growled like Grok, in timbre if not in happiness.

How come, she wondered, the romances never show the hard-bitten warrior as being up to her nipples in paperwork?

And how long was it since she'd been in the field, footloose, carefree, and destructive? A lousy week. Seemed like forever.

There was less than she'd have if she were still in the Alliance Marines, but still . . .

An unadmitted but experienced bureaucrat, Riss started flipping through reports. She frowned, went back through them, got on the com to Hore's battalion.

Hore's XO showed up on screen.

"Why isn't there any report on how well your training has been going?"

"We've been busy," the man said, a bit snippily. "But things have been going well."

"We've been busy, too," M'chel said. "That's no excuse. Can I expect something this decade, perhaps?"

"We'll see," the man said, smiled a distinctly unpleasant grin, and cut off.

"Aren't we the snotty little mercenary," Riss murmured. "What did I do to piss him off?"

She picked up a report, then stopped. She thought a minute, then went back to the com, and put in a 'cast to a Shaoki officer whose name she remembered.

Friedrich von Baldur got a com from the spaceport.

Someone named Miss Anya Davenport was at the spaceport, wanting pickup.

Von Baldur frowned. He knew no one by that—oh. Yes. That was the name of the lobbyist one of his contacts on Earth had recommended. She was supposedly expensive, but well worth the price.

But what the hell was she doing out here instead of hustling Omni Foods back wherever their corporate headquarters was?

A blank com answers no questions, so von Baldur grabbed the duty driver and headed for the spaceport.

"I do not understand what you are telling me," the Shaoki captain told Riss. "My brigade has not been having any training at all, ma'am. Unless being a stevedore is training."

"Explain, please," Riss said.

"Your Colonel Hore has had all available men putting an old arsenal back in service and transferring weaponry. Frankly, my soldiers are starting to grumble, saying they could have found jobs in a warehouse and gotten much better paid."

M'chel, even though she didn't know what anything meant, other than that Hore's troops were, at the very least, swinging the lead, was upstaged by Anya Davenport's arrival.

Riss knew Davenport was another kind of mercenary, but she hoped to hell she wasn't beginning to look as hard as the woman.

She was tall, could stand to put on about another five kilos, had clearly had at least one face-lift, as well as augmentation to her breasts, and was, naturally but unnaturally, blond.

Davenport announced to the assembled and very curious crew, over before-dinner drinks, as if it were a natural part of a résumé, that she'd been runner-up in one or another Miss Galaxy contest, as well as mentioning various politicos and firms she'd pumped for.

It appeared to M'chel as if Friedrich were thoroughly smitten.

Chas could have been, having never encountered a lobbyist before, but von Baldur appeared to have gotten in line first.

At dinner, Davenport asked if there was any of this wonderful *maln* tea about. Some was found and brewed.

Davenport tried it, smiling brightly, and only coughed twice.

"Very interesting," she said.

"You see," Grok announced. "There has to be someone besides myself liking it for it to be so successful."

"Fad freaks," Riss said, "never need a reason for liking something, other than other fad freaks do."

"I must say," Davenport said with a tinkling laugh, "it's as well you're not in Omni Foods' marketing division."

"That is the truth," Riss said, trying to sound friendly.

"Let me explain something," Davenport said, and the tinkle was gone.

"Omni Foods is divided, generally, into two divisions. The first is the Staples Market. This is rice, coffee, flour, and so forth. If your company is distributed by the Staples Division, or if your product is part of that network, you can relax, safe, comfortable, and very rich.

"The new foods—such as your *maln*—are in the New Products Division. That means Omni is taking a flier on them, on your company. If your product catches fire, as *maln* appears to be doing, then, after a suitable time, they'll move you over to the Staples Market."

Friedrich's eyes glittered a little.

"But if it's no more than a fad, a momentary interest, or if for some reason you cannot provide your product consistently, on a fairly massive basis, you're doomed.

"Omni's dropped hundreds of thousands of new products over the years. Do any of you remember *ralcat*?"

Blank looks from around the table.

"I didn't think so," Davenport said. "That is an example of just what I'm talking about. Gone and forgotten, and no one, including me, knows why.

"Now, from what Friedrich had sent me, you want me to convince Omni Foods that you are, ultimately, in control of the *maln* situation, as well as this cluster," Davenport said. "Which means no one need suggest the necessity of an Alliance peacekeeping force here."

"Just so," von Baldur said.

"The law gets in the way of our sort," Goodnight said bluntly.

"I hardly think that's the way to put things," Davenport said. "I wonder one thing, however, which you can correct me on. You are, let us say, advising the Shaoki here. Yet from what I've read, the other force in this cluster, the, uh, Khelat, have the majority of *maln* plantations. Am I in error?"

"No," Riss said. "But given the nature of things, that is not necessarily a permanent state of affairs."

Von Baldur looked mildly alarmed, as if Riss shouldn't have spoken.

"I gather by that," Davenport said, "you intend a swift victory."

Riss started to offer another option, kept her mouth shut.

"We anticipate an end to this frankly absurd war at any moment," von Baldur said, and M'chel knew why, way back when, somebody said she stood little chance of making general in peacetime, since that meant being most political.

"I'll be happy to provide a full briefing in my quarters," Friedrich went on, and Davenport dazzled him with a smile, her siren role coming back.

M'chel Riss decided she was going to bed early.

She was up early and heading out the door, buckling her combat harness on, when Anya Davenport, looking tousled, came down the hall from Friedrich von Baldur's suite.

That figured.

"How very interesting," Riss said as she eyed the manifest, authorizing the purchase of certain medium armaments, construction materials, and such, to be provided on a RUSH basis.

"Did I do something wrong by accepting this?" the worried clerk said. "Colonel Hore said he'd hand carried it to me, after you'd signed the requisition."

"No," Riss said slowly. "Nothing is wrong."

Everything was very wrong.

She'd never seen the requisition in her life, let alone signed it.

And she suddenly had a very good idea of what Hore was up to.

TWENTY-FOUR

It was Vian's death that saved Jasmine King's life.

When the patrol ship crashed, he went, very messily, into the control panel. Jasmine's seat broke at the mount, catapulting her into Vian's cushioning corpse.

The world went away as the ship pinwheeled, then settled, stern first, only thirty meters from shore.

She came back to a world of pain, hurting everywhere. There were various alarms, and King smelled something burning. She wanted to just lie still and go back to that place where it didn't hurt.

But she also wanted to live.

She managed to hit the quick release on her safety harness, rolled away from the mess onto the floor.

A port painted sunlight across her, then away, as the patrol ship turned in the surf.

She closed her eyes.

The burning smell got stronger.

Jasmine wanted somebody to help her.

But no one came.

Without opening her eyes, she ran her hands over her body. There weren't any bones sticking out. King forced herself to sit up, tried not to look at Vian's body. There were two more bodies in the cramped cockpit. She didn't need to get up to see they were as dead as their CO.

Hissing came.

King wondered, dully, what that could be, guessed it might be water hitting molten metal.

No.

She did not want to die.

She forced herself to her knees, then her feet. The overhead was very close to her, smashed down in the crash.

Still on the back of her seat was her combat harness. King stared at it for a time, then pulled it on.

She almost fell, caught herself on a bulkhead, staggered to the air lock. Jasmine hit the cycle sensor. There was a humming, then a grating noise, but nothing happened.

King hurt everywhere. There were tears running down her cheeks. That does nothing, she told herself, pulled the safety cover, and hit the emergency lock controls.

The explosive charges in the inner and outer doors blew the lock open, and she smelled ocean instead of the canned ship air.

The burning smell got stronger, and King heard, from somewhere near the ship's stern, the *whoosh* of flames. She felt heat, pushed herself down the small, twisted tube of the lock.

The ship rolled again, and slurped water into the lock. Jasmine let herself slide forward, out of the ship, into the water.

The salt burned her cuts, but it was cold enough to soothe her for an instant. King went underwater, curled, and brought herself back to the surface.

There was the ocean, a reef in front of her. She turned, wiped her blurred eyes, saw a rocky beach.

Jasmine discovered she could swim, and made for the shore. She feebly stroked, again and again.

It would be easier to just stop and let herself be swallowed by the cool greenness. It would be easier to let the combat harness fall away.

But she did neither, and then there were pebbles under her feet, and she was on her knees, crawling out of the tiny waves.

She wanted to collapse on the shore, but didn't, crawling toward brush. At least her near-indestructible ship suit wasn't torn.

She allowed herself to rest for a few minutes in the shelter of the brush.

Then she caught herself.

King stared out at the wreckage in the sea, realized anyone overflying it would assume everyone aboard was dead.

She fumbled in her harness for her SAR—search and rescue—com. Maybe the other two patrol ships were still in-atmosphere, and she could shout for help. Or maybe the SAR would reach beyond the atmosphere. She had no idea of its range.

The SAR com wasn't in its pouch.

Jasmine remembered where it was.

It was plugged into its recharger, where King had conscientiously put it the day before, back on the bureau in her suite on Irdis.

And she was the woman who was supposed to remember everything. . . .

There was a scream, and King got up. It had to be one of the patrol ships coming back to see if Vian or anyone was alive.

It wasn't, Jasmine realized, in time to flatten herself.

An in-atmosphere interceptor dove down.

Khelat.

Flanking it were three wingmen. Rockets spat from the lead ship, into the wreckage of the patrol ship, and it exploded, the shock wave rolling toward shore.

Jasmine found herself crying again, thought Goodnight would be snarling "What a baby" at her, forced herself to stop, crawled farther away from the ocean as the Khelat flight made another firing run.

An hour later, things looked a little better to her. She definitely had nothing but bruises, even though a few of them would make wonderful shades of purple.

All she was missing was the SAR com. Everything else was proper and well maintained.

Jasmine had some serious extras.

For openers, a lot more money than the standard survival kit suggested. She had both gold coins and Alliance credits.

Her emergency food packs had been tweaked by M'chel to be almost palatable, and she had tiny packets of spices to go with them.

Jasmine remembered the on-screen map of Khelat II quite clearly. Rafar City would be about thirty kilometers . . . that way. King didn't need a compass to find north. It was reflexive.

Her intent was to hike to the city, keeping away from the locals, since she would be hard-pressed to resemble them. She wished there really were bandits in the hills she could join up with until she was able to rejoin Star Risk, but knew better.

King guessed she'd work her way into the capital and try to join up with Ells and his maintenance crews. She doubted they'd turn her over to the Khelat. She was very unsure about the other mercenaries who'd remained with the Khelat.

It was a plan. Maybe not a very good plan, but a plan.

King put everything away in their little pouches in her harness, clipped it on, and set out, remembering the old cliché: "A journey of a thousand blisters starts with a single stumble."

TWENTY-FIVE

Hore and his ranking officers roused their battalion an hour before dawn, always a propitious time for a palace revolution.

In the hours before, the men and women had been armed, the supplies coming from the new arsenal to prevent suspicion, and told their duties.

The few mercenaries who still had any ideals were told that Star Risk had made a secret pact with the Khelat to doublecross everyone, including their fellow mercs, in the Shaoki worlds.

This was a deceit.

At the moment.

The more rational soldiers were told that Hore thought it was time to get rid of Star Risk because they weren't "winning the war by direct action," and, more important, were hogging the majority of the client's credits.

None of the various watching posts on Star Risk positions or soldiery reported anything untoward, although two LPs on the "mansion" said there'd been a flurry of ships that arrived after dusk on the roof landing platforms, but they'd trailed away within hours.

Electronic posts reported normal traffic from the high-rise.

The two critical units were Inchcape's destroyers and the three remaining patrol boats of Vian's unit.

All but one of the starships were comfortably grounded. Vian was dead, and Inchcape had just left on a five-day leave, according to reports from Star Risk Central.

Hore's XO and adjutant were beginning to gloat, but Hore reminded them of Shakespeare's lion hunter, and said the celebrations could wait until they had Star Risk's hide properly skinned and staked out for drying.

He reported to the Shaoki Council members who'd convinced him to betray his employers that his troops were on the move.

Hore intended to cause as few casualties as possible in his coup and make one quick strike against the mansion, wait until Star Risk realized fighting back was useless, and it would all be over.

Two cargo lifters had been fitted with 200 mm medium autocannon. Keeping to the streets, they closed on the high-rise. Behind them was the rest of the battalion, all in lifters.

Shaoki civilians heard the turbine whine, peered down, saw soldiers in the streets, and made for cover.

On signal, the two lifters came up from their concealment and took the mansion area into their sights. They each fired four rounds in less than a minute.

Masonry crashed, and glass sharded down. The outer wall of the high-rise cracked and tumbled, exposing Star Risk's innards.

The infantry lifters came in, surrounding the high-rise. There was only one slight problem:

There was no one, no one at all, in Star Risk's quarters.

Hore was still gaping at this impossibility when Inchcape's destroyer dropped down out of the clouds.

Two missiles spat out, were guided into Hore's artillery.

They blew, fireballs that left little debris to cascade down.

As the missiles struck, the other destroyers and the patrol boats lifted off from their fields. Her four destroyers linked with Inchcape, and each sent one missile arcing down on Hore.

The four Star Risk operatives watched, grim-faced, from Inchcape's bridge.

Riss had put sensors out around Hore's barracks, two days before, when she'd figured out what the man intended.

When the alarms went off the day before, as Hore concentrated his troops, Star Risk evacuated all their personnel from the hotel and let Hore walk into their trap.

The patrol boats flew up the streets, just over Hore's infantry lifters. There was no escape for the infantry— but the patrol boats held their fire.

Hore looked around, saw he was surrounded from above, took the obvious way out.

"Does anyone," he asked in an emotionless tone, "happen to have a white flag?"

Hore's battalion was disarmed, including the officers' individual weapons.

Hore started to say something about this being dishonorable, got a look from Riss that shut him up.

He was enough of a leader to be the last aboard the transports commandeered from the Shaoki, turned back at the entrance to the lock, and tried a smile.

"No hard feelings?" he asked.

"None," Friedrich von Baldur said in a friendly tone.

Hore nodded, went into the lock, and it cycled shut.

"Maybe not for you," Goodnight said. "But I'm looking forward to meeting him in a bar someday."

"Our blood requirements weren't satisfied," agreed Grok.

"Oh, well," von Baldur sighed. "At least they didn't ask for their back pay."

"Screw them," Riss said. "They're gone. Now we've got to figure out how to doublecross the Shaoki that tried to doublecross us."

TWENTY-SIX

Jasmine King glowered at the approach to Technician Ells's maintenance and supply compound. It was down a straight road with no hiding places on either side. The road was z'd with solid barricades to slow traffic. The razor wire fence around the dozen buildings was taut, well maintained.

The pair of Khelat sentries were sharply turned out, and there was a manned and alert AA site just inside the gate to deal with any attacking lifters.

Jasmine had walked around the compound looking for a weak point, and couldn't find any.

Why couldn't Ells have instructed his guards to be a little more sloppy?

She couldn't stay here and hope Ells came out. A roving patrol swept the outside perimeter every two hours.

She was far too tattered for that. King wanted a bath and a general cleanup.

The hike into Rafar City had taken five days. She'd been lucky in finding a strip of *maln* plantations to move through, which gave her cover and water.

In a shed, she'd found a worker's coveralls, which, though stinky, were far less distinctive than her ship suit and were large enough to hide her combat harness under.

King had been feeling a little clever by the time she wove her way around the city outskirts to Ells's compound.

And then the cards turned up zero-zero.

Very well, she decided. She would have to choose Option B.

Unfortunately, at the moment, she didn't have one figured out.

King muttered a few choice obscenities, feeling Riss would be proud of her for that, at least, and regretfully started away, into the city.

At least she had more than enough money. She could buy almost anyone on the planet, outside the royal family.

Maybe that was a clue to what she should be doing.

Instinctively, she headed for the poor section. Working sorts were somewhat noisy, but they weren't known as snitches.

Three hours later, she had an idea, sparked by the business across from her.

It was most prepossessing—a fairly large store, with not much of anything on the shelves.

The sign outside read:

BEYDOM & SONS—PHARMACEUTICALS AND BEAUTY SUPPLIES.

Inside, there was one clerk, a pudgy, defeated-looking man in his fifties, staring at a computer screen.

A possibility.

She went in.

"Mr. Beydom?"

The man looked up.

"I am he. Son, rather."

"I need some beauty supplies," Jasmine said. She named a base makeup, and a skin cream that would darken her face and hands to match the Khelat complexions.

"I can sell you one, but not the cream," Beydom said. "We're out of stock on that."

He looked around at the nearly bare shelves, was about to say something else, changed his mind.

This was going as Jasmine had hoped.

"May I speak frankly?"

Beydom looked worried, then suddenly smiled.

"Why not? What do I have to lose?"

"I've been watching your store for several days now," Jasmine lied.

Now Beydom looked really worried.

"I'm not from the police or anything like that," King soothed.

"No," Beydom said. "And you're an offworlder. Trying, I'd guess, to look like one of us."

King nodded.

"I'm looking for two things," she said. "First, a place where I can be, shall we say, incognito. Second, a place to invest in. You appear to be somewhat cash-short."

Beydom nodded.

"My father left me—and my brothers—with this, and no more. My brothers had the brains to find other work. Managing a *maln* processing plant. I should have gone with them. But . . . well, I always fancied myself as someone who could help people. . . . And this district has only a few stores. I'm as much a doctor as most of these people have. So I stayed. Along with the old people and those who couldn't afford to move."

King was mildly alarmed. She hadn't expected this fast a reaction.

"I have a great deal of ready cash, which I want to invest," she said. She reached under her suit and dropped gold coins on the countertop.

Beydom's eyes widened. He picked up one coin, examined it.

"Alliance credits," he said softly.

"Yes."

"Are you one of the mercenaries the king has brought in? I've seen them on the 'casts."

"No," Jasmine said.

Beydom looked at her closely, realized she wasn't going to volunteer anything more.

"I can't easily convert this to Khelat," he said. "But there's one advantage of living where I do. There are many people who deal in such things."

"Yes."

"How much are you willing to spend . . . and how can you trust me?" Beydom said. "I can't see drawing up papers."

"You do not need to know how much I have. . . . And the fact you brought up the matter of trust suggests I can," Jasmine said.

She brought out more coins, laid them out.

"I think you should close your shop now and buy the cream I need . . . as well as whatever else this store needs to be immediately profitable."

"I . . . I can do that."

"Now we shall see how far trust goes."

King sat down in a chair, smiled expectantly.

Beydom gurgled, said he could take care of things and could he get her anything, and he'd be right back.

He got a coat, went out of the shop hurriedly.

King waited until he was out of sight, left the shop herself, and went down the street to an alley she'd decided on before she'd entered Beydom's.

First contact was always the hardest and most dangerous in intelligence work.

She didn't like things going as fast as they were; she was worried about what could go wrong.

Not that she had that many options.

King went in the alley and crouched behind a large trash bin, her heavy blaster ready. If Beydom came back with the police, or with anyone, the question of trust would be conclusively answered, although Beydom was unlikely to benefit from the solution.

It took over an hour, and King's palms were very moist when she spotted the man coming back. He carried a large bag and was nervously looking about, as if expecting the heavy hand of the law at any moment. He clearly did not have the makings of a criminal.

Beydom ducked inside the store, then came back out, looking about for King, his expression worried.

King let him worry for a few minutes, then came out into the street.

Beydom looked massively relieved.

"I was afraid that—"

"I told you I'm not from the police," Jasmine said. "So I am now your silent—very silent—partner."

"I suppose so. What are your intentions?"

"I am not going to tell you. If the police arrive—or if you decide to sell me out—there'll be nothing they can beat out of you, is there? Besides, I have nothing but honorable intentions for the people of Khelat."

Beydom's disbelief showed.

"Now, I am going to turn myself into a Khelat," King said.

"I have everything you need," Beydom said. "Including some clothes. Don't look worried—I do better than most men. I used to shop for my wife . . . when I was married." His expression was massively forlorn. "You can wash and change upstairs. In my apartment."

King made an acceptable Khelat. The clothes were a little flashy, but nothing that noticeable.

Beydom offered to let her use rooms near his—he owned the entire building.

But Jasmine wasn't that trusting.

She went out at dusk, checked half a dozen rooming houses, found one where the owner didn't look as if she had the slightest curiosity about anything, and paid for a room by the week with Khelat coins.

Now she was ready to start work.

If the Khelat didn't really have bandits in the hills or in the city, they were about to now.

Jasmine's plans started with a large-scale map of Rafar City.

She had Beydom make a list of what he needed to put the pharmacy into profits, and sent him shopping.

King also included a few items of her own on the list, such as fuel for an emergency generator, red nitric acid, bleach, a salt substitute (potassium chloride), distilled water, a good filter, a battery charger, and salt. Harder to get were white gas and petroleum jelly.

Beydom desperately wanted to ask what she wanted with the latter two, but realized she wasn't about to tell him.

Working upstairs from the pharmacy, in a very well-ventilated room, King put what she'd learned from Riss and Goodnight to work.

Once a compound started hissing at her, but she quickly doused the budding explosion with a fire extinguisher.

Easier were the timers, after Jasmine found, in the bowels of Beydom's storeroom, old-fashioned mechanical timers, and some cheap electronic devices.

Hardest of all were the detonators. King took a very big chance and made up nitroglycerin, managing not to blow her fingers, head, or the building away.

She decided she didn't want a career as a budding saboteur, but didn't have much choice.

Over the following days, the store's shelves started filling up. . . . And there were thronging customers.

King insisted the retail price be no more than 5 percent above what Beydom paid for the goods.

Normally, ghetto stores are vastly more expensive than ones in plusher parts of town, their proprietors figuring, generally correctly, their potential customers didn't have the wherewithal to travel elsewhere to shop.

And so, between the prices and Beydom's rather sensible medical advice, business boomed.

Now it was time for King's own concerns to do a little booming of their own.

The first device, which she dubbed, having heard M'chel use the phrase, a "fiendish thingie," was planted outside what Beydom had told her was a police interrogation center.

Having no faith in her abilities, she used a bit more of what she'd made with the nitric acid and the fuel than the manual she'd memorized a year ago called for.

When it went off, it blew most of the station's facade away, and cheering prisoners escaped into the night.

An hour later, a pawnshop exploded.

Its owner's crime, Beydom had told her, was being a little too cozy with the police. Or so his money changer had told him.

Jasmine didn't really care if the man was innocent or guilty. The shop's main sin was being six blocks south of the first bomb.

Seven more to go.

Jasmine King hoped that Star Risk wasn't asleep at the switch.

TWENTY-SEVEN

M'chel Riss was glooming over a map of Khelat II's Rafar City. She was looking for revenge for Jasmine's death in general, and Dov's murder in particular.

She was trying to figure out a way to murder Prince Jer, Lanchester's killer, but nothing came.

Riss wanted to get him in a small room and thin-slice his guts, but was willing to settle for a nice, lethal air strike if that was all that presented itself. But she had no link to Jer, no way of following his travels.

It was not a good day.

It had started with von Baldur paying off the three remaining ships of Vian's squadron. Mercenaries have some virtues, but taking serious casualties is not one of them. In their tiny world, a single death is magnified, and the loss of Vian, and two ships, had hit them hard.

Von Baldur had decided—with no argument from the other three in Star Risk—that it was better to get rid of the soldiers rather than have them glooming around, ruining everyone's morale.

That was starting to leave Star Risk a little thin on the ground, after Hore's attempted mutiny. They were left with scattered odds and sods, with hardly anyone to cover their back. With the Shaoki's treachery in seducing Hore, that gave them a bit of an itchy feeling, about knife-size, between the shoulder blades.

In spite of her brave words, Riss hadn't figured out a way to double-cross the Shaoki, at least without it being a suicidal operation.

She was still unsure of what to do about Prince Wahfer and his two coms. She assumed his wanting to get in touch wasn't a case of lust, but couldn't figure any other obvious motives. Riss, like any experienced mercenary, knew better than to get away from her soldiery, even to meet with Wahfer on some neutral world, and wasn't about to commit at this stage of events. Mercenaries without swords around them tend to get assassinated, since a blaster bolt is a good deal cheaper than meeting the payroll.

Her map blipped at her, and Riss forced herself out of her brood.

Three red blots appeared on the map.

"What are these?" M'chel asked a technician.

"Uh . . ." The tech touched sensors. "Interesting. Somebody's setting off bombs in Rafar City . . . and it's not us."

Riss frowned. She didn't have the foggiest, and wasn't fond of anyone running a freelance operation.

Another screen blorped at her.

It was Friedrich.

"We have an inbound," he said, sounding happy. "Actually, half a dozen blips. Patrol ships, commanded by one Redon Spada."

Spada was not only one of the best pilots to ever be ignored by the Alliance, but someone who was known to make calf eyes at Riss.

"He's looking for a job," Friedrich said. "And I think we just might have one for him."

TWENTY-EIGHT

Riss met Spada and his ships at the port.

For some reason, there was a certain amount of tension between them. Riss cursed at herself, remembering the time she'd come home on leave from officers' candidate school, fresh in her new uniform, cocky in newfound self-confidence, and had encountered her old school boyfriend. One look, one embrace, and she'd been reduced to the sappy adolescent she'd been before joining the Marines.

But she'd never even kissed Spada, let alone anything better.

If she felt absurd, Spada seemed even more ill at ease.

"We are glad to see you," she said.

"Careful," he said with a grin. "Saying things like that drives my contract price up."

Grok and Goodnight were in space, off Khelat IX's primary world, aboard Inchcape's flagship, the *Fletcher*.

The *Fletcher* lay doggo, all coms silent, and only life-essential machinery turned on.

Two other DDs orbited nearby under equal silence.

The *Fletcher* was positioned just "below" the standard jumping-off point into hyperspace the Khelat used to reach the closest Alliance worlds.

Goodnight had learned the fine art of what he called lizarding while nothing was happening—to be awake, somewhat alert, but around him time simply flowed past, without notice.

Like he was a reptile on a rock.

For a time, anyway.

He was just starting to realize how bored he was, and how much it bothered him, when the watch officer buzzed Inchcape. "We've got activity on-planet," he reported.

Inchcape went to the bridge, looked at screens. "We do indeed," she decided. "Wake 'em up."

The general quarters siren screeched through the ship, and women and men came awake and, rubbing the eyes and yawning, went to their alert positions.

"What do we have?" Grok asked.

The watch officer said, "Four, no, six ships lifting off . . . big, suggest they're transports . . . and half a dozen smaller ones—escorts I'd guess—jumping off in front of them."

The officer consulted a screen, touched sensors, frowned, tried again. He hit another sensor, and a third screen lit. "They should be assembling about . . . here." He touched the screen.

"They think," Inchcape said. "Put all TA systems on seek around that point. And hook me up to the others."

She issued similar orders to the other destroyers. "I don't see any reason," she said, "for us to fardiddle around waiting to maybe get shot at."

"Against my religion," Goodnight agreed.

"Weapons, put me out about, oh, ten shipkillers, drifting them toward the IP so they'll get there in about twenty minutes."

She touched her throat mike.

"*Inch Two, Three,* did you monitor?"

Two affirms came in.

"You do the same. Hold the missiles in a orbit when they're close."

She cut her mike. "Now we wait."

They did, for almost an hour.

"Not very damned efficient, are those Khelat? They should've had them formed up and gone fifteen minutes ago."

"They're in range of our birds," the weapons officer reported.

"Have our babies acquired them?"

"That's affirmative," the officer said.

"Let 'em get a little closer," Inchcape said. "It never hurts to put 'em straight down the throat."

Goodnight was suddenly aware his lower lip was sweating.

"Fine," Inchcape said after a few moments, looking utterly calm. "Fire 'em up."

The blue dots that were the missiles began moving.

"On auto-home," she ordered.

"Yes, ma'am," the weapons officer reported.

"See if you can't get some good targeting on those incoming escorts," Inchcape said. "It'd be nice to have some icing on the cake."

Seconds passed.

The *Fletcher,* then the other two ships, reported targets acquired.

"Three shipkillers per target," Inchcape said. "On my command . . . fire."

She turned to Grok. "I should, if I was a professional, be scooting on home. But I'd like to see some blood."

"I also," the alien agreed.

Goodnight was watching a timer flash down.

"We should be seeing some explosions right about . . ."

"Hit!" weapons reported. "Hit! Hit!"

There were flashes onscreen. Then came three more.

"So much for those freighters," Inchcape said.

"Homing on one escort . . . three seconds to closing . . . hit!"

There was another flash.

"Three got lucky," Inchcape said. "Now, what about that other rascal . . ."

But there were no signs of another hit on the last escort.

"Just as well, I suppose," Inchcape said. "Somebody's gotta carry the message to Ghent. Now, let's go home and let them lick their wounds. Wonder what they were carrying?"

"This world is primarily agricultural," Grok said. "It could well be *maln*."

"I'd rather it were minerals, but we can live with the slow pain," Goodnight said. "It'll make sure Omni Foods is paying attention."

TWENTY-NINE

"We have something interesting," the technician back at Star Risk said.

Riss made a face. She was tired of screens, and thinking, and was thoroughly enjoying being out on a firing range working with Shaoki recruits.

"What is it?" she asked into the pocket-sized com.

"I think you'd better look at it, if you can find a larger screen somewhere."

M'chel grunted.

"Hold on. I'll get back to you." She turned to the Shaoki officer. "Take charge, sir."

The officer saluted.

Riss made her way to the range office, grabbed the com, and contacted the tech.

"It better be good, troop," she threatened.

"I don't know if it's good or not, M'chel," the tech said. "But it's interesting. I'm sending you the map of Rafar City you were looking at. See the three dots where someone has set off some bombs?"

"I have it."

"There have been four more bombings. . . . The Khelat press have admitted to a psychopath in the streets. I'm patching you the location of those four."

"I've got them, too," Riss said. "So what?"

"I'm now cutting the map into the background."

"Son of two bitches!" M'chel swore.

With the map subdued, the bomb locations made a very precise letter *J*.

"J," M'chel muttered. "Like in Jasmine, maybe?"

Hope came.

"No," she said. "Just chance."

"Probably," the tech agreed.

"I'm headed back right now," Riss said. "Get whatever firm principals are reachable, and tell them I want a face-to-face. Urgent."

"Right," the technician said. "I don't believe in chance, either."

Grok was helping the security crew make a routine sweep of Star Risk headquarters when he was commed.

"I shall be available in one E-hour," he said. "As soon as we finish checking the ventilation system. Out."

He cut the com, and eyed the cover one of his operators was unfastening.

"I shall never fit down that passage," he said. "But you are slender and young."

"And you outrank me," the operator said, grinning, lifting away the screen.

"I'll just slither up this one," the man said. "I think there's another outlet around the passageway . . . and HOLY GODDAMNED SHIT!"

"You have found something?" Grok said.

"You bet your furry ass," the operator said, wriggling back out. "Have a look."

Grok crouched and stuck his head in as the operator came out of the tunnel.

"Well, Bishop Berk with his hat on," the alien said

mildly. "Someone appears to have planted a bomb on us."

"This," Grok said, "is the detonator of the bomb I found just under your suite, Friedrich. The bomb, incidently, is about one kiloton in size."

Von Baldur eyed the device, as did Goodnight and Riss.

"Command detonated," M'chel said.

"One 'cast on its frequency and no more Star Risk, with a bomb that big," Goodnight said. "That'll take out this whole floor and then some. How very nice."

Behind them, ignored for the moment, was the map of Rafar City and the bomb site locations.

"I think we can assume," von Baldur said, "it has probably been planted by our employers. The Khelat do not appear to be very good at infiltrating."

"That's one of the problems," M'chel agreed. "It's the Shaoki's world, so it's hard to run an airtight operation. Not to mention we're too thin on the ground to provide anybody with any security, let alone us."

"First the bastards try a coup on us, next they're going to murder us," Goodnight said. "Nice sort of bosses to have."

"I wonder when they'll try to trigger it," Riss wondered.

"A better question," von Baldur said, "is why."

There was a blank silence. No one had any answers.

"I deactivated it," Grok said. "But I added a small device that will make a record if anyone tries to set it off."

"I'd suppose," Riss said, "whenever whoever has the bang switch decides we've become redundant, they'd want to wait until we're all together. So, no more family home evenings, boys and girls. We want to keep the fact that we know about their bombie secret as long as possible."

"We now have two things to discuss," Friedrich said. "First, and most importantly, what are we proposing to do about this bomb?"

"I have an idea," Goodnight said with an evil grin. "I just need to do a little research."

"I thought you might," Friedrich said. "But that brings up questions two and three: What are we going to do about ourselves, and what are we going to do about this mysterious *J*?"

Again, a silence. Finally, Riss tried one.

"If you've got some ideas on the bomb," she said, "I think I better get my young ass saddled up and go visit a certain prince. That might help us toward answering questions two and three."

THIRTY

The civilian Shaoki com operators routing the call were in awe. They'd never handled a com from the Alliance before, let alone one from Earth itself.

"This is Friedrich von Baldur." Freddie wondered who on Earth . . . literally . . . would be . . . oh.

"Scramble R342," a synthesized voice said.

Von Baldur nodded at the Star Risk operator, who set the appropriate key on a scrambler. It was a most sophisticated device, providing not a single scramble but synchronized with the sending com, changing both frequencies and code on a completely random basis at irregular intervals.

The screen cleared, and it was, indeed, their lobbyist, Anya Davenport.

"Good day," von Baldur almost cooed.

"I hope it is," Davenport said, in a far less congenial tone than she'd had before.

The very long subspace connection *blurp*ed occasionally, so von Baldur had to listen closely to the transmission.

"I have," she said without preamble, "established contact with the entity you wished."

Omni Foods.

"They are aware that you, essentially, control the supply of the item we discussed."

Maln. Von Baldur was impressed with Davenport's sense of security.

"Good," he said.

"I'm not so sure. The shipments have been irregular of late, and sometimes not arriving at all. The entity claims that you and your units are responsible for this."

"We are," von Baldur agreed. "We are fighting a war, remember?"

"I'm aware of that," Davenport said. "But is this wise? If you desire to be in the position you hired me for, at the conclusion of the fighting, wouldn't you be best advised to ensure regularity in the availability of the commodity?"

"Why?" Friedrich asked.

"The entity will, no doubt, think that if you can perform as promised now, they're more likely to have faith in you in the future," Davenport said.

"I understand your position," von Baldur said. "But, to rephrase what I already said, it is necessary to win this war first."

Davenport grimaced.

"I have only taken on people of your profession twice in my career, not with particularly happy conclusions. I took your company as a client because I was advised you are more subtle and aware of long-range consequences than soldiers are normally."

"That is, indeed, why you were hired," von Baldur said.

"Very well," Davenport said. "I'll do what I can to soothe the entity's feathers. But for the future, consider what I've said."

"I shall."

Without further chitchat, the screen blanked.

Von Baldur sat for a time, staring thoughtfully at the blank screen.

THIRTY-ONE

Riss chose her world, or rather worlds, carefully.

Her first com to Prince Wahfer told him the meeting was on a certain world beyond the Khelat-Shaoki Cluster, and to check into a certain hotel. There a message waited, saying that unavoidable circumstances made it necessary to change the meeting place to a second world a system away.

Not that she thought the Khelat were evil backstabbers who might have a hit team waiting for any member of Star Risk who materialized, but she thought the Khelat were evil backstabbers with hit teams.

The real meet was set on a small resort planetoid blessed with large mineral deposits, so it had E-normal gravitation.

The owner of the planetoid owed Star Risk, which M'chel thought meant that Freddie had lost large there.

And Riss called the favor in.

All she wanted was her choice of back doors to where Redon Spada's patrol ships waited, a plain-clothes security detail, and periodic reports on her in-coming guest.

The planetoid's owner told M'chel that she could have an entire casino hotel for her own. All other guests, other than Prince Wahfer and his retinue, would be local gunnies.

Riss wondered just how much von Baldur had lost on the tables there. . . .

Wahfer arrived in a sleek, gleaming, almost-Alliance-current-issue cruiser, with another one as escort.

Riss didn't get worried—princes do things like that.

The two met for dinner.

Wahfer's bodyguards had been stopped on their way in, frisked, disarmed, and escorted out. Wahfer started to protest, looked at Riss, said nothing.

"You are even more beautiful than I remembered," he gushed.

Riss thought he was debonair, impeccably tailored, charmingly accented, wonderfully mannered—and a frigging Khelat creep.

But this was business.

"Thank you, my prince," she said in a voice slightly oilier than his. "Please, sit down, and order us a drink. I know little about drinking."

She thought that if Wahfer held still for that one, he'd led an even more sheltered life than she thought. But he seemed to accept it, and ordered a magnum of Ganymede champagne.

It came, was loudly opened by the casino's sommelier, and poured.

Wahfer thought it wonderful.

Riss thought it not nearly dry enough.

Wahfer looked through the dining room, which was quite full, into the casino beyond, also filled with gamblers.

Riss thought too many of these phony customers were watching them, but Wahfer didn't seem to notice.

"Ah," he sighed. "I do love the riffle of the cards and the click of the dice. . . . But I'm afraid this trip must be held to business."

"Ah?" Riss thought about pretending disappointment, decided not to push her acting skills.

"Your com," Riss said, "told me there was some sort of terrible error made toward Star Risk."

"It absolutely was," Wahfer said. "Our accounting department became confused, which is why you had payroll problems. I do wish that you had come to me, or to the king, with your problems, rather than acting so precipitately."

Either Wahfer didn't know about Prince Jer having murdered Dov Lanchester, about the attempt to kill Goodnight and Grok in the warehouse, and possibly not about the Khelat pirating of Alliance supplies, or he was an excellent liar.

Riss put her money on the latter.

"And going to the Shaoki," Wahfer said in an almost moan. Riss thought his eyes looked like a spaniel's, and wondered if he was about to start crying.

"People value different things," Riss said. "With us, money replaces honor."

Wahfer took a minute to choose his response.

"Well, that is as may be. You may rest assured that whatever grievance you have against us has been more than repaid in blood and ruin."

Nice to hear, Riss thought. But she kept her silence and a neutral expression.

"That is the past," he said. "Let us set those matters aside and go back to the beginning.

"My king desperately wants to end this dispute between Star Risk and ourselves, and convince you to return to our service."

Now it was Riss's turn to be surprised. That, certainly, had been one of the possibilities she'd considered, and even hoped for. But to come this easily?

"I don't know about that," she said.

"King Saleph and Prince Barab have authorized me to offer you twice what the original contract was for. Paid month to month, or even day to day, in advance, to your bank." Wahfer's face looked like it was poisoning him to say this.

"Well, that is most generous of you," Riss said. "But that, quite frankly, doesn't match what we are currently being paid by the Shaoki."

"I don't suppose it matters to you that the Shaoki, as you know, are in the wrong in this matter, and are immoral dogs."

Riss sipped champagne.

"On my own word," Wahfer said, "I will increase our offer another one-third."

"Now, that might be worthwhile taking back to my colleagues for discussion," Riss said. "Of course, there would be additional fees required, since the war has grown more serious, and we shall have to take on additional personnel to be able to make the Khelat victorious. But it is interesting, and I suspect I would vote in favor of the measure."

Giving me, M'chel thought, a chance to get in a room with that murderous Prince Jer, tie his guts to a pole, and chase him around it.

"Good. Good," Wahfer said. "Obviously, there is no point in continuing this until the other members of Star Risk have a chance to think about things, although I know you will be most persuasive and I suspect, when the war is concluded, you will be eligible for a medal, and a bonus, which need not concern the others in Star Risk. You will not find us ungrateful.

"Now we can relax and enjoy ourselves, just the two of us, man and woman."

Wahfer smiled his sexiest smile.

M'chel Riss still thought he was a creep.

THIRTY-TWO

"So," Goodnight said. "We now appear to have a place to go."

"Assuming we are not doublecrossed by the Khelat on arrival," Friedrich said.

"I don't see any choice," Riss said. "Except getting the hell out of the system."

"Which means abandoning the slight possibility that Jasmine is still with us . . . which is, unfortunately, less than logical," Grok said. "Was there any mention of the J-bomber?"

"The subject didn't come up," M'chel said. "And I didn't bring it up, either."

"Probably just as wise," von Baldur said. "Grok, are you sure you want to be thinking Jasmine is still with us?"

Grok didn't answer.

"So the problem we have now is being able to make our exit gracefully," Goodnight said. "We don't want to alert the Shaoki, which would mean they'd set off the bomb. When it doesn't detonate as expected, I assume they'd send in the marching band."

"Speaking of which," Riss said, "did you figure out your end of the plot involving said bomb?"

"I did," Goodnight said. "Grok and I are going to shove it in its proper 'ole this very night."

"We are?" Grok asked.

"I volunteered you," Goodnight said. "I'm the beauty and brains, and you're the muscle."

Grok growled.

"So what we have to figure," von Baldur said, "is how we get ourselves, and what remains of our troops, out of here as quickly as possible."

"We could just worry about ourselves," Goodnight said. "They're big boys and girls. Don't you think the Shaoki would just let them wander off when they realize us villains are done gone?"

"You're assuming logic from the Shaoki?" Riss said.

"Strong point," Goodnight said.

"Actually, it should be quite easy," von Baldur said. "A little scheme, a little singing, a little music, and everyone's home free. Or, at any rate, in the Khelat's loving hands."

By the end of the day, von Baldur and Riss came up with a plan.

"All it takes to succeed is an amazing amount of stupidity on the part of the Shaoki," von Baldur said.

"I have full confidence in them," Riss said, just a bit smugly.

They began with acquiring, either through requisition or purchase, every recorder they could find.

Von Baldur commed Colonel Suiyahr, announced that he had some distressing news. Suiyahr, their main contact with the council, looked concerned. Von Baldur told the colonel that he'd sent Riss offworld on an espionage mission.

"We knew she had gone," Suiyahr said smugly. "We just were not sure what the reason was."

"Riss discovered," von Baldur went on, "that the Khelat have been buying large quantities of poison gas, and propose to make the first attack here on Irdis."

"The bastards!"

"Agreed," von Baldur said. "Fortunately, both Colonel Riss and myself are fully trained in the field of chemical weaponry, and feel that we'll be able to not only counteract their barbarity, but turn the weapon back on them."

"Good," Suiyahr said. "Our troops have no training in that aspect of soldiering. . . . We never felt anyone, even the Khelat, are dastardly enough to use such a weapon against us. Clearly, we were wrong."

Friedrich nodded.

"What we propose is, since many of our own soldiers are untrained, to run an exercise, then, after it's finished, to have a command-post seminar on what went right and what went wrong. Then we'll be prepared to train your troops."

"A CP seminar, eh? There at your central base?" Suiyahr said. She almost licked her lips. "I am glad," she said, "you are so concerned."

She blanked the screen.

Von Baldur got up from the com set, smiling.

"Hook, line, and sinker," he said gleefully.

"We want running feet," Riss said. "Right past the pickup, on to the next."

"What's this all about, M'chel?" one of the com techs asked. "You've had us chattering into the com, dashing back and forth, and shouting orders all damned day."

"Now, if I wanted you to know," Riss said, "I would've told you, wouldn't I? Now, hup, hup, huppity hup."

Goodnight was glad he wasn't claustrophobic.

The crawl space was not that wide, especially with him pulling at a tenth of a kiloton of explosives, even helped by an antigrav sled and Grok pushing from the rear.

If he slipped and fell, it would be an almost 25-meter drop, through the false ceiling to, most likely, impale himself on one of the seat backs below.

It was the second trip they'd made.

Grok had asked, "Is this trip necessary?" and Goodnight had wondered if he was making a joke. But no alien could be that antiquarian.

He took out the detonator that had been planted under von Baldur's suite, having replaced the small transmitter with some real, live primary explosives.

Goodnight knew nothing could happen. But at this stage of explosions, he always got sweaty palms.

"Colonel von Baldur," the rather shifty-eyed man asked.

"I am he."

"Do you have scrambling capabilities?"

"I do."

"On Alliance setting R09, up three, bassackwards, please."

The man hazed into interference.

Von Baldur puzzled out the hasty code, touched sensors on the com.

The screen cleared.

"I'm Hal Maffer," the man said. "Over here on Seth V. You haven't used me. . . . I run a hiring hall for people in your line of business. I'd like to do business with you someday, since I've heard your Star Risk goes by its word."

"We try."

"I'll make this fast, then," Maffer said. "Before your pals the Shaoki have time to figure out the scramble."

"You are keeping track of us?" von Baldur said.

"Nope," Maffer said. "I just happened to hear you're working the Khelat-Shaoki mess—I've put teams on both sides in there over the last few years— and heard something else that you might be interested in."

"How much?" von Baldur asked.

Maffer held up his hands.

"For free. But you'll owe me one."

"Depending how good it is."

"It's good. Day before yesterday, one of my competitors placed a battalion regimental team—the Malleus Maulers, they call themselves . . . armored lifters, some interstellar capability—with the Shaoki."

Von Baldur hid his surprise.

"Didn't figure you'd heard about it," Maffer said. "I dunno what kind of war you're fighting, but the client specified the team he picked had to have chemical training."

"I owe you one," von Baldur said.

"I thought you might," Maffer said. "Nobody likes competition when they don't know about it."

"So, they're getting cute," Riss mused.

"They're gonna bring in these Malleus clowns," Goodnight agreed, "right after they blow our asses away when we get together after the gas exercise, eh?"

"It appears fairly obvious," von Baldur said.

"Then we should active our drill immediately," Grok said.

"If not sooner," Goodnight agreed.

The night came alive with alarm shrills.

Befuddled officers and warrants were told to turn their men and women out, wearing protective masks.

The Khelat were attacking with poison gas.

Some of the mercenaries didn't have masks, or had forgotten where they were.

Umpires, wearing white armbands, started shouting, "You, you're dead! And you, you're another corpse," not adding to the peace.

The shrilling and shouting got louder, and the soldiers got more and more befuddled.

Especially when they heard the whine of starships on their secondary drives, and warships settled down beside their quarters.

Star Risk Command's hotel had a destroyer nose up to its building, and hover on antigrav.

"On board! Get your sorry asses to the ships," came the commands.

Redon Spada's patrol ships arced overhead, swept down to pick up stray detachments as soldiers were sardine-canned into ships.

A transport leased earlier by Grok settled down, picked up the last of the men, and then floated up.

Von Baldur was on the bridge of the *Fletcher*, linked to Colonel Suiyahr. He was visibly unhappy.

"Fifteen minutes to clear quarters. Not good at all."

"If this had been real, what would you do next?" Suiyahr asked.

"We would immediately go to the units we've been tasked to provide command responsibility for, evaluate the situation, and proceed to take action from there," von Baldur said glibly. "But that's for another drill.

"This night's performance was shameful! We shall be up at least until dawn dealing with this matter. I shall not allow such incompetence to happen again."

"No," Suiyahr said, holding back a tight smile. "No, you shall not."

The starships reversed their courses and lowered back toward barracks and the high-rise that was Star Risk's headquarters.

As they landed, or hung next to the Star Risk Command, the elaborate deceptions took over.

Remote-keyed recorders began playing the sounds of men and women disembarking, being ordered to the ballroom used as a briefing center.

Three remoted projectors whispered into life, showing, to the three eyes the Shaoki had installed in the Star Risk Command, soldiers filing toward the briefing room.

Appearing empty, the ships lifted away.

Coms went on aboard the ships and informed the mercenaries they'd seen the last of Irdis.

None of the Star Risk leaders paid the slightest attention to the howls that went up about lost and abandoned possessions.

"Tough titty, troop," Goodnight told one outraged sergeant. "You bought your gear to begin with. Now you can buy better."

Out-atmosphere, the destroyers, patrol boats, and the single transport jumped into N-space. Redon Spada's ship was the last to vanish.

There were no followers.

The small fleet made two more jumps, then set its

course for Khelat II and its capital world of Rafar City.

"Clean, very clean," Goodnight said.

"Finer than frog hair," Riss echoed.

"I am starting," Grok added, "to understand just how many varieties of your doublecrosses there can be."

THIRTY-THREE

About half of the Shaoki Council—those whom Colonel Suiyahr decided were either powerful enough to need kowtowing to or could be enlisted on her side when she determined a coup was appropriate—were gathered in the council chamber.

She held a small triple-frequency transmitter in one hand.

"Thank you for coming, my friends," she said. "This shall be very short.

"Some time ago, I determined that the Star Risk team that we had trusted with our worlds, our people, and our lives, had turned traitor, and were only secretly working for us. They had, in fact, returned to their true masters, the Khelat.

"This could not be borne by any decent, honorable soldier. Therefore, I determined to put in place an emergency device so that if they, in fact, behaved traitorously, retribution was swift. Today, using the mask of an anti–chemical warfare exercise, they are putting in motion their plan to betray all of us to the Khelat."

There were gasps, shouts of disbelief, anger.

Suiyahr held up one hand.

"Do not worry, my friends. The situation is well in hand. This device I hold will set off a large explosive charge I had prepared and planted in the midst of these turncoats.

"Now, here is full vengeance against those who would betray us."

She had a broad smile on her face as she pressed, in proper sequence, the sensors on the detonator.

The charge, planted just above the chamber's magnificent central chandelier, exploded downward, a one-kiloton blast and sheet of flame.

THIRTY-FOUR

Star Risk was staring at a large projection screen showing a pirated 'cast of the ruined Shaoki Council Hall. A propagandist raved mutedly about atrocities and such.

Star Risk and its people were now housed in a brand-new barracks instead of a luxury hotel, on Khelat II, which was just fine with them.

Hotels are impossible to secure.

Goodnight was seemingly hypnotized by the results of his and Grok's handiwork.

"What's the old phrase?" he said. "Hoist by their own . . . what is it? Dildo? That doesn't make much sense."

"The word you're looking for," a voice behind them said, "is petard. Like in fuse."

Goodnight spun.

"Jasmine!"

King ankled into the room.

"Any calls while I was out?"

THIRTY-FIVE

Friedrich summoned an aide, told her to get the best Methuselah of champagne in the Khelat worlds, and damn the expense.

"Come to think about it, make it a case," he ordered. "Tell anybody who coms us that we are in conference for the rest of the day."

It was Jasmine's turn to tell the war story.

She did, from the crash to her purchasing into a pharmacy to her discovery she sort of liked blowing things up.

"The only one that made me feel a little bad," she said, "was the one I needed at the end of the *J*. I had to blow up somebody's house. But at least he was related by marriage to the Khelat royalty, so I didn't feel too bad."

The champagne arrived and was poured.

"I *knew* you'd see the explosions and come back for me," King said.

"You have more faith in me than I have in me," Goodnight said.

"To slightly change the subject," Riss said. "And catching all of you at this emotion-drenched moment. Do you realize that we've never officially made our Jasmine a full partner?"

"Surely we did," Friedrich said, then thought. "No, we did not. I'm sorry, Jasmine. I formally propose, et cetera, et cetera."

"I fervently second the motion," Grok rumbled. "I think that's how it's supposed to be said."

"Are you sure," Goodnight asked, "you really *want* to be a partner with these degenerates? I mean, you've already been getting your twenty percent, and all a partnership is gonna get you is a fair share of the bills."

Jasmine nodded.

"Moved, seconded, and . . ." Riss looked around, saw hands—and a paw—lifted. ". . . Passed by acclamation."

M'chel kissed Jasmine, who sat, happily drinking champagne, oblivious to the tears runnelling down her face.

THIRTY-SIX

It was late . . . or, rather, early, but no one felt like going to bed, eating, or much of anything except more champagne and idle talk.

Jasmine was curled up next to Grok, who had one enormous paw around her.

M'chel wondered about the possibilities, might have had enough to drink to ask them, but suddenly and fortunately another thought came.

"You know what we're short of," she said, making sure she wasn't slurring her words.

"Inherited riches," Goodnight said.

"No," Riss said. "Well, yes. But more immediately, and I mean no offense, Freddie, but our forte so far hasn't been strategy. We're nibbling here and there, but what are we after?"

"More riches," Goodnight said.

"Shaddup, Chas," Riss said.

Von Baldur upended a bottle, tossed it carefully into the half-full trashcan, took another from an ice bucket, and started unwiring the cork.

"I take no offense," von Baldur said, appearing quite sober. "M'chel is correct. This is easily the biggest job Star Risk has taken on. We should have some sort of a master plan."

He shoved with both his thumbs, and the cork arced out of the bottle, ricocheted off a portrait of King Saleph, and away.

"Ask the wizard," Jasmine said, nodding at Goodnight.

"An idea," M'chel said. "Charles, let's hear a battle analysis. Go bester."

Obediently, Goodnight touched his cheek. His body started slightly. He sat, silent, for a couple of minutes, then he spoke, his voice metallic, as if synthesized.

"Since we've now sold both sides down the river, we should concentrate on winning this war as soon as possible. The longer things drag on, the more likely the chances will be that the Khelat will get tired of us, too, and try what the Shaoki did. One assassination plot per contract should be enough for us . . . unless we're mounting those plots.

"The most immediate thing that we should do is abandon this policy of being advisors and teachers. I think we should do more of the fighting ourselves, or at any rate by our direct hirelings, if we want to finish up this contract in an expected lifetime."

"Which means we need reinforcements," Grok said. "We are thin on the ground to be playing soldier."

"Already considered," Friedrich said. "I plan on contacting a man who we owe a favor to, on Seth V, immediately."

Goodnight nodded.

"Freddie, you'll be the grand strategist," Goodnight said. "Riss can implement his schemes."

"And Jasmine—"

"Jasmine will hold down the fort and run the center of things," King said firmly. "I've had enough adventure for a time."

"Finally, we should keep a back door open, in case

the Khelat move faster than we do. Also, we have to do something to improve the *maln* shipments, if we're to have Omni Foods making us rich and infamous.

"And since things are still pretty vague, that's about all I can suggest."

Goodnight touched his cheek, came out of bester.

"If I am to play admiral," Friedrich said, "I shall need a proper toy."

"Such as?" Riss asked, a bit suspiciously.

"A battleship," von Baldur said, a bit dreamily. "I have always wanted a battleship of my own."

"*That* will set easily with our Khelat masters," Riss said sarcastically.

"Not a very *big* battleship," Friedrich said, sounding a little injured.

"Well," M'chel said. "Since I've been acting paymaster while Jasmine was out playing, I guess we can afford a battleship. Or rather, the Khelat can. Get one now, while the Khelat are still feeling generous. A *small* battleship.

"By the way, Chas. You didn't say what you were going to do."

"All I know is a phrase came to me, just as I was coming out of bester," Goodnight said. " 'Singe the king's beard,' was all it was. I dunno what the hell it meant."

"I do," Grok said.

"Ah, the wonders of the subconscious. Come with me, my friend, and explain," Goodnight said, getting to his feet. "I need to rebuild my energy with a whoppin' great chunk of protein. Bloody protein. Plus, the booze sort of got burned up, and I'm sober now, and there's no bigger pain in the ass than being around a bunch of drunks."

But he staggered slightly as he got up.

"So we have a plan of sorts," Riss said.

"Of sorts," Grok agreed. "But we still don't have any sort of endgame."

"I suppose that will entirely depend on how things go, won't it?" Goodnight said.

THIRTY-SEVEN

Friedrich von Baldur was very grateful there was a screen and light years between himself and Hal Maffer on Seth V. Otherwise, he might have been kissed.

"M'god," Maffer whispered. "This is the biggest order. . . .Would you mind going through it again, uh, General?"

"First," Friedrich started, "we shall need eighteen battalions of infantry. We do not have time to train, so we shall want full units, with leaders, logistic trains, whatever.

"We are willing to pay the going rate, with a fulfillment bonus when, that is when, not if, we win.

"There is only a medium hurry for these units, since they will be used as fortress troops, one per Khelat System. They don't have to be elite, or commando qualified. We'll be content with competent infantrymen.

"Oh yes," he went on, remembering the mercenary units who'd been in place when Star Risk arrived. "We do not want any units or personnel who have been assigned here before."

Friedrich didn't mention that Goodnight wanted two shock battalions, since he'd told Freddie he'd recruit those personally, closer in toward the Alliance Worlds.

Goodnight was also prepared to pay top dollar.

No one in Star Risk had the slightest interest in going light on the budget. The Khelat were not their friends.

"A force that big will certainly need a significant payroll and supply section," Maffer said, not quite licking his lips.

"We have already provided for that," von Baldur said, wondering just how dumb Maffer thought they were.

There was room for only one set of thieves in this operation.

Jasmine had already contacted a perfectly straight accounting firm back on Trimalchio, who, once they were reassured there wasn't any real risk, was eager to see a little adventure.

"That's quite an order," Maffer said.

"It is," von Baldur agreed. "We shall pay a percentage of the first three weeks' salaries to the men, in advance, through you and their commanders. Otherwise, payroll is every two E-weeks."

Technician Ells had whistled at the number of ships Star Risk had in mind, said, a bit humbly, they'd have to increase the maintenance crews.

"Increase away," King told him.

"My metric ass," Ells said. "Up to the point we're not working around the clock?"

"Up to the point," King said, "where different shifts are working around the clock. And by the way, these ships will not be flown or crewed by Khelat."

"That," Ells said, "will reduce the workload by half right there."

"I'm not worried," King said. "I have full faith in your hem-hem efficiency."

Ells colored. Jasmine had told him about her inability to break through his perimeter, and he was still apologizing.

No one on his team, or with Star Risk, of course, ever intended to let him forget it.

Grok was left to keep a presence, being considered the least tired and the most reliable.

Riss, von Baldur, Ells, and Redon Spada went out to, as Goodnight said, "kick tires."

They kicked a lot of tires, and made Winlund, the rather attractive, if a bit avaricious, salesperson with Chamkani Starship Systems, almost as happy as Hal Maffer.

They leased twenty armed transports and forty small, Pyrrhus-like patrol ships for their escorts.

Fifteen destroyers went on the ticket, and while Ells stayed behind, making sure the ships were brought up to full operating readiness, or as near to it as the outback would allow, the other three went on to the planet of Boyington.

They took a lavish suite at the Bishop Inn, and announced they were hiring pilots and crews.

This time they didn't need to haunt the bars. The pilots came looking for them.

Riss wished they'd brought Jasmine to filter through the more-than-sometimes-specious flight records, but Spada said she wasn't needed—he'd spent enough of his life around pilots to have a built-in bullshit detector.

Spada took Riss out to dinner, reserving a private dining chamber at the Bishop Inn.

Even if he was an almost nondrinker, he'd learned about wines from somewhere, and a better vintage was served with each course.

Riss was first thinking that Freddie should have been along, since he was a much better connoisseur than M'chel, and second wondering if she ought to go along with Redon when he started making moves.

He was nice-looking, even if on the smallish side, and it had been a long while since Dov Lanchester.

Riss was just thinking it might be a perfect end to a wonderful evening, and deciding Spada's lips did look kissable, when the door slammed open.

Riss dove for her hideout gun, then realized the raiders were all pilots.

Drunken pilots.

They leapt on Spada, and, yodeling obscenities, hauled the cursing, struggling master pilot away.

"The tight-fisted bastard is always saying he'll buy us a round when we're back to civilization," one pilot explained as the swearing, struggling mass of flight-suited men and women disappeared down the corridor. "Now we're going to collect. You care to come along?"

Riss thought about it, shook her head.

Von Baldur chuckled when she told him about the non-evening.

"The gods of war evidently wish to keep you pure," he said.

M'chel growled.

"Would you care to go along with me?" Friedrich asked. "I am now ready to buy—or rent, at any rate—my toy."

Riss passed.

Friedrich went back to Chamkani Starship Systems and asked Winlund to find him a "proper" battleship.

She decided, after one week, she'd never had a bigger pain in the pilot's seat for a client.

Von Baldur looked at all the battleships in her yard, and rejected them all.

Winlund tried to explain that battlewagons were only built by rich, foolish nations, up to their necks in war and thinking they needed a fleet, and hence a ship to organize the fleet around.

Von Baldur listened politely, said, "If you cannot provide me with what I want, I am sure there is someone out there who can."

And so, in Star Risk's freshly leased yacht, they went afield.

This ship was in too bad shape.

The next was too old.

The next was too small.

The next was too big.

In desperation, Winlund seduced von Baldur, thinking that would make him more amenable to reason.

All that did was put her in a better, if exhausted mood, and a determination never to think that graying temples were necessarily a sign of reduced capability.

But at last, they found one.

Technically, it was a "very large, protected cruiser." But it was a kilometer long, sleek, fast, and very heavily armed.

Best of all, from von Baldur's position, was its enormous admiral's quarters, more than enough to hold the other members of Star Risk in comfort.

Von Baldur signed the papers, asked Winlund to find a crew for the beast, named it the *Pride of Khelat*, and went back to the Khelat System.

"I think," von Baldur announced, "what with one thing or another—"

"You mean finally having your own battleship." Goodnight snickered.

Von Baldur ignored him.

"I repeat, what with one thing and another, we are finally ready to clean up this mess."

A messenger from the communications center knocked, was admitted.

Von Baldur scanned the flimsy.

"We are summoned to an audience with King Saleph."

"Uh-oh," Riss said.

"He has an idea about the coming offensive."

"Uh-oh twice."

"Don't be so diplomatic about things," Goodnight said. "Put it a better way. The odds are, we're gonna be truly screwed.

"Seven to five. Any takers?"

THIRTY-EIGHT

"I think," King Saleph said, sprawled comfortably in the midst of what he'd dubbed his war room, "I have, with the assistance of Princes Jer and Barab, come up with the perfect plan to begin our offensive to utterly wipe out the Shaoki."

Both von Baldur and Riss kept poker faces.

They were still recovering from the room itself. It looked as if a pillow factory and an electronics firm had combined stock, and the warehouse had then exploded.

Khelat technicians scurried about, and there were uniforms aplenty. None of them, except for the two Star Risk operatives, were mercenaries.

"Indeed," Friedrich said.

"The Shaoki," the king said, "are girding for the great struggle. But they don't realize that there is a dagger aimed at the heart of their worlds, at the Shaoki III system."

"Your Majesty refers to . . ." von Baldur asked.

"To the world of Shaoki VI/III," Prince Barab said.

Riss thought, remembered it. Vaguely.

"That's an uninhabited system, correct? Except for some mining plants and ore processors."

"It is," the king said. "Although it's very recently

been garrisoned by some mercenary unit calling itself the Malleus Maulers. All that will be necessary is for us to occupy III, and use it as a springboard from there into the heart of the Shaoki system."

"How long ago did they put this unit on III?" von Baldur asked.

"Within the week," Prince Jer said.

"And how long, Your Highness," von Baldur asked, "have you been considering attacking the VI worlds?"

"About two weeks," Saleph said.

"Does not that suggest to you that there may be an intelligence leak here on Khelat II? The Malleus Maulers are highly regarded, from what I have heard, and we may be walking into a trap."

"Not to mention," Riss put in, "III has little or no atmosphere, as I recall, and fighting in a vacuum is a hard job, even for experienced troops."

The king flushed.

Both Barab and Jer started yammering in anger at von Baldur.

He held up both hands.

"Just a thought," he said. "I am sure I am incorrect."

"Even a better reason to attack," King Saleph said. "Have the two of you no confidence in the vast number of soldiers you've placed on my payroll? It shall be the Maulers who get mauled.

"Even as we speak, I've ordered a special training cycle to begin, training our noble warriors to fight under the most stringent circumstances."

"I have great confidence in our soldiers," von Baldur said quietly. "But I would have appreciated a bit of time to shake them out."

"That," Jer said, "is exactly what the Shaoki must be thinking."

"Yes," the king said excitedly. "We must seize the moment."

Von Baldur thought about arguing, realized it was pointless.

"I'll bring my staff in," he said, "whenever you're ready to give us a briefing."

"That's more like it," Saleph said in satisfaction. "The victory will be to the swift."

"No doubt," Friedrich agreed.

Leaving, M'chel and von Baldur encountered Prince Jer in the corridor.

"A word with you, sir?" M'chel asked.

"Of course," Jer said, stepping aside from his entourage and bodyguards.

"Actually, two words," Riss said. "Detachment 34."

She smiled, bowed, as Jer's eyes bulged.

M'chel took von Baldur's elbow, moved him away.

"Now, why," Friedrich said, "did you go and give the bastard warning? Machiavelli would have been horrified."

"I guess I'm just not the sub-tile sort," Riss said. "And I know what you keep saying about never wising up a chump. I just think it's more fun when they can see it coming . . . and can't do anything about it."

Friedrich shook his head skeptically.

"The damned marines never do anything other than frontal assaults."

THIRTY-NINE

"Nacherly, there's a bigmouth somewhere in the works," Goodnight said. "But whether it's a traitor or just a boaster . . . who knows?"

"And, really, who cares?" Grok said. "If we first convince the king someone is an agent, everyone will immediately start, as Chas might put it, jumping through his own asshole looking for the traitor, and meantime, nothing will get done."

"It's about your speech patterns," Jasmine said. "You have been associating with the wrong sort of people, Amanandrala Grokkonomonslf."

The furry alien might have been trying to look sheepish.

"We've had at least two hours to plot," Riss said. "Come on, people. Let's come up with something. Or, anyway, modify the something we've already got."

"First of all," von Baldur said, "this puts all of Chas's carefully figured strategy in a cocked hat, since we shall play hell changing the king's mind about his project."

"I think," Riss said, "our current tactics—tactics, not strategy—should be getting the king to delay his Great Plan until we get our troops here. Even a day or a week'll help.

"And I think there's at least one tactic that should stand: I think Goodnight should get out there and singe some beards."

"I wouldn't mind some action," Chas said thoughtfully. "Any particular places you got in mind?"

"As a matter of fact," Riss said, and indicated a hand to Jasmine, "our new partner has been doing some plotting. Take it, mynheer."

"When Freddie sent the com on the way back from the palace and said everything was up for grabs," King said, "I put Redon Spada and his patrol boats on standby. We can slave them to one of the transports, and jump toward the Shaoki worlds and take off from there.

"Take one destroyer along, for escort on the destroyer, with Grok and some of his people, and do some electronic deceptions while you're out.

"Grok and I figure you could rattle the Shaoki cages, and maybe distract them from building up this trap on VI/III.

"Hit, say, Thur, then make maybe a feint against Irdis. Hit Berfan hard, and by then we'll probably need you back for VI/III."

There was utter, stunned silence in the room.

Goodnight blinked. Thur, the capital world of Shaoki II. Irdis, the Shaoki worlds' capital, and the capital of the Shaoki III system. Berfan, the military capital of Shaoki III. It was nothing if not ambitious.

"We should let our Jasmine get chased around more often," Friedrich said admiringly. "That sounds very good."

"It should," she said smugly. "But all I did was look at what we had. . . . And Grok kept me honest."

"Well," Goodnight said, getting up, "leave the light on in the window, my friends. I may be out a little late."

FORTY

Goodnight, even though he wasn't planning on doing any work on the ground, wasn't happy his two battalions of shock troops hadn't arrived yet.

Maybe he'd been a little too picky, insisting on a recruiter well inside the Alliance and going with people from units whose reputation he knew.

Chas preferred operating under two conditions: either solo or with a hand-picked team of his own choosing, with women and men he'd already seen the elephant with.

But there was no choice now available at hand.

He had to get out in the field before King Saleph learned of his plans, since it would be almost certain the Khelat would object to anything not directly preparing for the invasion of Shaoki VI/III.

So he chose ten men and women, more or less as bodyguards, just to have someone at his back, smiling wryly at the thought. He had no plans of getting away from a nice, comfortable spaceship unless plans went seriously wrong. As deep as he planned going into in the Shaoki worlds, he'd need a prayer wheel, not a sprinkle of thugs.

Those ten were one of the best investments Goodnight ever made.

Goodnight checked out the transport, decided it was a little too wallowy, settled for the command suite aboard Inchcape's *Fletcher* for his quarters/operations office. If it had been built for an admiral, he thought, it had been a very short one with a minuscule staff.

Linked to the transport, hastily renamed the *King's Sword Bearer,* were ten three-man Pyrrhus-class patrol boats under Redon Spada.

Their crews, along with a maintenance team, rode aboard the *Sword.* The patrol boats were most cramped, and there was no particular reason to start living like an armpit until the shooting started.

Besides, it gave Spada time to get to know his new crewmen.

About the best troop, he thought, was an ex-Alliance ensign named L'hommage Curtis. Goodnight took notice, realized she was quite pretty, sighed at his personal commandment that you didn't screw in combat, and generally not at all with your juniors or anyone else on your team unless you were crazy.

Goodnight ignored his own periodic attempts, growing more and more feeble, to bed Jasmine King, and his halfhearted pass at M'chel.

The *Sword* and accompanying ships lifted off Khelat II in the middle of the night and jumped into nothingness.

Their next appearance in real space was to be off Shaoki II's capital, Thur.

Thur presented a host of targets. Goodnight consulted both the microfiches that Jasmine and Grok had reflexively prepared on all their friends and enemies.

A nice old-fashioned nuclear plant? Naw. That left the terrain dirty and hardly worth occupying; the same reason almost no one used nuclear bombs these days.

An orbital fortress or two? No. He had ideas about some of the ones on their next visit, which would be to the Shaoki III's military capital of Berfan.

Now how about this one? . . . Yes, indeedy.

Goodnight summoned Spada, issued his operations order, said he'd be riding along.

The target was a singularly juicy combination arms plant and starport, used almost exclusively by the Shaoki navy.

The *Sword* had come into the system unobserved, and no one reported the flurry of drives as the patrol boats cut away from the *Sword,* and, using one of the moons for a cover, crept up on Thur.

Spada had used an ancient trick and plotted the sun's position on his attack board, which completely perplexed some of his crew.

But not for long.

The ten patrol boats were broken into two fingers-five formations, and came in-atmosphere between the sun and the field.

The time was an hour after dawn, when Goodnight had calculated the crews down on the airfield would be just changing shifts and having breakfast and the workers in the plant were just showing up, thus creating a good-sized traffic jam.

The p-boats flashed down on the field, armed with kilotons of very primitive guided bombs.

Spada brought the ships down to one thousand meters, which would give the weapons officers time to aim.

Methodically, the officers focused their sights from

rank to rank of the parked ships, telling their bombs to "look around," and find targets.

Once targets were confirmed, the bombs were locked on and dropped, and the officers went on to pick new targets.

It was quite lovely—the Shaoki warcraft were neatly aligned as if for inspection, or for a beginner's bombing practice.

The second wave's target was even easier—anywhere and everywhere on that arms plant.

Bombs dripped down like a sower's casting, and the long industrial buildings erupted in flames.

By that time, the first wave had made Immelmann turns and were coming back on the field. This time, they came lower and strafed with their chainguns and dropped time-delay bombs.

The second wave did the same on the industrial plant, and the two waves lifted for space.

"Not too bad," Goodnight said. "Somebody's got a bit of a char on their beards, and we've got no casualties at all."

"Let's just hope my kiddies don't think this is the way it always works," Spada said soberly.

If they had, they learned better when Goodnight hit Berfan.

Napoleon, when about to promote one of his generals to field marshal, listened to a litany of the man's victories, then asked querulously, "Yes, yes. But is he *lucky*?"

And luck plays a greater part on the battlefield than generals are willing to admit.

Chas Goodnight was, normally, lucky.

Except when he wasn't.

There was no way the Shaoki could have known his

intents, since he had his minifleet set its course for jumps by the standard nav guides, plus or minus a few coordinates.

This time, when *Sword* and *Fletcher* came out of N-space, just off Berfan, they came out almost in the middle of a Shaoki formation, all destroyers or heavy corvettes.

Worse, the commander was alert and instantly gave the alarm and the order to attack.

At least Goodnight's patrol boats were manned and ready.

Goodnight ordered them dropped from their umbilical cords and to counterattack. The ten obeyed, and had only their maneuverability to help them.

The fight lasted only seconds.

Some of the missiles launched by the Shaoki were almost as big as the Pyrrhus-class boats. But the viciousness of the mercenary counterattack made the Shaoki formation jump back, and reform.

Spada ordered the patrol boats to jump to the already assigned rendezvous point. They obeyed, leaving one damaged Shaoki destroyer . . . and the smoking waste of five patrol boats.

"We have problems," Redon Spada said into the 'tween-ship com from the *Sword*.

"Tell me about it," Goodnight said, from the bridge of the *Fletcher*.

"No, I mean problems. Mutiny-type problems."

"Son of a bitch," Goodnight said slowly and distinctly. "Keep 'em off the bridge, and we're on the way."

He turned to Inchcape. "Keep a tracer on *Sword* in case these idiots take over and try to haul ass. If any of the p-boats do anything strange, such as hostile strange, feel free to hit 'em hard."

He hit the com to the small passenger space. The *Fletcher* was at General Quarters, so his bodyguards were still suited, waiting for whatever developed.

"Turn out to the starboard lock," Goodnight ordered. "We're going visiting."

They rode a small, skeletal ship's boat to the *Sword*. Goodnight went from man to man, giving brief instructions. Not that there were many orders to give, since he had no idea what sort of mutiny he was about to confront.

They braked the boat outside the transport's air lock, slipped through, securing the far side of the lock as they did. They went up the passage toward the control room at the double, blasters at port arms.

Goodnight heard the uproar well before he reached the control room. It was hard to believe that a handful of men and women could make so much noise.

Goodnight bellowed for order, got none, then drew his blaster. Aiming at a point he hoped didn't have vital circuitry behind it, he sent a bolt slamming up. Nothing stopped running, so it was evidently a safe shot.

There was a stunned silence.

"So what's the problem?" Goodnight asked in a mild tone of voice.

There was a yammer, then a woman wearing a sweat-stained flight suit pushed toward him.

It was L'hommage Curtis.

"We want out," she said bluntly.

"Out of what?"

"Out of our contracts," she said. "We didn't bargain to go up against battleships."

Goodnight didn't bother correcting her.

"I'm afraid that's not possible," he said. "Your contract says once you take on a mission, you carry it out. When we get back to Khelat III, you can all resign. But not here, not now. That's not how the world works."

"That's how it's *going* to work," Curtis said firmly.

"Once more," Goodnight said. "We're fighting a war. People get killed in war. Go back to your boats and make them ready for a jump."

Curtis looked stubborn.

"You all agree," Goodnight said, relaxing back against the bulkhead, his blaster still in hand.

There was a hubbub of general agreement.

"Tsk," Goodnight said, and his blaster blurred up and he blew off the top half of Curtis's head.

As her body collapsed, blood spraying across her fellow mutineers, there was a gape of silence.

"Now," Goodnight said, still sounding unbothered, "we'll try it again. Get back to your ships, link up with *Sword,* then report back here as we make the jump to Irdis."

This time, he didn't lower his pistol.

The fliers, most of whom had never seen blood up close and personal, stared at Curtis's unlovely corpse, sagged in surrender, and shuffled past him.

One flier started to say something, and two bodyguards lifted their blasters. He clamped his mouth shut and went with the others.

Goodnight went to the control room door, rapped.

"Open up," he said. "The excitement's over."

The port irised open. Spada, blaster in hand, and two crewmen, also armed, stood there.

"Have a couple of people dump the carrion out an

air lock," Goodnight said, indicating Curtis's body with a gloved thumb.

The crew of the transport, and even Redon Spada, looked at Chas Goodnight a little strangely after Curtis's execution.

It didn't bother him. He was used to it, after being one of the Alliance's assassins. Besides, most of his concern was wondering what might be waiting for them off Irdis.

The answer was, not much.

The five surviving Pyrrhus boats were unlinked from the *Sword* while it was still in N-space.

Four of them exited hyperdrive, and, a moment later, Redon Spada's boat and the *Fletcher* came into normal space just behind them.

The ex-mutineers had been told they'd be given targets on the spot, and for none of them to "get cute," as Chas put it, or else either Spada's craft or the *Fletcher* would happily missile them from the rear.

No one tried to disobey.

The targets were there, right in front of them: Two Shaoki orbital satellites, with a horde of light escorts and merchantmen orbiting about them.

"One pass," Spada ordered. "One target per missile. Fire what you have at anything you want, and come on back."

The p-boats obeyed, flashing at near light speed through the enemy.

Both orbital fortresses, and Goodnight couldn't tell how many ships, took hits.

The logical targets should have been the merchantmen, but Goodnight knew most of the demoralized p-boat crewmen and -women went for the escorts as being their personal enemies.

Missiles hit, exploded, and Shaoki ships blipped out of existence.

The orbital satellites were a gout of oxygen-fed flames for an instant, then boiling smoke.

The p-boats flashed back into N-space, where the *Sword* was waiting.

"I think," Goodnight commed to Spada, "the king's beard is now a fiery mess. Let's go on home."

FORTY-ONE

The royals were having what they called a gymkhana.

Riss wondered where they found the time to play, if the king was intent on battle.

Grok looked up the word, and desperately wanted to attend. "They compete on four-legged Earth creatures, which I've never seen."

"You don't want to," Riss said. "All they're good for is to shit and look pretty."

"Some say that describes humans, as well," Grok said.

He was terribly disappointed on the day, when he discovered this was a modern gymkhana using small lifters instead of animals.

Grok watched the various princes convolute around a course, whooping at each other, snorted, and went back to his computers.

Riss hung on, for some unknown reason.

She was brooding over the events, wishing she was in a lifter with half a dozen crew-served blasters, making a strafing run, when Prince Wahfer skidded to a halt in front of where she sat and asked her out for a drink and dinner later, having something important to discuss.

She turned him down, a little too sharply, she realized, seeing the rather hurt look on his face.

M'chel Riss was wondering if she was starting to get a little bigoted, something she'd never accused herself of in her most inquisitorial moments.

It was all because of Dov Lanchester, she thought. She hoped.

Riss decided it was time to clear up that particular matter, and then see if she still was being a racist.

Friedrich von Baldur was staring into a com screen, listening to a scrambled dressing-down from his lobbyist, Anya Davenport.

"I don't know about this entire contract with you," she continued, and there was not a bit of friendliness in her voice. "I've had to make explanation after explanation to Omni Foods, and now, when you're back with the Khelat—thanks for making it difficult to track you down—we've had a complete halt to *maln* shipments. Not good, von Baldur. Not good at all."

Friedrich couldn't tell her that the king himself was responsible—all nonessential commercial shipping had been suspended, and transports seized, to provide support for the upcoming invasion.

"I am going to wait until I calm down, make some apologies to some people who I told your Star Risk was reliable, and then think, very seriously, about whether I can continue this contract and keep my good name!"

The prince was well guarded, especially at night.

Too well, as Riss had discovered when she was casing his quarters a bit ago.

Guards formed up and marched around his manor, relieving each other at two-hour intervals.

It was a simple matter to slide into the rear of the

formation, dressed as a Khelat private, and drop out at a suitable place.

M'chel kept the uniform on as she went over two walls, avoiding one alarm and spoofing the second with a standard transmitter.

The Prince liked to sleep with a window open, which made things all the easier. M'chel made sure he was sleeping alone, took the panic button from his bedside, and pulled up a comfortable chair.

The sudden glow from a tiny light woke Prince Jer. He struggled up, eyes wide, fumbling for the alarm.

Riss held it up.

"Don't bother."

"You! You're—"

"An old friend of General Dov Lanchester, who you murdered," Riss said.

"I did not! I did no such thing! Those are all lies!"

"Lower your voice," M'chel ordered. "Or I'll have to kill you sooner rather than later."

"But . . . but that was fortunes of war," Jer sputtered.

"Call this the same, then," Riss said. She unsnapped the fighting knife at her waist.

Jer swung his legs out of the bed.

"Don't I get a chance to defend myself?"

"In court?" Riss asked, and laughed harshly.

"Then with a blade of my own."

He motioned to a wall where several knives and ceremonial daggers hung.

"Now, that might be interesting," Riss said, standing up.

Jer licked his lips, stood, turned toward the wall, reached for a near-sword.

Riss shot him in the back with a very small, very silent pistol she'd concealed in her palm.

Jer sagged, fell on his back.

Riss walked over, looked down at the complete surprise that had frozen his face, made sure he was dead.

He was.

Riss took a small Shaoki flag from a pocket, dropped it beside the body.

That would be the alibi.

She next thought about the Khelat and the Shaoki.

Did she now hate them, in the singular and the collective, a little less for being double-dealing bastards?

She did not.

Riss decided there were some folks the gods just didn't want anyone liking, which is why these two people inhabited worlds light-years from anyone civilized.

That was enough for her.

She put away her gun and knife and went back out as silently as she'd come.

FORTY-TWO

The Khelat fleet assembled.

Ships, sometimes singly, sometimes in small fleets, flashed into being off Khelat II.

King Saleph and Prince Barab were in martial ecstasy, and Khelat holo-casts were filled with footage of the ships, floating in vacuum, to solemn music.

The king dedicated the coming battle to the memory of Prince Jer, foully murdered by Shaoki assassins.

"I've decided the Shaoki don't have a spy in place," Chas Goodnight said. "They don't need one. The Khelat are posting their intentions on billboards."

"How badly?" Riss inquired.

"They've got a cluster of escorts, including a couple of ancient cruisers, off Shaoki VI/III, Grok told me," Goodnight said. "Shitfire, this is like the old, old, *olden* days. Twouldn't surprise me if old Saleph thought about sending an invite to single combat if there'd been another king to take him up on the offer."

Goodnight didn't sound disturbed. His two battalions of shock troops had arrived, been tested in maneuver, and were pronounced acceptable by Chas.

Riss, wondering if she would always be a sucker,

assigned herself to the Khelat lifter regiment that she'd ridden with in the battle on Hastati, instead of "in the rear, with the gear, the sergeant major, and the beer."

At least, she thought, she'd have a place to uncork her helmet. The poor damned crunchies'd be stuck in their suits until VI/III was captured. . . . Or until they were taken out of battle to the hospital or morgue.

She decided not to dwell on that.

War was killing, and that was her trade.

Self-chosen.

Shaoki VI wasn't an unusual system. There were five planets orbiting a dim sun. None of them had much of an atmosphere and were small, so that even their heavy metals didn't give the worlds much in the way of gravity.

Nothing had ever evolved in the system, like most in the universe, until the Khelat/Shaoki arrived.

The Shaoki got to the minerals first, exploiting them for their own use, then limited export.

If Shaoki VI hadn't been nestled in a nook surrounded by the settled Shaoki systems, it would have been peaceably hammered into rock, the rock cycled into raw minerals, until the system eventually vanished into the hammer mills.

But it was, and it wasn't.

It would, however, make a decent base for spacecraft, and could be easily leveled into landing fields.

Decent for starcraft, rotten for troops, who'd be confined to their ships, whatever housing could be brought in, or their suits.

Why its third world had been garrisoned, first by

the Shaoki, then by their hirelings, the heavy lifter unit the Malleus Maulers, was chance, the typical Shaoki strategic stupidity, or the knowledge the Khelat were coming.

Why, on the other hand, King Saleph hadn't chosen another arena for his Grand Offensive when he heard III was reinforced was another mystery.

Regardless, after a suitable passage of time, the assembled fleet jumped, in widely spaced increments, into the Shaoki System.

Riss got three separate messages that Prince Wahfer wanted to talk to her—"and it's not what you would think"—but didn't answer them, being busy with her own affairs.

Von Baldur, aboard the *Pride of Khelat,* jumped with the lead elements, escorted by Inchcape and twelve of her destroyers.

On the third jump, they entered the Shaoki VI system just as the shit hit the fan.

The Shaoki, perhaps at the Maulers' behest, had moved three orbital fortresses into position in a self-defending triangular formation, in a close orbit to III. Of course, there was now no doubt at all that the invasion was expected.

The fortresses had been observed by one of the Khelat cruisers on recon, whose captain had not reported their arrival. Friedrich wondered what had been passing through the woman's mind, but when he inquired he was told the king had already had her shot.

The fortresses were guarded by two dozen destroyers, and the landings were blocked.

Khelat ships swarmed to the attack, were drawn into range of the heavy missiles and supercaliber blasters of the fortresses, and smashed.

The Khelat, seemingly stymied, pulled back to the limits of the system, but were still occasionally hit by probing long-range missiles on by-the-grace-of-God missions.

"For the love of Henriette," Friedrich muttered. He was scanning King Saleph's plan for the attack on the Shaoki forts and ships. "Has this man no imagination?"

Redon Spada, Grok, and Inchcape were on the bridge of the *Pride*.

"It's not very creative," Spada agreed.

"We can do better than that," Inchcape said. "Let's get a plan together, get the king's approval, and—"

"We shall not trouble the king," von Baldur said, sounding regal. "We shall just deal with the situation."

Von Baldur's own scheme was very simple, if hazardous.

"Not good," Grok opined. "But not a frontal assault, either. Better than the royal scheme, at any rate. It even stands a fair chance of working.

"So I'll go now to put my own operation in motion."

Redon Spada pushed a couple of p-boats out toward the fortresses to check an idea all his very own.

The idea turned out to be correct.

The missiles from the Shaoki fortresses were not only cruising for targets, but they were seeding small spy satellites as they went, all in the direction of the main fleet.

So all eyes were on the king, who was making end-less open 'casts in all directions about what he was going to do to the rascally Shaoki.

Things looked a little better for von Baldur's plan.

Six of Inchcape's destroyers jumped behind one of III's moons, using it for a mask.

Redon Spada's patrol boats jumped to just out of range of the fortress's primary weapons.

The fortresses, regardless, launched at them.

The p-boats counterlaunched and easily destroyed the missiles as they arced beyond range of their controllers.

Inchcape brought the *Fletcher* and the other five, in an extremely hazardous jump, between the fortresses and III, an action that would've produced a court-martial for Inchcape, if this were peacetime and she were still an Alliance officer, for senselessly endanger-ing her ships.

If a navigator had dropped a digit and they'd come out of hyperspace in the middle of III, that ship, as well as a good chunk of the local real estate, would have been obliterated.

But she got away with it.

The fortresses went into panic mode, swiveling TA systems toward III, trying to acquire the destroyers.

Then Spada jumped his p-boats into range and launched heavy shipkillers at the fortresses.

The Shaoki ships covering the fortresses swirled, then counterattacked wildly, some toward the destroy-ers and others toward Pyrrhus-class boats.

Von Baldur held his battleship just out of range.

He sent a com to the king, aboard his own flagship, asking for backup.

King Saleph hesitated for a ship hour, then found a backbone somewhere and ordered half of the Khelat warships in against III.

Even on the *Pride*'s bridge screen, space was chaotic, a spinning whirlpool of ships fighting, sometimes alone, sometimes in pairs, sometimes in echelons.

Von Baldur had another real-time, real-view screen holding on the orbital forts.

He realized he wasn't breathing as the big screen showed friendly blips, darting close to the fortresses.

Spada's p-boats.

Two of them were hit by missiles almost as big as they were, and simply vanished.

One fortress bulged, reddened, and disappeared.

The com to Spada's ship came to life.

"I get five points for that one."

"Com discipline," Spada's calm voice came, just as three missiles ripped into another orbital fortress and it sprayed air and its guts into space.

Two destroyers ganged up on the last fortress, volleying missiles at it. A pair of Khelat ships appeared and launched at the damaged fortress. It hung in space, not fighting back, as missiles slammed home.

"It's dead," someone 'cast.

"All Wahfer elements," another voice said. "Break contact, break contact."

Now there were more and more Khelat on screen, and Shaoki blips either flared on-screen as being hit, fled into N-space, or drove toward III's surface.

The way was open for invasion.

Grok, however, had already made his.

Grok had carefully selected and modified his ship.

He'd originally thought of one of Spada's patrol boats, but was very tired of barely human accommodations, since he might be stuck in one spot for a lengthy period of time.

The speed and maneuverability of the patrol boats was an advantage, but Grok realized if he was caught, there almost certainly wouldn't be time nor enough room to do any serious running.

He settled on a medium-sized mining ship. Its hold was huge and was quickly converted to work area and, near the bow, a Grok-sized living area.

The half-dozen technicians were quartered where the processing machines had been.

The outer skin of the ship was first given an attractive, nonsymmetric set of bulges, so the craft didn't look like any sort of spacecraft, then tastefully anodized in a scheme not unlike that of a Gila monster.

Grok loved the ship, but no one else did.

The pilot he'd gotten from Spada had trouble not wincing when he looked at it, as did the technicians.

That didn't matter.

Grok named it, officially, the *Whitehead,* after a favorite philosopher, unofficially after his completely unpronounceable, at least by someone without two larynxes, home district.

While the modifications were being made, Grok went over recent aerials of III, selected a promisingly rugged range of hills not too close nor too far from the Maulers' base.

After the electronics array was loaded, circuited, and double-checked, the *Whitehead* jumped for the Khelat fleet.

The next two jumps led it behind one of III's moons, and then, once the battle started, the ship crept in-atmosphere and down to hover on antigravity just above the planet's jagged surface.

Grok could've done the piloting, but didn't see the need to do any more work than necessary.

The *Whitehead* flew to the mountains Grok had chosen, then maneuvered up a canyon to an abandoned quarry.

It landed next to an open mine shaft that, if utter ruin descended, could provide shelter and lay dead for hours. Everything aboard the ship had been shielded so it should be electronically invisible.

Grok distrusted electronics even more than he did people.

"And here we are," he said to his pilot. "Snug as a rug in a bug."

The pilot looked puzzled but didn't ask, since Grok was growling. He didn't know that meant moderate happiness to the alien.

A screen showed the battle raging above, around the orbital fortresses, but Grok didn't pay much attention. He was busy, still growling, putting the last details on his ideas.

Before the Shaoki could recover from the initial assault, fast transports, heavily escorted, darted down about a kilometer short of the main Shaoki position.

The ships grounded only long enough for troops—almost a thousand of Goodnight's hard chargers—to pour out. Still, one ship was badly holed, and limped away from III leaking fumes and various fluids.

Goodnight paid no attention. He was the first off his transport, which appeared heroic and leading from the front. In fact, Chas was deathly afraid of getting shot full of holes in a tin can that couldn't shoot back.

"Go, go, go," he and his officers were chanting into their coms.

The troops, heavily laden in their suits, stumbled away from the ships. Even with lighter gravity, they were staggering under the weight of personal weapons, air tanks, food, water, and the various crew-served weapons and missiles.

Goodnight had ordered the men not to turn on their small antigravs, for fear that could be picked up on Shaoki sensors and targeted.

Chas saw something flash overhead, went flat, as a missile impacted against a nearby crater.

Those who'd seen the incoming and reacted got up. The others, who'd not seen anything, were just bewildered. If they didn't learn quickly, they would be unlikely to survive the day.

Warrants were shouting the troops into widely dispersed assault lines. The objectives were half a dozen antiaircraft missile sites on nearby bluffs. The troops moved as fast as they could lurch while, above them, the Shaoki crews scrambled for weapons, having never thought anyone would attack them from the *ground*.

Soldiers went down, readied crew-served weapons.

The sights of the mortars and heavy blasters had already been adjusted for the gravity, and bolts slashed out as bombs arced overhead.

One site was firing back now, and Goodnight wondered if it might not be manned by Maulers.

Three p-boats shot overhead, and the site exploded in a flash of flames, swallowed by the near-vacuum.

Goodnight wondered who'd brought in Spada's ships, thought that if this were a normal army, somebody would have just deserved a medal.

The assault troops swept forward and went up the slopes to the sites.

Someone triggered a missile at the attackers. It

flashed out, hit the ground well back of the assault line, bounced high, spinning, and blew up.

Then troops swept over the missile sites, and the way was clear for the main landing.

M'chel Riss sucked air frantically. Even if it was fume-heavy, and smelled a little of garbage, it would be the only air she'd breathe beyond that from her suit or from the lifter's tanks, and she wanted something to remember, even if it was nothing more than ship air from the transport they were sitting in.

Her lifter was vibrating slightly—the power was on, ready to engage the drive at her order.

"Gunners?"

"Ready," came the two reports.

"Drivers?"

"Ready."

She checked the heavy blaster in her lifter's cupola. It was half loaded, a drum securely attached to the weapon's breech.

Riss felt the ship shudder as it jinked. Someone outside must've shot at it. . . . Or else the Khelat captain was getting a case of nerves.

M'chel closed the faceplate of her helmet, inhaled metallic, dead air as the transport slammed in for a landing.

The nose of the ship lifted up and away to expose the cargo deck, and she saw the desolation of VI/III.

"Lift it," she ordered, and the lifter came off the greasy deck of the ship.

Come on, come on, let's get out and doing something, she thought. She ducked down, pulled the cupola's hatch closed.

The two small lifters, scouts, near the bow were

airborne and slipping down the ramp, and the rest of her column was following.

Without needing orders, half of the troop broke left; the others went right. They grounded, waiting for orders.

Riss felt the ground shudder as her ship took off.

Behind it, other ships grounded and infantrymen poured out.

There was incoming fire—she saw men crumple, lie motionless.

She keyed her throat mike.

"All Lanchester units . . . commanders' option . . . take out those damned guns!"

She'd picked her own name for the twenty heavy lifters, their five scouts, and ten support lifters. Her radio jargon wasn't proper for Alliance armor, but then, she wasn't proper Alliance anymore.

If she ever had been.

Riss bent to her sight.

She saw movement up ahead, on a low rise, far ahead of the troops on foot.

"Gunner! Target! Gun position, thirteen degrees, five hundred meters. Shrapnel."

"Target acquired," the first gunner said.

"On command, shoot. Will correct. Fire."

"On the way—wait. Splash."

Dust and smoke lifted as the missile struck, missing by not very much. Riss swore. If there were good gunners up there with anything heavy, she could be one dead marine.

She corrected her aim.

"Fire!"

"On the way—wait. Splash!"

"Hit!" Riss said jubilantly as the missile blew up.

She saw no movement from the position.

"We got them all," her gunner said.

"Maybe," she said. "Or maybe they've got a trench to run away in."

It didn't matter much—that gun wouldn't fire anymore at the infantry.

She swept her sight across the battlefield, found another, multiple pom-pom position. It churned fire, and a scout lifter spun and blew up.

Another lifter unit swept forward, killed the pom-pom before Riss could fire.

"Press the attack," a Khelat voice came.

That was the landing commander.

More and more Khelat soldiers came on line.

Riss saw no signs of anyone breaking, although the infantrymen were a little reluctant to get up and charge.

"Lift it up," she ordered her driver. "Push them back."

Riss clicked her com to the unit frequency, gave the same order.

In the far distance, she could see the bulk of the old mine headquarters, supposedly now the headquarters for the Shaoki command and the Maulers.

Just for pure meanness, she sent a pair of rockets over the heads of the defenders at the mine.

She didn't know if it did any good, but it didn't do any harm, and made her feel better.

The Khelat kept pressure up all that day, into the night.

The Shaoki never broke, but they began falling back.

Riss allowed herself to feel a bit of hope. Maybe this idiot idea of the king's would work, and in a day or two they'd control III, and use that for a jumping off point to—

Her second gunner was the first to spot the hole in the lines.

Somehow, behind them, the infantry had left a gap, in spite of the fairly solid line the lifters kept.

Riss was just reaching for the com to alert the Khelat infantry CO's when somebody else spotted the hole.

From a draw, a dozen heavy lifters shot out.

They were about twice the size of Riss's, and two generations more sophisticated.

The Malleus Maulers were on the field.

Riss's gunner fired a missile at the lead lifter—Riss had a moment to see their ammo reserves were getting very low.

The Mauler's ECM "reached out" and took command of the missile, and sent it up and around in a series of loops before its self-destruct mechanism cut in and the rocket blew up.

A missile came back at Riss, and the second gunner managed to drop it with a countermissile.

"Zig left! Now!" Riss ordered. She spattered a burst at the oncoming lifter, saw bolts explode harmlessly on its compound armor.

To kill it would take a missile or a hit by Riss's secondary cannon.

"Back . . . now! Drop down into that ravine!" she ordered.

They were below ground level, as a second missile blew just above them.

Riss's com scrambled, went dead.

"Right down it, then back out when it shallows."

She heard a whimper from someone on her suit com, paid no attention.

Her lifter came out of the ravine, and in the few seconds she'd been blind, four—correction, five—of her unit's lifters had been hit, smoke coiling or oxygen gouting for an instant.

Then there were two slams against her own craft, and it skewed, grounded.

An instrument panel began smoking, then air hissed out of the lifter, and the smoke stopped.

Another missile hit her, rocking the lifter up, almost on its side.

"Come on," she shouted, dropped out of the cupola. "They've got us!"

She was at the rear of the lifter, smashed a gauntlet against the emergency button. Nothing happened, and M'chel had an instant to think of being trapped in this lifter while it was shot up, then the hatch dropped away.

Her second gunner pushed past her, ran into the open, and was cut down by a chatter of blaster bolts.

The first gunner was pulling at the second driver, who lolled, motionless.

The man's helmet—and head—came away, and the gunner was staring at the gore. Riss grabbed him, almost threw him toward the escape hatch.

The first driver stumbled up, and Riss saw, through his faceplate, a mask of blood. He sagged, and Riss had him over her shoulder, and had both their anti-grav units turned to high. It surely did not matter if they were observed or picked up on some Shaoki screen now.

She made it out of the lifter crouched, still carrying the driver.

The three survivors staggered away from the lifter just as two artillery shells crashed into the ruined vehicle.

They made it to a boulder, let blaster bolts crash around them.

The Maulers forgot about them, switched to other targets, and Riss pushed her men back, away from the battlefield, as other Khelat men and women began retreating.

A few had courage enough to fire, almost blindly, rounds back at the lifters and now visible Shaoki infantry.

There were bodies, smoking lifters, overturned SP guns, and then a line of soldiers, shaky but still holding, and they had antiarmor missiles.

The Maulers maneuvered around what was now their battlefield, took a couple of hits, then pulled back to cover.

They didn't have—quite—the firepower or aerial supremacy to drive the invaders back into space.

The Khelat may have held the original landing ground, but not much more.

Riss took her wounded driver to an aide station, reported in to her regimental commander, was told to take command of another lifter and assume command of a lifter battalion.

The battle would go on.

Riss's new lifter had only one drawback—it had taken a nice, neat hit through the spray shield that exploded just behind the late commander.

Blood and intestines had sprayed, instantly dried on the deck, bulkheads, and overhead.

Riss's new crew refused to reenter the lifter. She got her first gunner from her old lifter, and they set to cleaning. By midnight, they had most of the dried, caked mess cleaned up, and the old crew grudgingly moved back in.

*   *   *

Riss remembered the second day of the invasion because that was when the Shaoki first hit them from the air . . . or rather vacuum.

They managed to slip in ten—or maybe the number was twenty—patrol craft that swept across the battlefield, missiling everything in sight. Which included a formation of their own lifters, unfortunately not the Maulers.

Riss had cozied her new lifter up next to a very large boulder, and, unlike the Khelat, did not instantly return fire on the Shaoki ships.

They banked, made another sweep across the battleground, then vanished into space.

Fifteen minutes later, the Khelat air support arrived. Just a little late.

"How is it going?" Jasmine asked.

The hyperspace com hummed and hissed.

"I assume you are scrambling," von Baldur said.

"Of course."

"Lousy," Friedrich said. "I want you to contact Hal Maffer on Seth V and find out if he can hire, right now, a half dozen or more antiaircraft batteries. We seem to have come a little short.

"Also, anyone who is interested in fighting can get a most attractive contract from us."

Jasmine, as she made her farewells and cut off, noted that von Baldur looked drawn, worried.

The Shaoki tried again, but this time Grok was ready for them.

His ship was 'casting in all directions, on all of the frequencies used by the Shaoki, carefully noted by Grok during Star Risk's time with them. Commands, sightings, reports, all were lost in a cascade of static that did everything from buzz to yodel.

In addition, Grok was 'casting to all Khelat ships close to III signals to rebroadcast that turned radar, real-time screens, and even hyperspace com to garbled hash.

The Shaoki retired in bafflement.

Grok, even though he didn't believe anyone could pick him up in his cozy, was cautious, and had the ship moved to a new, hidden location.

Three days later, the Shaoki made their major counterattack.

M'chel's second lifter had been destroyed—she didn't remember how—and she was in her third. Her first gunner, who thought of Riss as a lucky charm, came along.

M'chel was thinking the same of him.

Khelat intercept teams had been recording an excess of chatter prior to the attack. Star Risk had a pretty good idea what was being talked about, having some familiarity with previous Shaoki codes.

Von Baldur had been appalled at the lack of security. But he was quietly appalled.

Jasmine ran the rough decrypts through a not-terribly-sophisticated computer, and Star Risk had the Shaoki codes, complete.

That, von Baldur thought, was a good, easy way to impress the client and assist in getting the final bonus they wanted.

King Saleph offered a plan for a counterattack.

But Star Risk had their own plan.

Goodnight took elements of his two battalions out just before dawn.

The troops were broken down into four-man groups: gunner, ammo bearer, and two gun guards.

They crept out, through the lines, found holes to hide in, and waited.

At dawn, the Shaoki attacked, sending heavy lifters in front of their infantry.

The lifters were met with a very nasty surprise—or, rather, many little surprises.

Goodnight's shock troops were armed with ground-to-air missiles, rather primitively brained.

But they didn't need much in the way of brains.

A gunner would take a Shaoki lifter in his sights, launch and forget the missile, his loader stuffing another rocket in the tube.

From the Shaoki side, it looked like more than a hundred sudden small spurts of fire, and then their sensors clanged into life.

The lifters had four choices: crash land, in which case they stood a chance that the missiles would go over them; go high and get hit with a belly-strike; maintain course and die; or pray.

This was a day when the gods weren't listening to prayers.

Lifters exploded, spun in, smashed into the rocky field.

Inchcape and six destroyers swept back and forth, parallel with and just behind the Khelat lines. They had the height advantage, and salvoed air-to-air and air-to-ground missiles.

They were just out of range of the Maulers' AA batteries, back of the Shaoki lines. A few fired, and their missiles were either taken out by countermissiles or the sites themselves were attacked with longer-ranged operator-guided missiles.

The Shaoki infantry went to ground, their assault stopped cold.

Prince Wahfer, seeing a chance for glory, broke orders and brought half a dozen cruisers in, holding at about ten thousand meters. It was too high for a proper attack, but the crashing bombardment didn't do the Khelat cause any harm at all.

Again, the Shaoki began to retreat.

Then the rest of Goodnight's battalions attacked, picking up their surviving rocket gunners and their escorts.

From cover, Riss's regiment of lifters rose to the attack.

They'd been badly hit in previous days, but there were still enough of them to turn the retreat into a rout.

Following orders bellowed by Riss, they ignored the running infantrymen and attacked over them, at the Mauler positions.

The Maulers, confused by the intermingle of Shaoki and Khelat forces, also fell back, but in an orderly fashion.

Khelat lifters came in on Riss's heels, hitting hard at their enemies.

Riss's own lifter commanders wanted to go after the Shaoki infantry, but she swore as she'd never sworn before, yammering at the lifter noncoms and officers.

More afraid of her than the enemy, they obeyed, and her regiment held firm to its goal: the now ruined mine, which had been the Maulers' and Shaoki defenders' base.

But the Maulers had pulled back, and the collapsed buildings were abandoned. The Shaoki had moved back into the mountains, into prepared positions.

The Khelat had the base.

But III was still held by the Shaoki. There were more than enough missiles to keep the planet from being developed into a stepping stone.

Riss had a good idea that either the Maulers or the Shaoki had air plants in their positions. Or else they could slip in enough ships to resupply.

The long, bloody day was a nice, meaningless victory.

Now the siege would begin

FORTY-THREE

The Maulers and the Shaoki were well dug in. Their lifters were turned into pillboxes—revetments were cut into the rock; the lifters would set down in them. Only the launch tubes and gun turrets stuck out, and these were camouflaged.

The Shaoki had a main base in the center of a broad mountain valley, and two large outposts to the east and west, guarding the valley's entrances.

The Khelat attacked twice, suicidal frontal assaults.

Riss lost another lifter and its crew, although her amulet-gunner survived.

Then, in the time haze, there was a request from von Baldur to her regimental commander that she be allowed to "conference" with him aboard the *Pride*.

Riss shuddered at making "conference" into a verb, but was very glad to get off of III for even a short time.

She was able to shed her suit and uniform and luxuriate in a zero-G shower, globules of water floating about her.

The suit went in for reconditioning; the uniform was burnt.

She ate food, real food, and immediately her bowels

growled at her, unused to anything but the constipatory field rations.

M'chel eyed the luxurious-looking cot in her cabin, decided she'd better go see Freddie before she allowed herself to lapse into unconsciousness.

Riss put on a pair of workout sweats, thought them the finest, most comfortable clothes she'd ever seen, and headed for the bridge.

An officer directed her to the admiral's suite. It was very luxurious, but she was most interested in seeing Chas Goodnight.

If M'chel looked as drawn and exhausted as Chas, she decided, it was time for major plastic surgery.

He was nursing a drink, and, unbidden, went to a bar and mixed her a brandy and soda, strong on the brandy.

"Hell of a way to make a living," he said.

"Ain't that the truth," Riss agreed.

"If we ate this combat shit up," Goodnight said, "we should've stayed with the Alliance and their shitty pay."

Riss nodded, sucked down brandy, as von Baldur came out.

He looked at the bar, visibly decided against a drink, and sat down, heaving a heavy sigh.

"I hate, hearing what you were saying as I came in, to be even more of a morale depressor, but I have to admit that this contract has me grinding my teeth," he said.

"Every idea I have seems to get stymied by fate. I do not like our current situation, even though Alliance Credit is most pleased with our bank balance."

"Income doesn't do us good if we're dead," Goodnight said.

"So far, that has not happened," Friedrich said. "I

called the two of you up here because, since you are at the sharp end of the stick, you might have some ideas on what could be done, remembering that we only break a contract if the money stops, the client loses or wins or goes after us."

Silence for a few minutes.

"We could just pull out, and the hell with our reputation," Riss said. "But we're supposedly winning. If we were losing, now, that might look better on the old résumé. But as it is . . ." Her voice trailed off.

Goodnight just shook his head.

"So I guess there is no other course but to continue," von Baldur said. "I suppose we can rationalize this nightmare by thinking of all the out-of-work soldiery we are employing."

"Or, in the rest of the universe's view," Goodnight put in, "the number of thugs we're keeping off the streets at night."

The three exchanged looks, and, without ado, left the suite.

Riss slept around the clock, then went back to war, feeling a little guilty about having taken one of rank's privileges.

No one still knew if the Shaoki/Maulers had an enormous store of ammunition and air or if they were getting secretly resupplied, but they showed no signs of running dry.

None of Inchcape's destroyers or patrolling Khelat ships found any signs of a supply convoy.

And the siege dragged on.

Sappers and some of Technician Ells's people came to III and put some of the abandoned mining machinery into life, added spatter shields and armor.

The sappers set to work, digging trenches that zig-zagged forward toward the eastern outpost.

The Shaoki brought in artillery, rockets, but the sappers kept digging.

Since the diggers were mining machinery, the trenches weren't the usual narrow workings but almost wide enough to accommodate one of M'chel's lifters.

Mostly Riss kept her lifters in revetments, since the Maulers, or somebody over there, were too damned accurate with their mortars and gun tubes.

Lifters, both heavy and scout, had an additional mission—taking air, ammo, and food to the forward lines.

That was another way for soldiers to die—lifter crews blasted out of existence, line soldiers by mortar if they dared group up for meals.

Everyone complained, but not very loudly unless they were line soldiers.

Now, *those* bastards, everyone agreed, had it *really* rough. . . .

Grok faithfully kept providing spoofery for raids, either aerial or on the ground.

Everyone knew it was getting bad—no one ever heard the alien complain.

Off-watch, he buried himself in abstruse philosophical works, and the gods help the poor crew member who bothered him with trivial matters like the war.

One thing working against Riss's personal morale was the combat armor everyone wore. The suits had been taken out of Alliance service a long time ago, and almost everyone figured it was just a matter of them being obsolete.

Riss knew better, having seen some of the suits in an armory once, and a gunnery sergeant who was slightly older than god told her why they weren't issued anymore.

The suits had been designed for combat, and were fitted with four "triage" units at the shoulder and hip. If someone was hit in an extremity, the triage units, which were unsightly lumps, came to life. They sealed the suit from atmosphere loss, automated jets injected opiates, and small laser units razored the limb off.

The casualty wouldn't burn his lungs out in a vacuum or human-hostile atmosphere, and medics could quickly medevac the wounded.

Of course, the shock of first the wound and then the amputation might cause death, but that was part of the price.

The triage units were guaranteed failure-proof.

The gunny sergeant had said the operative word was *almost* failure-proof, which is why they were taken out of service. Every once in a while, something went wonky in the units and an uninjured soldier would lose an arm or a leg.

The suits were now at least twenty years old, and Riss could never look at the bulge on her arms or legs without shuddering and expecting the worst.

Large freighters were commandeered by the government and brought in, far behind the lines, after having been hastily modified as troop-support centers.

The idea was Prince Wahfer's.

At first, mainly rear-area soldiers took advantage of the chance to shower, draw fresh uniforms, have a meal, and sleep in one of the holds, fitted with wall-to-wall mattresses.

The Prince heard about that, and sent in military police squads to make sure the first soldiers served came from the front.

His stock rose considerably.

Goodnight heard a rumor that he'd also wanted brothels established, but the puritanical king had vetoed the idea. Besides, as one of Chas's sergeant majors said, it'd be hell if some poor infantry type had encountered his wife, girlfriend, mother as one of the volunteers.

The battlefield was chewed up by artillery and destroyed ships and lifters.

Scattered here and there were the desiccated corpses of Khelat, Shaoki, or mercenaries that no one had time to pick up, or else the bodies lay in the open, with snipers around them.

At least there wasn't the usual corpse stink of rotting flesh.

The main trench was less than a hundred meters from the eastern outpost when Goodnight called, in code, to ask a favor.

Riss was happy to oblige.

She had her lifters register targets inside the outpost then waited a day.

Before dawn, she ordered all of her tubes unmasked, and barrage fire opened.

Rockets and shells rained down on the outpost as Goodnight's two battalions, now at half-strength, came out of the trenches and trudged forward. They were spotted within twenty meters of the trench, but it was too late.

The shock troops tumbled into the trench, blasters raving.

The Shaoki fought back hard, and then the weapons were knives, shovels, and even portable diggers.

Goodnight pushed them steadily back, and by noon the outpost had fallen to the Khelat.

But there was no sign of surrender.

There were, Riss thought, three levels of personal smell in combat.

The first was when the battle first began, and no one wanted to take his helmet off or let anyone realize how stinky he was.

The second was after a few weeks had passed and everyone smelled worse, and didn't care who knew it.

The third, and M'chel hoped this was terminal, was when a soldier wanted to hunt down some real echelon muhff, and open his suit under his or her nose.

Maybe this was one area where the infantry had a bit of an advantage over the lifter crews. You couldn't smell yourself after a while, so you stank in peace.

But in a heavy lifter, the crew compartment was about five meters by five meters by two meters, with various weapons and devices intruding. The four- or five-person crew could, when they weren't in combat, chance taking off their helmets and breathing compartment air.

And the smells that went with it: sweat, what was called ozoned air from the various instruments, urine, excrement, blood, halitosis, missile exhaust, burnt propellant, decaying food, machine oil.

Riss thought about the glamour of it all, realized if it weren't for her big mouth she could be sitting up on the bridge of the *Pride* or somewhere safer and less smelly.

M'chel discovered another danger of fighting in a vacuum—the silence.

An incoming artillery round, unless it was very, very close, could only be felt by the shock of its impact and explosion.

A round that missed you, missed you, and unless someone pointed out what had happened, you might not even be aware you'd been shot at.

That reduced combat fatigue—but it also made troops careless about their safety.

Riss had moved her regiment to cover the conquered outpost while it was reinforced, and the positions' firing ports were turned through 180 degrees.

Somewhere out there, she'd been told, someone, probably a Mauler, was using a sniper rifle. A big projectile sniper rifle, with 13-mm shells, probably recoilless.

After seeing a round splatter on rock or lifter armor, most soldiers developed a posture problem, walking hunched over and hastily waddling from cover to cover.

But still people were hit.

One of them was M'chel's "lucky" gunner.

He'd gotten out of the lifter through the cupola hatch and was stretching, glad to be in the open for an instant.

The round almost missed him, tearing past his leg, taking a chunk of suit and meat with it.

Then the triage unit went on, and Riss could hear the man squall as his leg was neatly, cleanly, cut off.

Then the man jerked, stiffened, and was dead.

Riss never thought she'd ever cry for any Khelat, let alone one who called her "ma'am," and whose last name she barely remembered.

But she did.

Then she found someone who'd seen a puff of dust

knocked up when the sniper's weapon recoiled . . . and who had taken a compass reading on the location.

Riss could have leveled the area with a missile or shell fire.

But that wasn't personal enough.

Instead, that night, her blaster sheathed, she went through the lines with a knife in her hand.

FORTY-FOUR

M'chel followed the compass heading inexactly. She would feel like a damned fool, not to mention being dead, if she was so intent on the swinging disc that she wandered into the sniper's lair.

So she hung a dogleg course north for a number of paces, then south for the same number, zigging across the heading, taking a great deal of time to consider the terrain in front of her.

She moved very slowly, one hundred meters in an hour, keeping her breathing quiet. Before she moved, she used a small available-light monocular to make sure no one was lying in ambush.

It was getting near dawn when she came on a small rock nest that she would have chosen as a post if she'd been a sniper.

Riss examined the ground carefully, saw, by the dim moonlight, some bipod-sized scrapes in the soft rock.

Very good.

She found a hide a few meters from the nest, laying her blaster on the rock in front of her.

If the sniper was really good, he—or she—would never return to this position.

Riss was counting the shooter wasn't perfect.

She was right.

Crouched low, just before first light, she saw four space suits moving toward her from enemy positions.

She puzzled, then realized one would be the triggerman, one would be backup cover, one would be a spotter, and the fourth would be, considering the weight of a 13-mm rifle and its rounds, the ammo bearer.

She hoped.

M'chel was utterly motionless as the men found a position, and she saw the long rifle being put together, and its bipod and monopod positioned.

She braced for her rush.

A very large, probably multiple-vision telescopic sight went on top of the rifle, and Riss had seen enough.

Her blaster came up, and she shot the cover man, then the spotter.

The ammo bearer was looking about wildly, and she put a bolt through his faceplate.

The sniper himself had forgotten about the blaster holstered at his waist, was trying to get the big gun around.

M'chel dropped the gun, came across the ground between them in a waddling attack.

She brushed the rifle aside and dove on top of the sniper. Her knife went under his helmet, into the expansion-contraction joint, and through into softness.

The sniper jerked, his heels thrashed twice, and he was dead.

Riss wanted to gloat over the body, wished she was primitive enough to collect ears, instead went back to her position, feeling a great deal better about the world.

A transport landed, and its passengers and crew were bustled to positions about two kilometers behind the Khelat front lines.

Star Risk now was truly in debt to Hal Maffer.

Somewhere he'd found an entire 200 mm multiple-launch rocket battery, and enlisted it. There were ten launchers in the battery, and a full complement of rocket men.

They went into action that first day, firing ten rockets at a time per launcher.

The rockets were simple solid-fuel devices and had no guidance after they left the tube. They weren't terribly accurate, but ten of them landing in approximately the same place at a time was impressive. Not to mention lethal if you or your lifter or your pillbox happened to be in that same place.

The ground rocked under the rockets' impact, and obliterated positions.

Little by little, the Shaoki lines were being driven in.

The next victory went to Grok.

He and his technicians had been trying to decode whatever secrets were hidden in a burst of what appeared to be static, but failed utterly.

Then Grok rethought the matter.

He had Freddie detail him a couple of destroyers. Against practice, considering Grok knew far too much to be allowed in combat beyond what was utterly necessary, they picked him up and lurked on a position just beyond the atmosphere, trying to get a fix on where that static burst was coming from.

It took two tries, but then they homed in on the signal and found a pair of Shaoki transports nestled snugly into the broad mouth of a cavern, almost impossible to see unless you were right on it.

Grok now knew why the Khelat had been unable to figure out how the Shaoki were able to resupply. The transports would have jumped to a nav point very close to III, picked up the transmission, perhaps triggered by a com on one of their ships, and darted for the surface before they could be detected.

There were antiaircraft missiles around the site, but the destroyers spoofed and then toppled them.

Two barrages of rockets went into the cavern, and, later, four of Wahfer's cruisers were put in synchronous orbit over the mine's remains.

That was that for Shaoki resupply.

"If these Maulers had any brains," Goodnight said, "they would be starting to think about the virtues of a good, honest white flag."

Some had brains.

One section did find white, or rather whitish, flags, and began waving them about.

The shot was patched through to the king's command ship.

Three lifters went out to accept the surrender.

The Maulers—about twelve of them—clambered out of their semiwrecked lifter, hands held high. When they were all in the open, the two Khelat lifters opened fire.

They killed all twelve.

In the shriek of self-congratulations, Friedrich made sure his people had seen the footage.

"Nice," Goodnight said. "Very nice, indeed."

Sarcasm dripped from his voice.

"It certainly is," Riss agreed from her position with the tracks. "It'll be a cold day in hell before anyone else thinks of a little sensible cowardice."

"Are you humans entirely mad?" Grok wondered.

"No," van Baldur said. "Just our leaders."

"Shit!" Riss said, and that ended the conference.

*   *   *

Goodnight didn't need to trigger his battle analysis to know what the Shaoki would do next.

There were only two options: to abandon VI/III and its soldiers and mercenaries, or attempt to reinforce or relieve them.

Intercepted holo-casts from the Shaoki worlds said what that would be: reinforcement.

Shaoki ships swarmed off Irdis, ready for the Grand Fleet Action.

King Saleph said that he was prepared for battle, and told his ships to englobe VI/III.

It was to be a battle of total destruction.

Friedrich von Baldur gently tore his hair, then asked the king for his permission for a "spoiling attack, just in case."

Saleph, busy moving model fleets in the air around his control room, gave his assent.

Von Baldur asked if he could use his mercenary ships, and possibly Prince Wahfer's cruiser squadron.

The king was glad to give up the latter for what he was very sure would be a no-action piece of foolery by the mercenaries.

Wahfer had been getting entirely too much attention on the holos of late.

Von Baldur, feeling like a very grand admiral, took Grok off III and transferred him to the *Pride.*

He put a pair of Redon Spada's scouts near each standard nav point in the VI system, figuring that the Shaoki were as likely to be as lazy as the Khelat when battle was met.

He was right.

One of Spada's p-boats reported a steady stream of ships pouring out of N-space. They weren't coming out in any sort of coherent formation.

This had to be the Great Fleet of the Shaoki.

Von Baldur had figured that, too.

Given the fairly high degree of incompetency/inexperience Star Risk had witnessed when they were on the Shaoki payroll, he didn't figure it was likely the Shaoki Council would fly tight formation and chance collisions.

The Shaoki paid no attention to the small p-boats skittering for shelter, but concentrated on their battle formations.

Von Baldur had more than enough time to position Wahfer's cruisers above the Shaoki and send for Khelat reinforcements. He was careful, in com, to praise the king's intelligence and masterly strategic abilities in allowing von Baldur to lurk.

He thought, as he watched the Shaoki move toward III, they were almost stately, even though they were hurtling forward at several times light speed.

If he had a battleship—and he did—the Shaoki could move in a stately manner . . . if Fleet Admiral von Baldur determined it was.

He felt like he was Nelson at Trafalgar . . . Togo at Tsushima . . . Nhrumah at Deneb Four.

But he didn't let himself get ego driven into a direct confrontation.

Von Baldur sent Wahfer down in a bounce attack. That caused several squadrons to hive off.

Friedrich took the *Pride,* escorted by a dozen destroyers, in to mop up on the stragglers, then jumped well before Shaoki heavies could complicate the issue.

About the time he came out of N-space, the Khelat fleet had arrived.

It was a swarming melee.

Inchcape wanted to get in on the action; von Baldur forbade it.

"There'll be enough blood to drink in a few hours," he told her.

There was.

The Shaoki command broke, ordered *"sauve qui peut,"* and, obediently, every man took off for himself.

At that point, von Baldur ordered his destroyers and patrol boats into action.

They assyrianed the fold, holding themselves to one missile, one target, and if that didn't get him, the next ship would.

It was the only real victory of the VI/III battle.

"As long as those fools upstairs are dancing about," Goodnight said, "what do you think of us doing our share for the war effort and all?"

"Good," Riss said. "Let's get this nonsense over with. I'll need to soak for a week to get the dirt off my dirt."

Riss's regiment went forward the next dawn, and Goodnight's storm troops swept on the remaining outpost's flanks.

That battle was over within the day, hardly a crushing victory, but, like infantry battles, one trudging step forward.

By rights, the Maulers at least, trapped in their hopeless valley, should have surrendered.

But they didn't.

Riss, cursing King Saleph's trigger-happy goons, took one medium lifter and a driver, after plastering the lifter with white plas banners front, rear, and dangling from the autocannon.

She hoped the Maulers would think kindly of her.

If she were in their position, after the murders, she might not have.

And she really hoped she was closing on a Mauler, not a Shaoki, position. She had no idea what they might do, considering the defeat going on overhead.

'Casting, on the standard emergency frequency, that she came in peace, she told the pilot to ease the lifter forward.

No one answered her. But no one opened up on her, either.

Two well-camouflaged chainguns swiveled to cover her, and then the emergency frequency came alive.

"Far enough. Ground it."

She told the driver to obey.

"One person out, and advance."

Riss almost grinned. This was one of the formal dances done by every military since spears went out of fashion.

She obeyed.

There was no blaster at her waist, for the first time in many weeks, and she felt naked. She didn't think about her lack of grenades or even a hideout gun.

Two soldiers came out, keeping out of the chainguns' line of fire, checked her for weapons or transmitting gear beside her suit com, and then covered her faceplate with something opaque.

Fingers fumbled at her belt, turned her suit radar off, led her forward.

She felt smoothness under her boots, heard a lock door open, close, and the lock cycle.

Riss was led forward, around a corner, another corner, and a third. She assumed this was misdirection.

A 'cast came on the emergency frequency: "You can doff your helmet now."

She obeyed.

The first thing that hit her was the smell.

Riss thought she managed to cover her reaction.

She thought she, and her men, were in sad shape, which they were. But facing her were two women and a man who looked like they'd been dragged, sideways, through the bowels of hell.

The woman, in front, had a plas bandage on one cheek.

"You are?" she demanded.

"M'chel Riss," M'chel said. "Star Risk, limited."

"You want?"

"You—if you're with the Maulers—to surrender."

"After what they did to our boys," one of the men said bitterly, "what chance do we have."

It wasn't a question.

"Come on," Riss said. "Mercenaries don't fight . . . unless they have to. I'll give you my own—and Star Risk's—guarantee. Nothing will happen to you. Hell, if you want, you can even keep your personal blasters."

The woman stayed expressionless.

"Put her in that chamber," she ordered.

One of the men obeyed.

Riss didn't wait long. This time, she was escorted out as if she wasn't a prisoner.

"You have a good reputation," the woman said. "If any of us do." She smiled, a wintry expression.

"I'm Malleus," she said. "We did a fast check. . . . And I remember you actually let Mik Hore walk after he tried to doublecross you."

"We're sentimental," Riss said.

The woman laughed, not humorously.

"And there's one of us—a man named Erm—who spoke well of you."

Riss didn't remember him.

"All right," Malleus said. "We're yours. We're not

stupid enough to ask for conditions. Other than our lives."

"You'll have them," Riss said. "Take your personal gear, and leave everything else."

Malleus nodded.

"We'll have a transport—or two—down here," Riss continued. "Tomorrow, if you want."

"We won't need more than one," the man who'd spoken before said.

Malleus's face twisted, then she regained control.

"By nightfall tomorrow," she said.

"I'll need to get on the com," Riss said.

Friedrich von Baldur brought a transport down, escorted by the *Pride*, and two destroyers.

The Malleus Maulers, silent, sullen, and exhausted, filed aboard the transport.

Riss stood beside her lifter, not feeling any particular sense of victory.

When the last mercenary had boarded, one of the two chainguns that had greeted her suddenly elevated to vertical. Everyone jumped, but the gun made no further movement.

Two people in suits came out of a lock.

Riss went to them. She saw, through the faceplate, one was Malleus.

"You keep your bargains," the woman said.

"We do." Riss said nothing about the lack of trust, pretty sure if the situation was reversed she would've done something similar and been the last man out, with a gun. At least, she hoped she would have had the courage.

Malleus nodded, and without saying anything else, went up the transport's ramp, into the lock.

Moments later, it lifted away.

*   *   *

With about half of the final base now unmanned, the Shaoki soldiers began surrendering en masse.

Grinning Khelat accepted their surrender.

Riss, watching, thought their faces looked like dogs in a fowl run.

"You did not have my permission to treat the foreign soldiers as you did," King Saleph said, keeping his temper under control.

"What would you have done, Your Highness?" von Baldur said.

"Treat them as the criminals—the murderers—they are," he said. "Just as I shall treat the Shaoki, now that they have begun surrendering. I will set up prison planets where these fools can expiate their crimes."

Von Baldur nodded curtly, cut the com.

"Goddamnit," he complained to Goodnight, who was also on the bridge. "I cannot save everyone."

The two of them stared at each other, both dumb with fatigue.

And the battle for Shaoki VI/III was over.

FORTY-FIVE

The troops stumbled back to their bases, were peeled out of their suits, and collapsed.

Even the mercenaries took one look at the parade field and exercise yards, said stuff it, later for getting back in shape, had a couple of drinks, were besotted and asleep.

Star Risk, so tired they could cry, did everyone a favor and hired civilian contractors to launder or burn the suits the infantry had worn.

Then, having done their bit, they thought, to prove the imperviousness of leaders, they died as well.

Everyone knew that, with Shaoki VI/III conquered, the next step would be the invasion of the capital, Irdis.

And no one wanted to think about that, because it was guaranteed to be twice the bloodbath they'd just been through.

Eventually, Riss woke up, took a very long bath, looked at her hair, and shuddered.

That would come before anything military. She found a salon, and had her hair cut very, very short.

Style comes second to dirt in a prolonged campaign.

She treated herself—of course, at the Khelat's

expense—to a full massage and facial. Then she found a boutique and treated herself to some new outfits.

Dressed, she considered herself in a mirror, and decided while she still looked like the ravages of hell, in her opinion, she wouldn't frighten small boys and dogs to death.

Feeling a bit cheerier, and determined to surround herself with many calories, healthy ones that didn't cause pimples, she headed for the Star Risk barracks.

Jasmine was there, looking impossibly unscathed. Her hair was also trimmed very close.

"I hate you, woman," M'chel managed.

Jasmine grinned, preened.

"Buzz Goodnight," King said. "He wants to confer. We seem to have a problem."

Riss obeyed.

Both Chas and Grok answered the call.

Friedrich drifted in from his own quarters.

"We have," Goodnight announced, "not just a problem, but a very large problem. We seem to have a case of journalists."

"So?" Riss said. Unlike many soldiers, she didn't care about the media one way or another until she'd decided whether or not they were going to get in the way.

"Yes," Goodnight said with a scowl. Clearly, he was with the military majority.

"A team of four, representing themselves as free-lancers, working for some independent outfit I've never heard of has shown up," Goodnight said.

"I figured they wanted to cover the blood and slaughter, which is always marketable, as long as the consumers' blood isn't what's leaking.

"But they didn't show any sign of wanting to tour VI/III, or more than token coverage of how the Khelat forces are fighting for freedom, et cetera, et cetera, et cetera.

"What they were interested in, quite intensely, is the *maln* plantations, which, according to Prince Barab, are just coming into flower."

"That's . . . odd," Friedrich said.

"Certainly is," Goodnight said. He bowed to Grok. "Your cue, sirrah."

"Chas brought me in," the alien said, "because these journalists were sending their reports back into Alliance territory coded."

"That's very strange," Riss said. "Never heard of that, although maybe, if there's a couple-three fighting for the same story . . . which there doesn't seem to be."

"No," Grok agreed. "Even more unusual is that the code they are using—which I haven't broken as yet— is a three/five/three, sprinkled with two-character groups."

Jasmine's eyes went wide. "That's the pattern Cerberus Systems likes."

"Indeed it is," Grok said. "And I can add that Cerberus, during the time that I was with them, frequently used journalists for their cover IDs."

"So why is Cerberus lurking around Khelat?" M'chel said.

"I do not know," von Baldur said. "But always assuming Cerberus is never up to any good, especially as far as we are concerned, I think we should have them chased back where they came from."

"I can take care of that," Riss said. "Prince Wahfer wants to talk to me in the worst way. Which means he wants something. And a favor for a favor . . . hmmm. As long as I don't have to go to bed with the bastard."

"If you will take care of these reporters," Friedrich said, "preferably without us having to show our faces, I shall do some inquiring with our pet lobbyist and ask who on Earth—or in the Alliance—has the curiosity bug."

The dining place Wahfer chose was quiet, romantic, but most of all, secluded.

Riss wondered if Wahfer had a jealous wife, who was more closly connected to King Saleph than the Prince.

Or maybe wives.

She knew little of the social customs of the Khelat, hadn't particularly wanted to learn.

Riss told Wahfer about the journalists.

He said they were easily taken care of, and would be deported tomorrow. They would never know that Star Risk was behind their being declared persona non grata.

She was not to worry—and he actually used the hoary phrase—her pretty little head about it.

Riss hid her wince, and asked how she could return the favor.

Wahfer grew kittenish. Riss couldn't look under the tablecloth to see if he was digging his toe into the carpet.

"I was not particularly pleased," he obliqued, "with the way the most recent battle was conducted, in spite of our success."

"The old saw has it, 'One more victory like that and I am undone.' "

"Then you—which means Star Risk—agree."

"We think," Riss said, "the campaign might have been conducted a bit more subtly."

Wahfer smiled at Riss's careful words.

"What I wanted—want—was to ask, in a very casual sense, how attached Star Risk is to King Saleph."

"He pays our bills," Riss said.

"Suppose a client happened along that offered you a better deal?"

"Star Risk," M'chel lied, "tends to keep its word. But we also have a reputation for keeping all options open. This is, after all, a very tough universe."

"It is, is it not," Wahfer agreed. "Perhaps, in the weeks to come, I might have an interesting proposition for your team. I would appreciate your silence—to anyone except your fellows—until I come to you with something definite."

And he changed the subject.

He also made only a token pass at her, when he returned her to her barracks, which surprised Riss.

The next morning, she reported fully to the others.

Von Baldur clicked his tongue severally and thoughtfully against the roof of his mouth. How very, very interesting," he said. "I would suspect Prince Wahfer of ambition.

"Jasmine, could you do a bit of research, and find out how often—and how violently—Khelat changes its rulers?"

"I shall," King said.

"I would suggest," Friedrich went on, "keeping in mind Machiavelli's caution about a mercenary ever straying from his swords, that each of us start practicing extreme caution.

"Further, I was finally able to make contact—gads, but that is an intolerable verb—with Anya Davenport, to inquire about Cerberus's presence. She knew nothing, at great length, and was *terribly* astonished at Cerberus's presence.

"As I said, watch your backs."

FORTY-SIX

"Well," Redon Spada said to M'chel Riss, "if you don't have anything better to do than wait around to get killed, you want to go adventuring with me?"

"How romantic," Riss said.

"It is," Spada agreed. "Or will be, rather. Moonlight on the waters . . . raiders from the deep . . . tiny islands lapped by waves."

"Translate, please."

"I have discovered," Spada said, "Irdis has a lot of little tiny islands, and lots—so to speak—of war plants."

"So?"

"So they send a lot of stuff by sea to the bigger spaceports."

"So again?"

"While they've got AA up the wazoo," Spada said, "how much you wanna bet they've never even thought about what's under their oceans?"

"Which is?"

"Me . . . and some other p-boats. Starships make great submarines."

"Ah," Riss said, thinking about the state of the world. She hadn't really determined on what unit she'd be with for the coming invasion of Irdis, and didn't much care about making herself useful on Khelat.

She realized she was still recovering from the nightmare of Shaoki VI/III. But Riss being Riss, she never considered throwing her com in the nearest body of water and disappearing somewhere nonmartial for a few weeks.

"Raiding?"

"Sure," Spada said. "It's got to be safer than tarting around the approaches to Irdis. Who knows from submarine raiders?"

And so M'chel Riss went raiding with Redon Spada. It almost got her killed.

The sea wasn't Earth green, but not far distant, and the swells rolled three thousand meters below them.

"These reaches don't have many islands to break up the wave heights," Spada's navigator—weapons officer said. "Which is why we chose this area."

Spada nodded.

"A good place to make entry," he said, and touched his throat mike.

"Take 'em in," he said.

The two Pyrrhus-class starships obediently dove, Spada's ship in front.

Riss, even though she knew better, braced as the ocean rushed up toward them.

Spada braked slightly, keeping his speed below Mach numbers. These waters should be deserted, but who wanted to take a chance?

His ship hit, and there was only a slight jolt. Then they were underwater.

Spada checked a screen that showed the other two ships flanking him, then cut his speed to less than 100 kph.

M'chel was wondering why she'd forgotten about her fairly recently developed sense of claustrophobia.

"Now we turn south and east," Spada said. He nodded at the navigator—weapons officer, and a large-scale chart appeared on the center screen.

"Here's the port city of Lafan, with manufacturing plants all to hell and gone behind it. Goodies . . . everything from unfinished ship hulls from a big casting yard to missile tubes gets shipped to Berfan, then finished up, and shipped offworld to designated systems," Spada said.

"How official briefing you sound," Riss said.

"I do, don't I?" Spada said, catching himself. "What we propose to do is hang off Lafan until we spot a convoy, or a target of opportunity, anyway, and then count us some coup."

"Coo?" Riss puzzled.

"Spelt C-O-U-P," the navigator said. "Old Earth custom. One tribe made points by whacking a member of another tribe with a stick, preferably when that other person had a lance or something."

"I assume," M'chel said dryly, "we can dispense with following primitive customs that precisely."

The three ships moved closer to the city, keeping close watch on the screens. Nothing moved on the oceans.

"Clean, clean, clean," Spada chortled.

At his signal, the three ships grounded, very deep, more than five hundred meters down.

"Now we wait for targets."

Riss volunteered to take the predawn watch, what Spada was calling the "dog watch."

She found out that was an old water-sailing term, and instantly started aye-ayeing and telling Spada how the deck was, how everyone's timbers were shivering, and other nauticalisms she made up.

Before she relieved the navigator on watch, she had him show her all the little toys of the control board.

One particularly fascinated her: a small rocket that could be put in a particular orbit and then used as a silent, nearly undetectable observer in many different wavelengths, including normal visual.

It seemed to her that rocket might be interesting underwater.

Once everyone was asleep, she dimmed the lights of the control board and launched the rocket upward.

A storm was raging on the surface, and she let the rocket drift, wearing the observer's helmet.

This was better than any holo, any projected experience she'd known, and she let the rocket be carried by the tidal current toward shore, then submerged it and sent it hissing back to its proper position, just above where the p-boat lay, many meters below.

Waves washed over the tiny projectile, and she fiddled with the control panel, found a microphone control, and let the winds whirl into her earphones.

She sent the rocket arcing out of the water and into the face of waves. If there were any Shaoki ships out there, she thought they'd be concerned with their own survival, not some strange fish leaping about.

Sometimes she let the rocket ride a wave, near the crest, where foam boiled.

She decided if this contract paid off properly, she would need one of these rockets on her island, much better, in the stormy season, than a windsurfer.

For the first time she could remember, she actually regretted being relieved at the watch's end.

Two ship days later, the engineer, standing his watch, reported contact.

With a minimum of communications, Spada brought his three starships close to the surface.

His engineer, muttering, was fussing with the filters on one screen.

Radar already showed three large blips.

The screen burped and showed, in real time, three tankers, each about two hundred meters long. They were strange-looking, twin-hulled catamarans whose decks overhung their cargo tanks between their hulls.

Spada searched, found nothing else on the water. High above, almost invisible against the cloud cover, were two ships, possibly escort against the tankers being hit from space.

"Wonder what they're lugging?" the navigator said.

"Shush," Spada said. "I'm figgerin'."

He touched keys, then got on his throat mike.

"Spada elements," he cast. "Transmitting firing solution. Fire two missiles each in five minutes."

There were mike clicks of acknowledgment.

On time, Spada nodded at the weapons. "As they used to say, you may launch when ready, on the time tick."

"Yessir."

Five minutes ended.

The weapons officer touched a sensor, and Riss felt a slight jolt, then another, as two missiles slid out of firing tubes, floated, not under drive, toward the surface.

The weapons officer put on a gunnery helmet.

"Firing," he said.

On a screen, the two blips of the missiles went vertical, shot upward.

The gunnery program muttered to itself as the missiles, not caring whether they were fired in space, air, or water, focused on their targets.

The tankers never had a chance.

Six missiles closed on them.

Two struck the lead ship at once, which mushroomed into flame and black smoke. A third missile, seeing nothing much but destruction to impact on around the first tanker, shifted its aim to the second ship, blew its bow off.

The ship veered, out of control, almost ramming the third tanker, just as two more missiles slammed into it.

It, too, exploded.

"Now," Spada said, viewing the shambles with evident satisfaction, "where did number six missile get off to?"

The helmeted figure of the weapons officer shook its head.

"Number two target's probably for it," Spada said. "Having no bow and all. But put another one out there, just to mak' siccar."

"Yessir."

The seventh missile struck the last tanker just aft of a five-story island that must be the bridge.

Obediently, the tanker blew itself apart.

"Hell of a way to make a living," Spada said, his voice somber. "Riding those matchboxes.

"Let's go deep. I don't want to find out what those aircraft are for."

They hugged the bottom for a day, with remote sensors above them.

Riss didn't dare play games with her rocket now;

instead tried to concentrate on the new globular mathematics text she'd brought along.

But the sounds in the p-boat were off-putting, neither the hum of deep space nor the silence of inaction.

They came to the surface at twilight, and saw, in the distance, lights.

Spada ordered the patrol boat to speed, and, with its fellows, sent his ship skating around, far faster, to the front of a two-ship convoy.

Both of them were medium-sized merchantmen.

Overhead flew some sort of escort aircraft, and, surprisingly, two very small ships.

"They learn fast, don't they?" Spada said, and launched a pair of missiles.

Both struck home, as did follow-up strikes from the other two ships, and the p-boats went deep again.

Spada, having seen lifeboats launched, was fairly cheerful.

But Riss kept thinking about those escort vessels, if that was what they were.

She managed to get Spada alone that night, although there was no clue, this deep in the ocean, as to the hour.

"About those two little ships," she said.

"Maybe escorts?" Spada nodded.

"Suppose they're not particularly fast learners around Lafan," she said. "Any more than the Shaoki have showed themselves so far."

"Awright," Spada said amiably. "I'll make that assumption. Where does it get us?"

"Maybe," Riss said cautiously, "that they've had problems with sea raiders before and already have an SOP figured out."

"What? Pirates?"

"Call them what you will."

Spada started to make a joke, saw M'chel was serious, and thought for a moment.

"Given that," he said, "that would mean that we'd better not think we're in killer's heaven for very much longer."

"That was my thought."

"Tell you what," Spada said. "We'll hit them again, tomorrow or the next, and if they're showing any signs of being ready for us, we'll get out of here. This was, after all, just supposed to be a little rest and relaxation for you."

Two days later, Riss's fears were realized.

And then some.

Half a dozen large merchantmen set out from Lafan.

Spada planned a nice, conventional approach, straight down the throat at them.

He and the other two p-boats maneuvered into attack position, crept toward the oncoming ships. He was about to bring his ship to the surface and prepare for firing when a superficial overhead sweep saw three ships in the air, dancing close attendance on the convoy.

"I'd guess destroyers," he said, lips pursed. "So we'll launch from deeper, just in case they've got magnetic anomaly detectors or sonobouys or like that. But between you and me, Riss, I think maybe we should've gotten some hat last night."

He thought some more.

"No. Wrong way in. They'll be expecting something from in front, since we done that before.

"Navigator, put me around behind these bastards,

and let the other two know we're going in from the rear."

Riss didn't know enough about ships to be afraid, but she saw the expression on the navigator–weapons officer, and then figured out that if Spada was going in behind the convoy, that would put the patrol ship in shallow water, which meant less hiding room, and with the shore closing off half of their possible escape routes.

But no one said anything, and there was the hum of the drive for over an hour.

"We're looking up their butts, sir," the navigator reported.

"Come up on them . . . say, about ten klicks faster than the convoy," Spada ordered. "And have the weapons ready for launch. We'll hit 'em and get out. One launch, no time to police up the wounded.

"Pass the word."

They crept up on the convoy.

The four of them aboard the patrol boat spoke in whispers, as if the Shaoki ahead of them could hear.

When the three starships were in position, Spada waited for almost ten minutes.

But nothing happened.

"Make your firing calculations," he ordered, even though those had been done, and were being redone every few seconds.

"I wish," he said, "this was a submarine, with one of those periscopes. I'd like to see what's going on up on those ships, like gun crews and such."

But blips and interpreted images remained as they were.

"Ready to fire," the weapons officer reported.

But Spada seemed reluctant to make the launch.

"All right," he said finally. "Launch two."

His other ships obeyed, as well.

"Fire them."

As the missiles started toward the surface, nav-weapons jerked.

"There's a pair of ships—little ones—coming out of nowhere. Coming fast."

The image on-screen showed six new, tiny ships near the merchantmen.

"Hovercraft, maybe," Spada said.

"The merchantmen have countermissiles up," nav said.

"Too late for one . . . a good, solid hit on its stern . . . two of our birds are out . . . jinking . . . I have some kind of launches from the escorts."

An alarm shrilled.

"Overhead," the man said, voice still calm. "Coming in on us."

"Ambushed, by the Lord Harry," Spada said, equally calm. He keyed a mike. "All Spada elements, take independent action, break contact, and reform at rendezvous point."

That point, determined before they entered Shaoki space, was somewhere just inside the Khelat worlds.

Riss, with nothing to do, felt like chewing on her seat's armrest.

Spada hit controls, put on power.

"I can't jump out of this," he said over his shoulder. "Those goddamned ships up there'd take us out in a second. And if we try to run . . ." he touched sensors.

"Ambush, indeed," he said. "There's five biggish ships coming out of Lafan. I think we stuck around too long."

There were dull thuds above them—the hovercraft were dropping explosives.

"Any idea how much water we've got under us, navigator?"

"It just deepened out. Maybe . . . a thousand meters."

"Well, God bless that. If we'd hit them in shallow water . . ." He let his voice trail off. "I knew there was a reason I was sitting on my thumbs."

Spada sent the starship deep.

"Now where do we want to go?" he asked.

"Our target's sinking," the navigator reported.

"Forget about . . . no. Wait."

Spada's smile was meant to be fiendish, looked skull-like. "We'll go under the bastard, which ought to foozle them. That'll give us a straight shot at the open sea, and we can do our vanishing act."

He put on more power.

One screen showed the looming bulk of the merchantman as it went underwater, turning upside down as it did.

Another screen lit, showing the sinking ship just overhead.

"A close one it's going to be, yes, indeedy," he said.

Then there was a scraping crash, and the patrol boat rocked sideways, then, stern first, started sinking, its drive screaming uselessly.

FORTY-SEVEN

Grok didn't hang about waiting for the invasion, either.

His analytic work was pretty well finished for the moment—he didn't anticipate intelligence suddenly discovering the Shaoki happened to have an extra fleet or assault army, just waiting around for something to do to worry him and Friedrich.

And he was feeling very, very stale. Plus, he'd picked out a very lovely target.

There was an easy entrance/exit: a large bordering lake and wilderness.

He'd found, and "borrowed," an obsolete Khelat three-man ship, intended for covert operations. After some ripping, tearing, and rewiring, it just about fit Grok with his suit on, although the lock was a tight squeeze.

Grok had a pair of destroyers escort him to just off Thur, then made a solitary entrance as night fell on his target below, trying to think and look as much like a largish meteorite as possible.

Just in case anyone was tracking him, he put on a burst of power at about five thousand meters and zigged down to submerge in the lake.

Step one.

Step two was pushing himself out of the lock and surveying his transport.

It lay half-buried in the mud, and he'd stirred up enough silt in his landing that the ship should be covered within the day.

Very good.

He took various packs out of the ship and went on his way.

He was too heavy to float, so he waddled ashore and found the cave he'd been pretty sure about from aerial holos.

That would make a more-than-adequate hide.

If it was discovered while he was out, an alarm would alert him on his return, and he'd simply go back to the lake and home.

If searchers came on him while he was in the cave . . . Grok made an unpleasant face intended to mimic a human smile.

Heaven help them.

Grok's target was Thur's main military base, which handled everything from basic training for half a dozen systems to range qualifications, to officer candidate school to command and general staff school.

It stretched for thousands of square kilometers and covered every sort of terrain from desert to jungle. There were chambers to teach combat in space and underwater.

The main gate was dominated by a huge statue, called the Warrior, a particularly odious bronze of a man brandishing a sword in one hand, a blaster in the other. No one seemed to know what, if anything, it represented.

About two million men . . . against Grok.

The alien was almost sorry he had them so badly outnumbered.

The first order of business was to prowl the base. One thing Grok found very helpful in his nightlong wanderings was the military's fondness for labeling things.

He paused at the assistant base commander's house, noted some species of pet animal yowling to get in.

That was as good a place to start as any.

He waited.

In about an hour's time, someone inside got tired of listening to the complaints and came to the door. It came open, and a muttering, balding man with atrocious taste in pajamas came out.

He didn't even have a moment to realize what was looming up at him before he was silently dead.

Grok put the body over his shoulder and loped away.

He'd already noted where one of the post garbage recyclers was, and didn't think anyone would consider the indignity of having the body of a colonel or general deposited in it.

He took care of the corpse, thought about calling it a night. But there were still a couple of hours before dawn.

Grok went to the armory for the Crew-Served Weapons Training Committee, and made an unobtrusive entrance. He then picked the lock on the weapons bay and went down the line of racked medium blasters.

Each barrel got tweaked very slightly, enough so at best it would explode, at worse none of the trainees would be able to hit anything, which would not increase their faith in Shaoki arms.

That was enough. Yawning, he found his way to his cave. Grok slept deeply, content in the knowledge of a job well done.

When he awoke, he treated himself to an excellent meal of frozen grubs, imported from his home worlds. He normally didn't eat them around Star Risk, because they had a certain . . . aroma about them. But here, among the enemy? Just another reason to find the Unknown Monster, for such he'd dubbed himself, truly loathsome.

He dug a minuscule radio out of his gear and tuned it to what seemed to be the base audio station. It would be no fun at all if no one screeched at his depredations.

That accomplished, he went forth into the night.

One of Grok's virtues was that no one could believe a being that big, that bulky, could move as silently as he did.

This night was for the general's mess.

He pried open the back door, after having curled a massive lip at the nervous trainee walking sentry back and forth in front of the building, and put certain additives in various staples, from sugar to tea.

Some would merely make the consumer violently ill. Others would turn his teeth bright yellow. Still others would produce parabolic vomiting, or defecation.

The largest bulk of substances would kill, slowly, painfully, leaving no trace behind.

Grok spent the rest of the evening vanishing a sentry here and there, then went to his cave.

By noon his radio was screeching with panic-stricken news about Khelat assassins and murderers. There must be at least two full platoons of them, killing sentries and colonels and hiding somewhere on Thur.

Before sleeping, Grok rumbled unhappily at what he considered the underestimation of his talents.

He'd found it more convenient, years earlier, to adjust his metabolism to that of the humans around him, although he could easily function for over one hundred hours without food or sleep.

But that made life easier.

He awoke to more howls from the radio. Little by little, he pieced things together.

A Khelat saboteur had been caught. He'd been posing as a trainee. During flamethrower training, he'd torched six recruits and three cadremen.

Grok puzzled about that, guessed that some poor idiot had panicked and frozen at the nozzle. And now he was a saboteur.

Grok almost felt sorry for him.

This night, he went out to the officers candidate school and crept into one building.

The candidates were paired up, two to a room.

Grok slithered into each room, a knockout spraygun in one hand, a knife in the other.

He slit every other candidate's throat, then was gone.

He hadn't had to use the spraygun at all, and felt a little proud.

Those prospective officers would not only have nightmares when they woke, seeing their assigned partner's gore, but wonder why the murderers had only chosen one man or woman.

He burbled happily on the way back to his cave, and, full of benevolence, let two dozing sentries live.

Grok had an uncomfortable feeling, with no logical explanation for his paranoia, so he decided to trust it and moved to the back of the cave to sleep.

In the afternoon, he was wakened by the crash of branches, the subdued shouts of men.

He lay quite still, thinking neutral thoughts.

The sounds came closer, even into the mouth of the cave, then away.

Very good.

But he did think it was time to be moving on.

As soon as one—no, two—small tasks were accomplished.

The first was easiest, and, somewhat lightened, Grok went to the second.

That was at the commanding general's home.

It was old-fashioned, lavish, two-story.

Grok almost thought the Shaoki believed their own scare tactics, for there was a grounded heavy lifter at each of the four compass points.

Men in pairs walked the rounds between them.

Grok sneered.

There was a light on.

Grok lifted himself up to one of the second story's decks, which groaned alarmingly, but Grok thought it would hold him. A nearby window was latched, but not locked.

A thin, angled blade slid into its jamb, pried, and the window creaked open.

Grok froze, waiting to see if someone had heard the slight noise.

Nothing.

He looked inside, a little afraid that he'd pried into one of the bedrooms, and was about to leap in on someone's chest.

It was a storeroom.

Grok went into the house, padded down a corridor, hearing three snores from as many rooms, went downstairs, toward the light.

The door was open.

It was a study, impressive in battle trophies, computers, and maps.

Inside, puzzling over a book, was a man who had to be the post general. No one less than that could look that imposing.

Grok was halfway across the room before the man looked up.

He scrabbled a desk drawer open, reached for a blaster, and slumped dead as Grok broke his neck.

Very good.

Grok pondered his next step.

He thought about going back upstairs and murdering the snorers—probably the late general's wife and children. But he decided not—Goodnight was always cautioning him on overdoing things.

Still.

He took out his large combat knife and sliced off one of the corpse's hands. That got a respectable spray of blood.

He painted, across one map, FREE THUR LIBERATION, then, on another chart, a rather abstruse symbol from his childhood.

That would add a certain confusion factor to the equation.

Then he carefully dissected the body.

Grok thought about eating some delicacies, such as the general's liver and lights. But human flesh really didn't agree with him. So he simply put these various parts in a pouch and decided those who came on the body could think anything they wanted, knowing humans always preferred the most vile.

And that was that for Thur.

He went back out the way he'd come, past the lifters and into the night.

An hour later, his ship blasted out of the lake and into space, far ahead of the AA batteries that fired wildly at nothing.

An hour after that, four shaped charges went off, and the statue of the Warrior toppled facefirst into the square it imposed on. The statue's head snapped free from its neck, bounced twice, and demolished a guard shack and its occupants at the main gate.

Grok decided his small vacation had been time well spent.

FORTY-EIGHT

The engineer reached to cut the power.

"Carefully," Redon Spada said. "We might need that sooner or later."

The engineer reacted, then gingerly slid the drive pot about two-thirds back.

Riss hoped she didn't look as scared as he did.

Redon Spada's expression suggested he was taking a walk in a rather boring park.

He moved controls back, forth, but the tiny patrol ship continued—as far as Riss's seat of the pants told her—sinking as it jerked to and fro, but remained still pinned.

Eventually, it *sqwushed* down on something—M'chel hoped it was the ocean floor—and something very large and heavy crashed down atop it.

"We appear to have arrived," Spada said. "Somewhere. And it might appear that something is on top of us."

Riss involuntarily glanced up.

"It won't squash us, whatever it is," Spada said. "The hull's far too resistant for that. However, I do wish," and his voice turned plaintive, "we had some sort, any sort, of gauges that might suggest what the blazes just happened." He scanned the control board. "Ms. Riss, take a letter. Dear sirs, why don't you people put depth gauges or sonar or radar sets that show things in millimeters away from the hull. I remain your dissatisfied customer, sincerely, and so on and so forth, from full fathoms five."

"I've a theory," Riss said. "Which I don't like."

"Try it."

"Could that damned ship we sank have sunk on top of us?" M'chel asked.

"That's foolishness," Spada said. "But it's the only sort of foolishness that fits."

He unbuckled his safety harness, stood. The ship's antigravity kept down firmly where it should be, even if that might not be the case on the outside.

"I suppose I should suit up and take a stroll to see what fix we're in," he said. "Unless someone happens to have an advanced degree in using space suits for diving?"

There were shakes of the head.

M'chel, wanting to stay a nice, comfortable coward but thought she was too afraid to do that, held up a hand.

"I've got a few thousand hours in suit drill." She realized to her horror what her mouth was saying. "I'd better go."

Now she wished for the old sexist days, when someone might stop her for gentlemanly reasons. But none of the other three in the p-boat's control room moved.

Riss grunted, got up, and eeled herself into space gear.

"And here I go," she said, moving into the lock and sliding the hatch closed behind her.

She cycled the lock, and its outer hatch came open with a great gush of water.

M'chel held on to a stanchion until the lock was flooded, then slowly moved outside.

She didn't have to go far.

The patrol boat sat firmly on the bottom, half embedded, at a forty-five-degree angle.

The merchantman hadn't gone down exactly on top of the p-boat, but when the missile hit, its anchor had come unstoppered and crashed onto and, somehow, around, the starship.

"Wonderful," Riss muttered.

Then the ship had sunk on top of her.

All that would be necessary was to take a cutting torch to the anchor cable, and then the p-boat could bull its way to freedom.

Spada eyed Riss's sketch of what lay outside.

"How nice," he murmured. "Take another letter. Dear sirs, how dast you send out your little pickle boats without even the hint of a good argon double-throw-down anchor-chain cutting torch. . . . Well, at least one thing. We'll die of boredom or starvation before the life-support systems run out.

"Anyone got any ideas?"

There was utter silence.

Riss had this sudden idea of herself, gray-haired and hobbling, taking her shift outside to work away with a hand file on that damned chain.

Then she had it.

It was an idea so stupid, so horrible, she frightened even herself.

She lined it out, and was not pleased to see equal looks of dread on the other three faces, even Spada's. They sat in silence for a while, mulling her idea.

"I don't see anything wrong with it," the navigator–weapons officer said. "The fumes from the missile will gas us, the explosion will hull us, and that frigging chain will crush us.

"Come on. Let's get on it."

It took about two hours to slide one of the missiles out of its launch tube.

Using maintenance tools, they unshipped the warhead and then suited up. Using hand tools and terror, Riss, being the most experienced with explosives, cut the back of the warhead open.

Knowing little about whatever put the bang in the missile, she found a plastic bar that looked nonmagnetic and not sparky, and set to work, gingerly digging the explosive out and rolling it in sealed tubes.

While she was doing that, the other missiles were pulled from their launchers, and their command detonators removed. One command det trigger and one tube of explosives were combined.

Riss went back outside and clambered up on the hull, and found a kink in the chain.

She hooked her tiny bomb—the detonator was almost as big as the charge—up, and climbed down. She decided to stay outside, and backed off a suitable distance.

She had her radio on.

"Firing one," she said, and could hear herself breathing very loudly.

She hit the detonator trigger inside her suit, feeling it slip on suddenly sweat-slippery fingers.

Riss saw a puff of sediment, felt a slight wash of seawater.

She climbed back up to the hatch, and then on up to the chain. There was a noticeable gouge in the metal.

M'chel allowed herself to feel a bit—just a bit—of hope, and packed another charge in place and turned the detonator on.

Again, she went back, after reporting progress on her radio, and set it off.

Another puff . . . but this time, nothing seemed to have changed.

She wondered what the hell the difference was, tried a third charge.

This time there was not only a puff, but the anchor chain slithered down, crashing on the hull, no doubt scaring the hell out of the three inside.

Now all that was holding the p-boat pinned was a bit of the sunken ship's upper hull.

"Anytime you're ready," Riss said. "Sir."

Spada shrugged, fed power to the drive.

Through the hull, they could hear, could feel, scraping, and then the boat surged away.

"That did it," the engineer announced unnecessarily.

"Take me home, Captain Spada," Riss said, trying to avoid a sag of relief in her voice. "And never, ever, ever take me messing about with boats again."

FORTY-NINE

Signal intelligence from Irdis said that the Shaoki rulers, the somewhat reconstituted council, really did believe in killing the messenger.

When reports of the "Free Thur Liberation" group and the depredations on Thur came back, there were wholesale reliefs and several executions of officers assigned to the great military base, which wouldn't do Shaoki morale any good whatsoever.

But Grok's glee was a little buried under larger events.

King Saleph was finally ready for the assault on Irdis.

As horrified as anyone was at the debacle on VI/III, he was now ready to listen to advice from his mercenaries, so long as they didn't rub things in.

"One of the reasons I decided to become a war leader," Friedrich said, sotto voce, to Riss, "was to stride nobly down the corridors of power, looking regal, while generals and admirals cowered out of my way."

M'chel looked at him oddly.

"Of course," von Baldur said, "if I had a brain, I

would have realized the same effect can be realized
with a sour expression and a clipboard."

Riss hid a snicker.

"Your forces appear to be assembling quite in order,"
von Baldur told King Saleph, who preened.

His chief advisor, Prince Barab, did the same.

"I think the only thing that needs your approval is
the exact role Star Risk and its employees might
profitably play in the coming days."

The king looked a bit alarmed. "I assumed that you
will be beside my fighting men and women, ensuring
their tenacity is strong."

Riss wasn't sure tenacity could be qualified, but
said nothing.

"Of course," von Baldur said soothingly, "but there
are additional tasks we might be qualified for."

He passed a fiche across, and the king fed it into a
viewer and scanned it. Then he scanned it again.

"This . . . this is irregular . . ." he started, but Barab
politely interrupted.

"I think some of these are most meritorious, and
you and I should provide our input, Your Majesty."

"Oh. Yes. Of course," the king said.

"I think we just won," von Baldur said as they left
the palace.

"Appears so," Riss said. "Assuming someone
doesn't get a wild hair."

"Always assuming that."

Shortly thereafter, one of Khelat's most noisome gos-
sip artists had the hot flash that the famous Star Risk
warriors would be mounting a special attack when the
assault on the evil Shaoki's capital began, and that the

clever king would be leading diversions instead of the main thrust.

Credence was led to the story by the seizure of all copies of the holo, and the whisking off to detainment of the erring hack.

Riss got a message from Prince Wahfer:

> *WHEN TIMES AND CIRCUMSTANCES CHANGE FOR THE BETTER, YOU AND I ARE FATED TO BE TOGETHER.*

The message gave her chills, and she determined she had better not take Wahfer casually. When the current mess was over with, she would have to have a long talk with the man.

"I'm not happy," Redon Spada said, twirling his first, and only, glass of wine.

"Why not?" Riss asked. "Haven't your paychecks been clearing?"

"Man cannot live by bread alone," Spada said.

"No," Riss said. "A little unsalted butter and caviar makes a nice addition."

She nodded to the cut glass tray and bowls in front of them.

"I think it may even come from Earth," she said. "What the hell. My palate just says, 'Fish eggs,' and then 'yum.'"

Spada obeyed, and spread butter, chopped onions, caviar, and lemon on a toast point.

"Don't laugh at me," he said.

"I won't," Riss said, seeing how serious the pilot was.

"I don't think I'm going to make it through this next one," Spada said.

"Oh, piddle," Riss said. "Do you know how many times someone has crept up to me and said how mortal he felt . . . and how alive and healthy the sniveler is today?"

"I've never had this feeling before," Spada said.

"I could, were I a suspicious woman, think that you were hoping to rouse up my womanly instincts, and I'd take you home with me and let you screw my little lights out."

Spada brightened, tried to hide it.

"Sirrah," M'chel said. "I thought you were a perfect gentleman."

"Great gods," Spada said. "I hope not."

"So do I," Riss purred.

It was just dawn when M'chel Riss kicked Redon Spada.

"Wake up and get dressed, and take your sorry ass back to your ship. Love's for later. Now it's time to make war.

"And stay alive, hey?"

Jasmine came into Friedrich's quarters with a quizzical expression.

"Boss, I got something I don't know how to handle."

"Go," von Baldur said, turning from his computer.

"I sent the monthly retainer to Anya Davenport. . . . And it was returned, marked ESCROW ACCOUNT CLOSED."

"Hmm," Friedrich said. "Well, she said she was going to fire us. I guess she's honest."

"That's not the problem," Jasmine said. "I tried to com her, to get a complete explanation."

"And?"

"I got somebody who said he was taking care of her accounts while she was offworld. I asked where she was, and was told, and I quote, 'Some faraway cluster called the Khelat worlds,' end quote. No other details were offered."

Von Baldur stroked his chin thoughtfully, then shook his head.

"I'm damned if I know what it means, either. I guess we'll just have to wait and see."

The fleets from the other Khelat systems drifted in to Khelat II and were escorted to parking orbits by Spada and Inchcape's ships.

Then, secretly, the destroyers and p-boats loaded up Goodnight's battalions of raiders and vanished from the Khelat worlds.

At about the same time, Grok, King, and von Baldur disappeared.

The Shaoki agents Grok had discovered were carefully fed the news about von Baldur's disappearance, and that several new divisions of Khelat had vanished with him.

Then King Saleph, on the bridge of his warship, flanked by the might of Khelat, went off to the final battle.

FIFTY

"The only nifty thing about this operation," Chas Goodnight told M'chel Riss, "is that it ain't in our contract to pick up the pieces after we go and break them. No peace plan, no negotiations, no foreign aid."

"It's nice to lead a simple life," Riss agreed. "But how much you want to bet they'll find some way to make it complicated again?"

"No takers here," Goodnight said. "But I better get back to my troopies. We'll be on the ground in another hour."

Slightly against policy, which dictated there never should be more than one general in one spot at a time, to avoid catastrophic damage, the two had jumped out from Khelat on a single transport, the rest of Goodnight's battalions trailing behind on other ships.

There was a time tick on the control panel of Riss's transport showing the time until landing—or, rather, assaulting—Irdis.

Riss wondered why she never lost the symptoms— dry mouth; sweaty palms; the desire, heavily suppressed, to babble nervously; the constant feeling of a full bladder, without being able to empty it—before an attack.

She checked her blaster, her ammo pouch, and her emergency pack.

She was as ready as she could be.

At least this time, she thought, we're not landing in goddamned suits.

She went down into the troop holds, made sure officers and noncoms were checking their men and women.

Another blessing, she thought, was that most of the raiding force was mercenary rather than Khelat, which suggested a bit more professionalism.

"Strap down," the intercom brayed. "We're coming in fast and hard."

M'chel found an open bulkhead with an emergency landing harness, obeyed the command.

There was air scream as the transport entered atmosphere, hard bumps from maneuvering, atmospheric conditions, or near misses.

Riss preferred not to think about the last.

If a transport, on final, took a hard hit, that would pretty much be it for its passengers, and she despised the thought of dying helplessly.

At least the antigravity was full on, so her stomach wasn't changing places with her tongue every few seconds.

"Landing in four . . . three . . . two . . ." And the crashing thud and bouncing didn't need to finish the countdown.

The ship stopped moving, and the large clamshell doors on each hold crashed open.

Riss flipped open her landing harness, and ran down a ramp into rubble.

The landing ground had been well fired up by the rockets and chainguns of the transports.

The city—Riss didn't even remember its name—had a large spaceport on its outskirts. The city center was on flatland, and then the land rose to a minor peak.

Here, a few of the colonels on the Shaoki Council lived. There were also the sensors for the port's anti-aircraft system, a com center, and so forth.

The Shaoki might have been expecting the port to be hit.

Instead, Goodnight put his troops down on the crest of the hill, with orders to ruin anything and anyone they came across.

The AA systems below were useless, and the mercenaries set up precision short-range rockets, and destroyed ships, hangars, and control towers.

Within two hours, the alert came: The Shaoki reaction force was lifting off from its various bases to come after them.

Moving fast, but without haste, the mercenaries reboarded their transports and the ships lifted away.

Below them was a city in flames.

They'd taken less than two dozen casualties, most of them wounded.

"Now *this*," Goodnight said, "is the way to fight a frigging war, not padoodling around on some vacuum-packed nowhere!"

Riss couldn't argue with that.

Other raiders were hitting in various places around Irdis, and Wahfer's cruisers were smashing orbital stations.

All this was intended to confuse the Shaoki, and Grok judged, from his monitors, that it was succeeding very well.

Riss and Goodnight's second target was the seaport city of Nonat.

Again they used indirection.

Rather than attack the port itself, which would have meant coming in from the seaward side of the city, where most of its aerial defenses were located, the raiders came in from the landward side.

Their landing ground wasn't the spaceport near the city, but directly in the warehouse section that reached for kilometers.

The soldiers' orders were simple: Burn what you can, smash the rest. And don't worry about the Shaoki unless they put up a good fight.

They didn't.

Most of them were what Grok had deduced, from SIGnal INTelligence, to be reservists, and rather sullen ones at that.

They fled, when they could, and the mercenaries set to work with the torch.

The full warehouses went up with roars, and the soldiers were forced to pull back.

The Shaoki aerial units were closer, and managed to attack just as Riss's and Goodnight's units were heading back to their transports.

But waiting overhead were two flights of Star Risk patrol boats that slashed down into the attack.

Riss watched one boat blast a wallowing Shaoki destroyer out of the air to smash down in the center of the city. She wondered, as the p-boat flashed overhead, if Redon Spada was at the controls.

That's the problem with having gonads, she thought. You start worrying about people who have proven capable of taking very good care of themselves.

She put that, and Spada, out of her mind, and concentrated on chivvying her troops into their ships.

This time, there were less than twenty casualties.

"I think," Friedrich von Baldur said from the bridge of his ship to King Saleph, "we have the Shaoki sufficiently confused. If you wish, Your Majesty, you may land the landing force."

FIFTY-ONE

Khelat's invasion fleet was stacked over Irdis. At the lowest level, within Irdis's atmosphere, keeping at about ten thousand meters, were the assault craft, hammering away at the ground defenses.

Some were huge monitors with tubes firing monstrous missiles one at a time. Others were darting small ships, almost as small as Spada's patrol craft, hitting targets here and there. Over them were the Command and Control ships, vectoring the small ships to ground targets or the Shaoki aerial formations.

The troop transports were the next in the layer, escorted by Inchcape's destroyers, in holding patterns until ground fire was suppressed.

Some of the Khelat generals, seeing the patterned hell being leveled against Irdis's surface, thought they might make an unopposed landing and began to act cheerful. None of the mercenaries with any experience who overheard this cheeriness bothered to argue with them.

The generals would find out in due course.

Beyond the destroyers was the main battle fleet, including Wahfer's cruiser squadron. Among them were the supply ships, hospital ships, maintenance craft.

Further out were light escorts, making sure no off-world Shaoki reliefs or attackers got through to the fleet or the transports.

King Saleph, from his battleship just outside Irdis's atmosphere, gave the landing order, and the transports swooped in.

Now all of the Khelat and mercenary attack ships were striking anything that resembled a target. Shaoki AA missiles launched, and were acquired, diverted by the electronic countermeasure ships, and destroyed.

Then the sites themselves became targets—small ships dove on them before they could reload and salted the sites with small antipersonnel missiles and even dumb bombs. Even the handful of Shaoki mobile launch sites were hit as they hastily packed up launchers and guidance trailers.

The first wave of transports zigged toward their landing grounds. Wahfer brought his cruisers low, savaging the Shaoki infantry and lifter units, backed by Inchcape's destroyers.

Here and there a transport streamed fire, smoke, and dove toward the ground. Then the first wave was down, and Khelat infantry swarmed out, their lifters close behind them.

And, from the ruins, Shaoki infantry fought back. The soldiers may have been badly led, indifferently trained. But they knew how to die.

The battles were fierce and bloody.

"I have an intercept," Grok announced, "that one of my underlings sent on to the *Pride of Khelat*. Actually, it's a series of intercepts."

It was the second day of battle, and the ground attack was going trudgingly well. There'd been five landings, and all of them had at least found a foothold.

The four other members of Star Risk waited, knowing whatever Grok had wouldn't be commonplace.

"Shaoki Command keeps querying its intel where are the foreign mercenary commanders, and ordering any station who has data to report with the highest priority. With, of course, no responses."

Jasmine King accepted another cup of coffee from Goodnight.

"This is coupled with rather panicky requests for reinforcements from various ground units," Grok continued. "Invariably, the reply is that without reporting the presence of the mercenaries, Shaoki Command assumes that all of the landings are nothing but feints, and until we foreigners are reported, none of the reserves will be released."

Goodnight lifted his cup in a toast to Friedrich.

"It is nice to belong to a unit so feared that its very absence wins victories."

"So far," von Baldur said, a bit cynically.

The first wave of Khelat infantrymen had been not the bravest of the Khelat, but deliberately chosen sacrificial and penal units. They were hit hard, and were beginning to fall back.

King Saleph landed the second wave, his regulars.

Now there were no more suicidal, frontal attacks.

Saleph had learned from the catastrophe on VI/III, and landed his soldiers here, there, and ordered their officers to always look for the flanks and attack there.

"Never send a man where you can send a bullet . . . or missile," was one of his standing orders, which had been given him by Riss, and hardly original with her.

The Khelat secured their footholds and began spreading out.

* * *

"I have a somewhat jubilant message here," King said. "Two of the invasion points have just linked up."

"Progress," Riss said. "I wonder what the casualty count is."

"Who cares," Goodnight said. "As long as it isn't one of us."

Friedrich stood, stretched.

"I suppose we might as well involve ourselves in the vulgar fray," he said.

"Might as well," Goodnight agreed. "We do need to look heroic, so there won't be any argument over the victory bonus."

FIFTY-TWO

Star Risk was loading its gear for what it hoped was the final offensive.

Jasmine King, always being efficient, had her ditty bag already aboard von Baldur's *Pride of Khelat.*

She was ready to roll . . . but two things nagged at her. First was what Riss had said Prince Wahfer had messaged; and the second was the still unexplained word that Anya Davenport, their lobbyist, question mark former, was headed toward the Khelat System for some unknown reason.

Jasmine had figured out, long ago, that unanswered questions tended to turn around and bite freelancers in the butt. So she accessed a series of computer commands that Grok and she had prepared, set them in motion.

If not canceled, the program would query her in a week, on a daily basis. If the reply was not what had been set, or if anyone else tried to access the program, it would take instant action.

And both Jasmine and Grok doubted any third party could either stop it or figure out what its end use was.

"Are you coming out to play?" Riss asked, sticking her head into Jasmine's room.

"On the way," King said. "Just setting up some backdoor investment opportunities."

"We are proposing to support your landing, at . . ." Friedrich flipped three coins, considered the result. ". . . at Point X-Ray Tardis."

"Excellent," King Saleph enthused. "You have picked one of my weakest areas, that could desperately use your reinforcements."

"Attacking now," von Baldur said, nodding at the watch officer.

The *Pride of Khelat* cut its speed, used steering jets to drop out of its orbit around Irdis.

The great cruiser was heavily escorted with Inchcape's destroyers and half of Spada's p-boats.

What the king didn't know is von Baldur had specifically used a coded channel that Grok knew had been broken and was monitored by the Shaoki. Now their council would know Star Risk was in the picture, and commit its reserves accordingly.

"I went and said it very clear/I went and muttered in their ear," Friedrich muttered.

"Pardon, sir?" the watch officer asked.

"Nothing."

Von Baldur planned to make one sweep over the contested area, then divert to a second landing zone.

He smiled, thinking of all the lovely confusion he would be wreaking below.

Reinforcements boiled out of the small transport. One of them was Grok. He'd transshipped from the *Pride* on the way down, wanting a more immediate experience than just strafing and missiling.

Soldiers goggled at him, not knowing what to make.

The gigantic alien had puzzled on how to keep from

being a blue-on-blue casualty by his own men, decided to have a shirt made out of the Khelat flag. That should slow any attackers down so that he could either reason with them or kill them if they didn't listen to logic.

"Come on," he bellowed. "For Khelat and freedom!"

Officers looked at each other.

The stranger seemed to know what he was doing—which he did. He'd been studying this particular city, and the problems the Khelat were having, since the landings began.

"In the name of God and the Continental Congress," he shouted, having no idea what that meant, but thinking it sounded martial as all hell.

The Khelat came out of their positions and followed him.

Grok spotted an entrenched crew-served weapon, dug a grenade off his harness, and lobbed it an impossible distance to land just under the horrified gunner's nose.

Not waiting for the explosion, Grok ran on, looking for another target.

Within the hour, the Shaoki defense had broken and begun falling back.

"Spada One this is Star Risk Two," Riss said, peering over the commander's hatch at the twisted landscape in front of her. "I have a target."

"This is One. Go," came back.

"On the map . . . from Helet, down one zero left two five."

"I read back, from Helet down one zero left two five."

"Target, cluster of bunkers, with some light artillery hiding behind it."

"This is One. We're coming in."

Riss involuntarily ducked as a flight of three Pyrrhus boats crashed down at her, pulled out bare meters from the ground, and rockets shot from their exterior tubes.

The rockets slammed home, and the ground roiled and became even more surrealistic.

"That's on it, One," Riss 'cast. "Stand by for another mission."

Goodnight's mercenaries debouched from their lifters.

The road was quiet, and only a few craters pockmarked the low hills around it.

On the other side of the hills, about five kilometers, were the outskirts of the capital.

The men came off their transport with their blasters at port arms, and without needing to shout a lot, formed up in platoon formations and trotted toward the city.

Goodnight and his command group were just back of the point company. Chas, to his embarrassment, found himself breathing hard after only a couple of kilometers. I gotta keep remembering to work out, he thought.

Then a scatter of mortar rounds crashed into the side of the road, and he forgot about being tired.

Grok allowed himself to pose nobly atop the hill, looked about for more Shaoki to kill.

He didn't see any.

The Khelat were busy looting the bunkers or making sure all Shaoki casualties were corpses.

That didn't bother Grok—he always thought the human fetish for prisoners to be absurd.

*   *   *

Three Shaoki ships, large destroyers, came out of a canyon toward the *Pride*.

"Target acquired," a weapons officer reported.

Friedrich nodded. "Stand by for launch, on my command—"

All three Shaoki exploded, one wheeling down into the ground.

"What the—" Friedrich managed.

A speaker blared.

"This is Inchcape One. Thanks for the setup."

Von Baldur allowed his pique to pass.

"You know," he said to the watch officer, "I think this war might be just about over."

The streets of the capital were hung with white flags, made from everything from sheets and towels to shirts.

Goodnight ran past the ruins of the council building he and Grok had blown up months earlier, that the Shaoki hadn't had the time or capital to rebuild.

"Well, sir?" Goodnight's second in command asked.

Goodnight thought.

"Fine. Looting by squads. And no goddamned rape. I shoot rapists. No burning. No drunkards. They'll lose their share . . . if some frigging Shaoki doesn't backstab 'em."

The officer saluted, and doubled away.

"All Star Risk elements," von Baldur broadcast on a frequency only monitored by his fellows, in a rather singular code.

"It is all over. I say again, the war is over except for the police call. Pull back and out. I say again, pull back and out and stand by for pickup.

"There's no point in being the last man killed."

FIFTY-THREE

Prince Wahfer waited until his agents reported that the Star Risk principals had returned to Khelat II. He didn't think they had the slightest idea of his plans, but they were gifted with battle luck, and he needed no intrusions.

Below his squadron, in low orbit over Irdis, was the king's cruiser, waiting for the last holdouts below to give up so he could graciously accept the final surrender of the Shaoki worlds, the ultimate triumph.

The king, according to Prince Barab, was busy planning just what he would wear to the ceremony, and figuring out what ultimate abasement he would inflict on the Shaoki, as well as who else, besides their council, he should have executed immediately.

The king thought . . . the king planned . . . ran through Prince Wahfer's mind in a merry chorus, as so many wistful dreams that would never happen.

Wahfer grinned, turned to his watch officer, who had been one of the first to be involved in Wahfer's plans.

"Execute Plan Triumphant," he ordered.

The officer grinned.

"With pleasure . . . Your Majesty."

"Careful," Wahfer warned. "The gods tear the glass

of exultation from the lips of those who drink too soon."

"Aye, sir." The officer privately thought the prince was a pompous ass, but a winning one, so he kept the smile broad. The man seemed to get everything he wanted, down to the smallest item.

The officer went to the confidential-materials safe at the rear of the bridge, touched sensors.

It swung open, and the officer took out a fiche.

But Wahfer needed no reminders on the first step.

The crew of his cruiser was already at General Quarters.

"Contact the flagship," he ordered.

In a few seconds, Prince Barab's face was on-screen.

"I have had an idea," Wahfer said. "Rather than lessen the attention paid the king, I propose that my squadron should take care of that damned island that's still holding out."

Barab could barely hide his smile.

"That is most honorable, sir."

"And I have some other targets that should be disposed of at the same time," Wahfer said. "May I approach your ship and transfer the list?"

"Why . . . yes. Of course."

"I shall not need to come across," Wahfer said. "And will send no more than one messenger."

Barab agreed, and Wahfer cut off.

"Bring our ship within contact range of the flagship," he ordered. "And take command. I shall be in the gunnery compartment."

The watch officer saluted, and Wahfer left the bridge, having trouble keeping his pace down.

It has been so long, he thought.

In the main weapons room he ordered a gunnery officer away from his post, and put on the man's control helmet. He knew that trusted men were already securing all vital departments on his cruiser.

Wahfer waited until the bridge reported that the king's ship was less than a thousand kilometers distant.

"Prepare to launch," he ordered. "I'll take the missile on individual control."

The gunnery commander looked puzzled, but he'd learned long ago to follow the prince's orders exactly.

"Yes, sir."

Wahfer touched the synchronize sensor, and his senses swam for an instant.

Then he was outside the cruiser, in space, and then in a sealed tube.

Wahfer let his fingers, back in the gunnery room, ghostlike, touch the LAUNCH button on his board, and the tube came open and he was in space again.

He "looked" around, saw a handful of destroyers clustered around a much bigger ship.

Wahfer applied power, armed the missile, and at full drive shot toward the king's ship, correcting his aim.

If anyone gave an alarm, he didn't notice, hypnotized by the onrushing target.

A second or two before it struck, he cut contact with the missile and jerked off his helmet.

He looked for a screen, found one, just as the missile struck and exploded, exactly as planned, on the king's compartments just behind the bridge.

Flame gouted, then the entire nose of the flagship detonated, spraying men and flame and oxygen into space.

Then the ship blew up, and the screen blanked for an instant, sought another pickup, and when it cleared, the king's ship was a dead hulk.

Wahfer smiled.

"I *said* I'd only send one messenger."

He got up from the gunnery station, ignoring the shocked—or smiling—faces in the compartment.

"Now for *my* triumph," he said. "And to secure my companion."

FIFTY-FOUR

"I am going to take a shower," Redon Spada announced. "I still don't feel clean."

"You, Sir Pilot, are light in the ass," Riss announced. "If you were line slime like I am, you wouldn't whine about being four days or so out of a fresher."

"But that, my lady love," Spada said, "is the differments between us. I always had brains enough to keep away from the trenches."

"Hah," M'chel said. "And have I ragged you sufficiently about your mistaken ideas of mortality?"

"Only about lebenty-leben times."

They were curled, naked, on pillows on the floor of the living room.

"Mmm," Riss said, rolled over, and watched Spada go into the bathroom. She decided he had a nice ass, even if his legs were a little too short.

Riss yawned, thought about turning the 'caster on. But she wasn't interested in martial music, some braying announcer talking about how noble the king was and how the evil Shaoki would now be paying for their sins and so forth.

Why, she thought, was she messing with success?

She and Redon had stayed incommunicado, except for periodic orders to the kitchens, for almost two days.

She was starting to decide she was almost human again, and was looking forward to her island on Trimalchio IV, and maybe buying one of those rockets Spada had used to watch the waves from underneath.

And she was wondering if she wanted to take Redon with her to her island . . . or let things just be solo. Maybe the latter would be a good idea, while she sorted out just what she felt, beyond good old-fashioned lust, for the pilot.

Speaking of which, she sat up and thought about joining him for a shower, and whatever else arose.

The door to the outside world banged open, and Prince Wahfer was standing there, wearing full dress uniform.

Which left Riss at a bit of a loss.

"M'chel," he said, "I have come to ask you to join me."

"Get the hell out of my quarters," Riss snarled.

"I want you for my consort," Wahfer said grandiosely, as if he weren't listening. "My partner. To join me in ruling the Khelat Cluster!"

M'chel was wondering what the hell he was talking about when the fresher door opened, and Redon Spada, wearing only a towel, came out, having heard the voices and looking perplexed.

Wahfer's eyes goggled.

"You! Who are . . . what are you doing here?"

"None of your goddamned business," Spada growled.

"I told you to get the hell out of my—" Riss started. Wahfer's hand was on the flap of his holster.

Redon Spada saw the movement, dove for the pistol in his belt over a chair.

Wahfer's pistol was sliding out of the holster.

Spada wouldn't make it in time.

Riss moved very quickly.

Her pistol was beside her, on the nightstand, about which Spada had chided her for her paranoia.

It came up smoothly, the safety slid off, and Riss fired three times.

The blasts were very loud in the room.

All three hit Wahfer in the chest, and he made a choked noise, his arms windmilled, and he dropped limply.

Behind Wahfer, in the doorway, was some aide or other. He started to move for his own gun, saw Riss's leveled pistol, froze, and backed out into the corridor, his hands raised chest high.

Riss kicked the door closed in his face and made for the com.

"I think," she said, dialing, in a classic of understatement, "things may have changed a little while we were cuddling."

She looked over at the sprawled body. "The king is dead. . . . Long live the king. Poor sorry bastard."

FIFTY-FIVE

Star Risk was glooming in its quarters the day after the king's memorial service.

Prince Wahfer's body had been ceremoniously cursed, since his coup collapsed instantly. No one cared about the circumstances of his death.

In addition to Star Risk's other moils and toils, the Shaoki, emboldened by the royal deaths and the rather confused directorate that the royalty of Khelat had cobbled together, had gone back to shooting a mean almost guerrilla war on Irdis, and open warfare on the uninvaded worlds.

There was only one bright note. Jasmine's program had run its course very smoothly:

Star Risk's, and its employees', paychecks for two months in advance, plus the contracted victory bonus, had been neatly and automatically lifted from the Khelat national treasury and bounced through six worlds' state banks before ending up in a nice, anonymous number-call bank account on a seventh world—not Trimalchio IV.

"So we should just say stick it, and go home," Goodnight said.

"I vote we remain here. There are still Shaoki to kill," Grok said.

"Enough slaughter for the moment," Jasmine counseled, patting Grok's paw. "Practice peace and philosophical ponderings."

"If I have to," Grok grunted. "But I do not have to like it."

"We signed a contract," Riss argued. "And it's not fulfilled."

Goodnight snorted.

"This from the woman who started all this double-doublecrossing. How pious!"

"It is not piety," von Baldur said. "It is a matter of common decency and moral justice. We have never broken a contract—yet—without cause."

"True," Goodnight said. "Looks like crap on the old résumé."

"I suggest," Riss said, "that we all think about this situation a bit, and meet maybe tomorrow and vote on it."

"I do remind you," King said, "that if we decide to be upright and moral, we'll have to give the bonus back."

"Gad," Goodnight drawled. "Do you think we are but whores for the common day, concerned only with our bankbooks?"

"I do indeed," King declared.

Late on the second day—the meeting had been pushed at von Baldur's request to give him another twenty-four E-hours to reach his decision—the five were brought running by a 'cast being monitored by their com center.

". . . will be met with a proper response."

A blare of static, then the message started over:

"All combatants, Khelat, Shaoki, and their hirelings.

This is the Alliance Peacekeeping Force, now entering your cluster.

"It has been determined by the Alliance that your increasingly bloody struggle is imperiling the peace of your sector.

"A truce is declared, to take effect immediately. Alliance peacekeepers will be landed on both Khelat and Shaoki capital worlds. All soldiers are ordered to disarm immediately. An Alliance commission will determine proper justice and reparations due.

"Final peace has come to the Khelat Sector. Any continued violence will be met with a proper response."

A pause, then the message began once more.

Von Baldur waved to an officer, and the com was muted.

"What, in the name of Socrates, would bring the Alliance into this?" Grok wondered.

Very suddenly, Riss got it.

"Freddie . . . remember Anya Davenport's representative told Jasmine that Davenport was headed to our cluster?"

King got it first.

"Omni Foods!"

"Just so," von Baldur said. "A dangerously clever woman. We were not providing the *maln* on schedule, so she got Omni in her pocket and they called in enough votes in Parliament to authorize intervention. Now Omni will be able to get its *maln*. . . . And Khelat has a new master.

"And Anya Davenport will get very, very rich. Clever. Very clever." There was nothing but admiration in his voice.

"We have been doublecrossed," Riss said, and started laughing.

"Aren't we assuming a lot?" Goodnight asked.

Without waiting for an answer, he motioned to the com officer. "Gimme a mike, and patch me in to whatever frequency the Alliance is 'casting on."

"Yessir."

"You don't think," Riss asked, "that anybody with the Force will admit to Davenport being there, do you?"

Goodnight motioned her to silence.

In minutes, there was an Alliance officer standing by.

"Star Risk, this is Peacekeeper Seventeen. You should be advised that we have every intention—"

"Screw all that," Goodnight said. "The only question we've got is, What the hell took you so long?"

Chris Bunch became a full-time novelist following his twenty-year career as a television writer. A military veteran, he is the *Locus* bestselling author of *Star Risk, Ltd.*, and such popular works as the *Sten* series, *The Seer King, The Demon King,* and the *Last Legion* series. He lives in Washington State on the Columbia River.